The Test of the Magi

Johannes Bergmann

The Test
of the Magi

⊕   ⊕   ⊕

Angelico Press

First published in the USA and UK
by Angelico Press
© Johannes Bergmann 2014

For information, address:
Angelico Press
4709 Briar Knoll Dr.
Kettering, OH 45429
angelicopress.com

ISBN 978-1-62138-083-2 (pbk: alk. paper)
ISBN 978-1-62138-084-9 (ebook)

Cover Image: Detail from
Mary and Child, surrounded by angels,
Mosaic of a Ravennate Italian-Byzantine workshop,
completed within AD 526
by the so-called "Master of Sant 'Apollinare"
Cover Design: Michael Schrauzer

CONTENTS

For my mother, Ellen,
who still shares her fascination with
the Three Wise Men.

...behold the star which they had seen in the east,
went before them, until it came and stood over
where the child was.

And seeing the star they rejoiced
with exceeding great joy.

And entering into the house, they found the child
with Mary his mother, and falling down they adored him;
and opening their treasures, they offered him gifts;
gold, frankincense, and myrrh.

Matthew II: 9–11 (Douay-Rheims 1899)

prologue:
The World of the Magi

HALF A CENTURY BEFORE the birth of Christ, a war with Persia ended in what may have been Rome's most humiliating defeat, and a Cold War began. The Republic had been toppled, although many Romans hoped in vain for its restoration, and their fast-growing empire was ruled by three triumvirs: Julius Caesar, Pompey the Great, and Marcus Licinius Crassus. The latter, although Rome's richest man, was last among equals. Old and half deaf, he craved ever more power, recognition for his military prowess, and, of course, gold. Opposed by his more successful rival, Pompey, he nevertheless formed a vast army of more than 50,000 men and marched forth to conquer Persia.

Persia herself had been seized by Parthians a half-century before, and her exquisite culture—ancient Classical Persian, blended with Greek Hellenism since the days of Alexander the Great—was under threat from political turbulence within. However, her new kings, whose allies were coarse and uneducated compared with many of their new subjects, brought technological improvements, especially in the arts of horsemanship and archery. Hence the smaller and weaker, but more skilled, Persian force clashed with the massive Roman army and feinted and withdrew again and again, drawing their enemies deeper and deeper into waterless deserts.

Finally, they struck with all their might, deploying a secret weapon that terrified the invaders, made them break ranks and run. Above the heads of the Romans danced and sparkled flashes of coloured light: silken banners. The Battle of Carrhae was the first time that any Europeans had seen silk. In nearly equal portions, the Romans were slain, enslaved, and driven into the deserts to die of drought and madness. Crassus was killed and, according to legend, in death he was reunited with the greatest love of his life: molten gold was poured down the throat of his corpse. Several gilt-bronze eagles, on Roman regimental standards, fell to the Persians, and memories of that bitter humiliation festered for centuries. There began the great Cold War between the Classical world's two superpowers.

Soon after Rome's army first saw silk, Roman elites could not resist it. By the birth of Christ, the Emperor Augustus objected bitterly to the quantities of gold flowing east out of the empire, chiefly to pay for imported silk. The price of an ordinary house, he complained, could be spent buying only one silk dress. Soon after the death of the Republic and the quickened spread of empire, colonies had already begun to be bled dry to quench the increasingly Lucullan appetites of the capital. The trade-routes that pampered the Roman rich were far older than Rome herself. Much earlier, precious lapis lazuli had come from modern day Afghanistan to adorn the Egyptian pharaohs, and caravans had borne glass goblets, bronze trinkets, rare spices, and medicinal herbs over long distances. However, the booming trade in Cathay's exclusive luxury cloth increased trade exponentially and served to give the Silk Road its name forevermore. Along its several paths to different markets, caravans paid duties to the nations through which they passed, leeching away a vast empire's gold and sprinkling it liberally over bazaars and towns and desert hostelries from modern Italy to China. Afghanistan's gentle Kushans, who lived by trade and not conquest, melted down Roman gold coins by the bucketful and then struck anew the more crudely-rendered faces of their Zoroastrian and Buddhist kings. Quite apart from the haemorrhaging of gold, that, too, must have rankled the haughty Romans.

Into this tempestuous world came the Wise Men, in the Gospels mentioned only by Saint Matthew, and only briefly. In Western Christian tradition there were three, identified with their three famous gifts. But in other Christian traditions there are twelve or even nearly twenty. They are known as magi, originally a caste of Zoroastrian priests that by the time of Christ had lost its sacred monopoly; also as kings, chiefly by way of inference from Psalms (72:11), in which kings fall down before the new-born Messiah. Different sects give them different names and origins. Chinese Christians, for example, claim one as their own. Circa 400 AD, Saint John Chrysostom believed them to be the Jewish kings of Yemen. But the usual Western tradition, based on an Alexandrine manuscript of 500 AD, recognises Melchior as the oldest and a scholar from Persia; Caspar as the youngest and a scholar from South Asia; and Balthazar as an Arab or African sage.

While there seems little doubt that the Magi were astronomers and astrologers, the Star that drew them to Bethlehem remains a matter of far greater controversy. Ancient theologians and modern historians, astronomers, and every planetarium curator at Christmastime, even television preachers and newspaper editorialists, disagree vigorously, calling it either a nova or an asteroid or a comet, or else a propitious conjunction of stars already known. Eastern Orthodox Christians and Seventh Day Adventists believe it was "a company of shining angels" of which the Magi were somehow unaware; Jehovah's Witnesses believe it was a product of Satan, luring the Magi to Herod, who longed to kill Jesus. Some think the Star traversed the firmament on high, others that it hovered only a few feet above Bethlehem's manger, making it rather tiny indeed. In 1611, the renowned German astronomer, Johannes Kepler, thought it was a series of conjunctions of Jupiter and Saturn, while similar theories involve Aries or the star Regulus in Leo. Conjunctions held a greater appeal, because they would have conveyed additional meaning to ancient astrologers. Also meaningful is the image of a king and a star depicted on coins from Parthian Persia, accommodating almost any explanation without contradiction. Perhaps the simplest theory is that it was a purely miraculous occurrence. Considering that it must be preceded by belief in one God-Creator, who has a Son and sent Him to earth as a man to live and grow and die among us, perhaps one unique star neither strains the capabilities of our Creator nor Christian belief.

A decade before Rome's defeat to the Persians at Carrhae, their proconsul (later triumvir), Pompey the Great, won a war, put down a rebellion, and re-secured Judea. Herod the Great, from a family of ethnic-minority converts to Judaism, routed the ruling Hasmonean Dynasty and seized the Judean throne as Rome's puppet king. He was reviled by his subjects as a great villain and murderer of rabbis, as well as winning renown as "the greatest builder in Jewish history" with his famous Temple in Jerusalem but more numerous glorifications of Rome. Following the Star along the Silk Road, the Magi reached Jerusalem, where, in their distinctive Persian clothes, they would have inspired gossip and controversy among its no more than 35,000 inhabitants. Entering a Roman province dressed distinctively as that empire's worst enemies would have been tantamount to uniformed Soviet officers arriving uninvited at NATO headquarters at the height of the 20th Century's Cold War. Herod's spies had no doubt told him what the suspicious visitors sought. So, while fearing a usurper in the infant king of the Jews, Herod summoned the Wise Men. He asked the Magi to report back, intending to murder but one more rival in his long reign.

At Bethlehem, the Magi met the Holy Family and presented their three gifts to the infant Messiah—except in one Persian legend told to Marco Polo, in which they began a scientific test instead. Once bidden to choose, they reasoned, if the Christ Child selected the gold, then He would become a great king or emperor; if He took the frankincense, a mystic or the founder of a new religion, like the Persian Zoroaster nearly a millennium

4

before; and if the myrrh, a healer, for these were the greatest types of men known to history. But a miracle made the Magi abandon the experiment.

According to Saint Matthew, they then went home on a different path, avoiding Herod, and there the Scriptural story ends, but the legends continue. To some, the Magi swiftly became Christians and were gloriously martyred, although perhaps not too swiftly, because Christianity did not exist until after Jesus reached manhood. Others believe that one or more of the Magi was converted by an early missionary, possibly Saint Thomas the Apostle, on one of his legendary journeys to India.

Their bones were supposedly acquired by Saint Helena, the mother of the Emperor Constantine, himself a Christian convert and later a saint, who gave her free run of the Imperial Treasury to buy relics while on pilgrimage to the Holy Land in 326–328 AD. These were venerated first in the Basilica of Sancta Sophia in Constantinople, were then moved to Milan in 344, and finally to Cologne Cathedral in 1164. There they remain in a splendid medieval gilt reliquary behind the main altar, where they have attracted pilgrims for 900 years. A century after the relics arrived at Cologne, Marco Polo reported being shown their tombs in the Persian city of Saveh south of Teheran, where "the bodies are still entire, with hair and beard remaining," perhaps raising questions of what was sold to St Helena as opposed to what was shown to Marco and at what price.

The earliest known depictions of the Magi, from the Third Century, show them wearing the day's distinctive Persian clothing: stovepipe trousers and Phrygian caps, like Lady Liberty or French Revolutionaries. Similarly, old depictions in Bethlehem's Church of the Nativity, believed to be on the original site and rebuilt by the Emperor Justinian in 565, survived the Persian-Byzantine War of 614, when the invaders spared the church after recognising the Persian national costumes.

Now, on every Sixth of January, concluding the Twelve Days

of Christmas, the visitation of the Wise Men is celebrated in northern Europe, in Poland, in Austria and Hungary, and in Germany and the Low Countries especially, just as it is in Spanish and Portuguese-speaking lands. It signifies the revelation of Christ to the Gentiles, offering salvation to all mankind. There and elsewhere across Christendom, after being portrayed in medieval illuminated manuscripts and stained glass windows and later in Renaissance and Baroque paintings, their likenesses are now among the favourites in Christmas tableaux. In King's College, Cambridge, beneath "The Adoration of the Magi" painted by Peter Paul Rubens in the early 17th Century, gift-shop workers report that various Christmas cards depicting the Three Wise Men outsell all other images by a considerable margin.

JOHANNES BERGMANN
Mayfair
2014

Chapter One

I WAS NOT THERE when they came for the old man. I was not there and I cursed myself bitterly.

I cannot recall why I was not there, for it was very long ago. I might have been on an errand, buying a chicken for one of the evening meals, which so often we took together, or ferrying his charts or my manuscripts from the copyists in the bazaar. It was surely something mundane that does not matter anymore. But it mattered to me then, because I was not there when they took him away.

They bound his hands, you know, and it was all so unnecessary. He had long, frail hands, and beneath his parchment skin you could see all the workings—the bones and joints and sinews. They would have been elegant hands, were they not always spotted with ink from hours spent with the bottle, the brush, and those vast, yellow sheets of vellum on which he charted all of the Planets of the Spheres and all of the Stars of the Outer Heavens.

They bound his hands, but not because he would have fought them or even tried to flee. He was far too old and frail to fight, and an *Achaemenid* never runs away. They are all gone now, the *Achaemenidae*, but they never ran. He was one of the last.

No, they bound his hands, you see, because they were police. Temple police, as it happens, but no different from the rest of the breed anywhere that I have ever been—strong-armed, weak-brained, and fervently loyal to the power of the state, which awards them their small, sole, simple pleasure in life, that of humiliating their betters. He went with them quietly, without so much as a harsh glance at the calloused illiterates whom our new masters see fit to employ as guardians of the state religion, then as now and now as then.

I had gone off on some errand or another, I am now almost certain of it. I might have been buying ink. We bought a lot of ink, it seems. But, when I returned, Bilquis told me that he had been taken away. I was angry with her, because she had done nothing, but in hindsight there was nothing that she could have done. Mostly, I suppose, I was angry with myself, for, in failing to be there, I felt that I had somehow betrayed him. The old man was gone, and I was not, and it was all so permanent and so very, very unfair that I wept. He never learnt that I had wept. As long as he drew breath, he never learnt that I had wept. And that is a good thing, for he would have thought it unbecoming.

It all happened so fast—that was my first thought after Bilquis told me the news. I thought neither of how he was nor of what to do next, but only of how rapidly it had all come to pass. In a sense I was paralysed. I was, of course, not much older than you are now. And at such an age the days drag long and life seems to stand stock-still, until you sometimes think that you shall go mad from anticipation and boredom. But then something cracks like the lash at the start of a race. Then, ever after, nothing remains the same. So at least it was for me.

It all happened in fewer than eighteen months. A lifetime, a thousand lifetimes, swept past in scarcely more than a year. We saw the Signal. We prepared the Experiment. We mounted the Expedition and crossed half the earth to Jerusalem and back. We were traduced by the despot, looked into the eyes of a living god, and were rescued by winged *apsaras*, which in itself is quite amazing. Scarcely anyone has seen an *apsara*, you know. We witnessed the end of a Great Birth and the beginning of a Great Death.

Moreover we lived to tell the tale, and now Melchior was doomed only because the tale had been told too well. And, throughout it all, time had gone from a standstill to a headlong dash, as if an ox had leapt to its feet and run like a cheetah. Time never flowed so fast again, but neither did it ever slow to the leisured pace of my youth. Would that I could once more make it so.

We had not wished for this, not a piece of it. Neither did the old man deserve to die, nor we to lose him and be thus condemned to grieve so long as we lived. He would, we both knew, be put to death. In some dark place, at some appointed hour, he would be garrotted with a silver chain—the last so-called honour afforded the old families by the barbarian kings who displaced them.

Any why? Not because we dreamed. Not even because we dared to look upon the face of a god. Merely because we dared to look. Because we hoped to see, and see not as animals see, but as men see. Our only sin was looking. And we looked, because we hoped to learn as I learnt from the old man and as you learn from me. As his fathers learnt from the ancient *Unani* and as your descendants and students shall one day learn from you. Assuming, of course, that you pass your exams, and that is an assumption, quite frankly, that you ought not to make too hastily. But that is another matter.

They bound his hands and led the old man away. But I said that, did I not? It was a very long time ago.

We were in his tower when I heard the news, four storeys built of mud-brick and always in danger of toppling down. Eventually they razed it along with the whole block and built the great *dakhma*, the Tower of Silence, where the corpses are placed. No one wants to live there now because of the proximity of death and the stench of rotting meat and the sky black with clumsy vultures always dropping gruesome morsels onto the rooftops and into the kitchen gardens below. So the surrounding streets have filled with tanneries and abattoirs and crude foundries, and the drains run foetid with poisons. But it was green enough then, with tiny, mud-walled gardens crammed with saplings, slashed by dusty, narrow lanes, dappled in shadows with white ducks paddling in the ditches alongside.

The tower, Melchior's tower, was the tallest building in the neighbourhood, and he needed the height for his work. Mathematicians have low operating costs, he used to say, for they can live and work in a drain, while astronomers are helpless without their towers. His was old and made of mud brick and tilted slightly to one side. Transfixed, I stared blankly out of the window, the west-facing one that was his favourite, but soon enough I regained my senses. Or so it seemed, but I was nonetheless still deranged. I was mad with a plan and thus dangerous to myself and to everyone around me. If the world is ever destroyed, it will be accomplished by madmen with plans.

I told Bilquis that I would go first to the *serai*, for by then it was sufficiently dark. I would try to find Daoud. He had led our expedition and many caravans before it. Moreover he knew enough *Yehudi* drovers, small, burly men accustomed to fending off desert bandits. Turkomens too. They had wicked daggers and knew how to use them, if not precisely in the manner of the palace fencing masters. No, they preferred to work quickly and, if possible, from behind. With a dozen of them I thought we could free the old man and make haste for Baghdad before the moon rose and revealed our tracks.

Bilquis said that I was out of my mind, and, although I started to protest, I soon realised that she was right. Even had we cut our way through the temple police—a foolish prospect that in my youth I frankly rather relished—the old man would see his escape as running away, and an *Achaemenid* never runs. He would have refused to flee, and our lives, like his, would have been forfeit.

She said that she would bring him food in prison that evening, for, as his niece, it was her right. She added that I could not accompany her, for I was no blood relation. Such is the tradition and such is the law.

There was nothing for me to say, so I gave her a few coppers to buy one of the yellow, thin-skinned, *kharbouza* melons that he liked so much. She tied the coins into the corner of the old man's favourite woollen shawl. He once said that it had belonged to his father—dust brown, worn threadbare in places, but woven of best Kashmiri *pashmina*—so fine that it could be drawn through a wedding band, yet warmer than a shepherd's heaviest cloak. It had been expensive once. She gathered it up and left without a word.

The streets seemed unearthly quiet after she had gone, as quiet as the night on which we had first seen the Signal. But on that night I had not been left alone.

IN TIMES OF CRISIS, it is odd how swiftly the mind digresses and remarkable how rapidly it completes the thought and returns to the problem at hand. Before the journey, I had paid little attention to Bilquis. She was his niece. She killed and cooked the chickens that I bought in the bazaar, and, so far as I knew but never cared, ate the scraps after we had finished. I thought her sharp-tongued and dull-witted, but I was wrong. I soon learnt that she was both competent and clever. Of course, I had no inkling of how she felt toward me, no idea of her animosity, because she cloaked it so ably. She was, after all, part *Achaemenid,* as was the old man. But I digress.

They bound the old man with hempen rope and they took him to the prison. Apart from the temple compound and the Palace of Elders, it was then the only other major building made of stone, and, despite long generations spent living in tents, our Parthian overlords soon learnt the utility of stone gaols.

Bilquis saw him there. His chains were slack enough to let him sit or stand, an act of kindness by some anonymous gaoler. She fed him, and, although he had not been formally charged, he knew what the allegations would be, just as he knew what would be the arguments of the prosecutors, the decision of the tribunal, and the sentence. Alone to be decided was his own defence, a formality preordained to fail but the last real choice that a prisoner can make affecting his own fleeting life and one that, if done and done well, just might see him dispatched to the next world with a shred of dignity left intact.

Bilquis said that she had asked who should represent him before the tribunal, what information might be amassed for his defence, and who might be called upon to testify on his behalf, but he only smiled faintly and shook his head very slowly from one side to another.

She suggested selling the furniture, even the tower itself, then visiting his few surviving classmates and many friends and former students, raising perhaps enough silver for a timely donation to the temple. I thought it showed sense—I would have given all that I had, and others would have given more. But he said nothing and only laid his hand gently upon her hand and continued smiling while looking away intensely, as if at something barely visible and far away.

"Bilquis," he said softly after a while, "realise that mine has been a good life." She began to argue, but he silenced her with a gesture. "I have well acquitted myself to my ancestors, and to you and to my students," he whispered. "I have wanted for nothing. I have beheld wonders and told the truth, always. Now I am old. Is there more that you would have me do?" She wept and pleaded, but he comforted her and remained unmoved.

"What can I bring you?" she asked him at length.

He thought for a time. "Some pomegranates," he said. "Bring me some pomegranates. The season is over, but I believe that the shops may yet have a few. If there is a choice, I prefer those from Mashad; the climate is drier there, and the fruit is thus sweeter. But you know that already." After a moment he added, pointedly, "And send me Caspar."

It pains me still to recall the look of resentment, when she told me this request. To her I was a *kharegi*, an outsider, not only not of the family, but also a foreigner. Moreover, I was, in her eyes, an unbeliever, although she was no bigot. I think she resented me as an interloper of sorts, in competition for the old man's affections. She failed to appreciate, I sometimes think, the bonds that develop, when one is first the student of a man and then, dare I say it, a colleague. Such ties differ from the bonds of family and boon friendship, but they are forged of much the same strong stuff, maybe stronger, since they include no material desire. And then there was the whole matter of our expedition together.

Bilquis was a bright girl then, with a good heart, but those sorts of inchoate resentments are only overcome by people who are the most extraordinarily wise and kind, and even then only with the greatest difficulty. Not wishing to deepen her wounds, I only nodded and said that I would, as always, obey his request.

I did not sleep on that night when the old man was taken away. Sleep was unwelcome. I sat on his favourite cushion, a tattered old gift of astronomers from Balkh, of wine-red velvet shot through with fraying golden threads. I looked at his room, at his few things, at the shelves piled high with his stacks of scrolls so neatly tied with green ribbands, scrolls that he might well never open again and some of which we had once made together. And when the lamp guttered, I did not bother to call the boy to refill it. I simply sat in the dark and through the window watched the old man's stars. They rose and brightened, whirled and danced in their appointed paths, then dimmed and died. I left before dawn, just as we had always done.

Do you know, it cost me two pieces of silver to bribe the guard? Two pieces! Even today you could visit any prisoner in the empire for one. The captain was a fat man, horse-faced and undoubtedly the son of shepherds. He was no moon-faced nomad khan, rather an offspring of the Persian poor and unlettered who so eagerly appropriated the next rung on the ladder, not to mention the invaders' silver. And my silver too. He cleared his throat, spat in the corner, grinned, and said that a higher fee was required to visit *Achaemenidae*, because there were so few left anywhere in Iran, and even fewer in our prisons. While corrupt, at least he had a sense of humour. Of course I paid.

Have you any inclination to the contrary, you would be well advised to stay out of Persian prisons. I need not describe them, but the old man was not in the worst of cells. In those, they take pains to breed insects and serpents to, shall we say, distract the prisoner from the fate that awaits him. Melchior's cell was merely wet and dark. It was also cold, which is probably a blessing in the summer, but was not so in those late autumn months almost a year since we had set out on our expedition. Fortunately, he had his shawl.

I venerated the old man. But I had spoken to Bilquis, and, clearly, this was no time for me to play the junior colleague. Whoever we are, we sometimes need direction. So before I entered his cell I resolved not to let him descend into that form of martyrdom that is sometimes confused with dignity by the well-born. After all, I am a foreigner, and the chief advantage of being a foreigner is that one is never obliged to fully adhere to local rules. You know this, of course, because you come from my homeland, and we have a certain practicality that people here sometimes lack.

"You have spoken to Bilquis?" the old man asked. He remained sitting and chose not to rise to embrace me, undoubtedly because of the chains. I said that I had spoken to no one else. He looked old and frail, but somehow, thankfully, less miserable than I might have otherwise assumed, given his age and the circumstances of our meeting.

"Then you understand that I will conduct my own defence?" he asked in the way that he, always the professor, often asked questions that required no answers. It confirmed what his niece had told me. He had purposefully chosen a doomed strategy, and I would not let him off that easily.

"I have read the philosophers," I replied, tight-lipped and perhaps too evenly. "Indeed I have read them in your own library. If you choose to die like Socrates, might it not be wiser to also select a country that will later venerate your bravery?" I was angry at his surrender and scarcely realised that I had insulted his forebears, however true the charge.

For a moment he stared at me with pale blue eyes. Then he erupted into laughter that disconcerted me even more. "Fair comment! Then whom shall we recruit as my defender?" he asked, eyes dancing.

His question stopped me cold, for I had not thought of a candidate, only that one should be selected. "I do not know," I admitted.

"Think," he said, "then speak." I was annoyed, although he meant nothing by it and had used the same phrase many times, when I was his student. Still, I thought and spoke in haste.

"It must be someone of obvious virtue," I said rapidly. "Given the tribunal, someone well-lettered, well-bred."

"A Parthian?" he asked.

I immediately knew the answer: "No, for they will seek to mollify their kinsmen and keep order above justice. Not a Parthian," I answered, as though I was his student once again.

"So an educated man, well-spoken," the old man prompted. He was being helpful.

"Indeed," I replied hastily, "an academic, of course, but preferably not a religious elder. Still, someone conversant in theology."

He did not hesitate. "Here, apart from a few Medes and not many others, the only well-bred men left are *Achaemenidae*. Our new rulers and their nomad mercenaries killed the rest or drove them away," he said. "We could take months to import a *Yehudi* rabbi or a Roman. But the *Yehud* do not understand our religious traditions. Neither do the Romans, who are, as well you know, our sworn enemies. Thus it must be an *Achaemenid*. There are perhaps forty of us left in the empire who are neither so old, ill, or inbred to be of help. Of the remainder, how many are landlords beholden to the Parthians and are thus owned by them? And how many are scholars? Of those who are scholars, how many are practitioners of the Temple Rites, which makes them potential enemies of the message, and how many are true scientists but who still have respectable religious credentials?"

I was quiet as I pondered his point. I finally answered: "I see what you mean." No one could better represent him than himself.

"I thought so," said Melchior, betraying a hint of triumph, but he reached across from his wooden bench and touched my arm. "I want my niece to expect the worst," he said, "to avoid unpleasant surprises and in so doing strengthen herself for what may well prove to be inevitable. Besides, the worst is often the most likely. But you are my friend," he continued, "and from my friends I expect strength." The old man had never so described me, at least to my knowledge. I averted my eyes and looked across the cell—silly, because there is little to look at in a prison.

"My end is virtually assured," he said. "We spoke of this, as we returned from the expedition. It was all foreseen, and I kept my part of the celestial bargain, did I not?" It was true; nonetheless I felt tears well up in my eyes.

"Caspar, even if things go badly," he continued, "is the truth silenced or have they silenced but one speaker of the truth? Did you learn not even this from my lessons?"

My shoulders started to heave, but, suddenly, I pulled myself up and looked him in the eyes. I nearly shouted: "And did you not tell us all, every damned one of us, to be fearless in defence of the truth? Then what are you saying? Can you not hear the admission of failure in your own words? Is it your age? Or is it pride? Or convenience? Do you think yourself too highborn to fight? Or are you merely too old and weak?"

The old man looked at me, blinking, but displaying little emotion. I continued: "Or have you learnt surrender? If so, when did you learn it? Not in your youth! How many Roman standards did you take then? How many eagles, nearly fifty summers past?"

He tilted his head quizzically, as he answered, as though he were surprised by the memory. He murmured: "Many we took on those plains of Carrhae." He paused in reverie, as if by magic his gaze had pierced the stone walls and revealed some portion of the old battle re-enacted before him. The gilt-bronze eagles, still on their regimental standards and prised from the hands of the greatest army on earth, had been the nation's foremost victory in many centuries.

"Of course, our foolish leaders gave the eagles back many years afterwards," he grumbled. But then he brightened: "But only after we sent their Senate the severed head and the right hand of Crassus. That earned the attention of Rome, oh, how it did!" His eyes danced, recalling how he and the other Persian youth had humiliated the invading army so many years before.

"And were you given then to surrender?" I blurted, but soon regained my composure.

Melchior hesitated not one moment. His blue eyes twinkled. "Perhaps I should have given you better marks as a student," he said, suppressing a smile. "You have learnt well. I may be lost, but before we mount a defence, I need to know if my friends have sufficient determination. I am now convinced. You have reassured me."

"I have things for you to do," he continued, "but you must realise the small chance of our victory. First I ask you to discourage my niece from holding unrealistic hopes." I nodded dumbly.

"Then you will not give up?" I asked hopefully.

"Not yet," he replied with a faint smile. His eyes widened and shone brightly, and, in almost a conspiratorial whisper, he added: "I may be an old horse, but with your help I hope to give these upstart rulers and their nomads one last ride that they might not soon forget." He was no longer a frail old man in prison, but again the one who had led the expedition and on whom I would once more hang so much hope.

That is what Caspar recalled that night in his study, and his dark brown eyes so sparkled, and his eyebrows so rose, and his timeworn hand so clutched my shoulder then, that I shall never forget it. I saw the old servant woman behind the curtain, bearing the tinned copper tray containing his simple evening meal. She had a kindly face, but shot me a stern glance, making it clear that I was soon to overstay my welcome. As she brought his food, she covered him gently against the evening chill in an old and threadbare brown shawl of fine Kashmiri wool. It had been, I suppose, bequeathed to him by his teacher, Melchior. I swiftly made arrangements with him for my next tutorial and then bade him farewell in our common tongue.

Chapter Two

THERE. TAKE SOME MORE BUTTERMILK. Now where was I? I had gone to see Melchior, had I not? Well, it was difficult seeing the old man in prison. It was not that I had known him so very long, but rather we had been together through so very much in the course of such a very short time. It was a slow-growing affection that I developed for the old man, and I did not fully realise its intensity until very late. Until almost too late, it seemed. But the expedition was another matter entirely.

Looking back, I suppose that I was initially inspired by the adventure of it all as much as by the scholarship. After all, few from our city of Nagarahara have ever ventured much further west than I had already, here in Persia, and wherever the star led us was, to me and to our people, *terra incognita*, as the Romans might say. Of course the interests of Melchior were purely inquisitive. Or so they seemed at first.

And as for Balthazar, who could ever know? What inspires a river or a cyclone or a cloudbank? Perhaps it was in his case destiny, for our *Yehudi* friends have a prophecy about a foreign king coming to pay tribute to the birth of their own king in a town outside of Jerusalem. Yes, I am quite certain of that, despite it being, as I said, so very long ago.

How I came close to the old man was a fairly straightforward matter. I was one of his students, of course, as almost everyone was. And I was not one of the better ones, judging by his comments at the time, but not too bad a one either, I suppose.

I had no intention of becoming an astronomer and never

became one. I studied it, because you simply cannot claim to be educated without a basic working knowledge of the subject. Indeed, had I wanted to be an astronomer, I would probably have studied somewhere many leagues to the south and east of our city, for there are very good schools of astronomy down in Hindustan, and the science is there much purer than in Baghdad to the west. Indeed I sometimes suspect that, wherever one goes, everything is purer than in Baghdad. Melchior used to talk at great length on what crimes the Babylonians perpetrated in the name of astronomy. For two coppers or a pound of cheese, he would say, a Babylonian could find anything in the heavens, and for a drachma the stars could spell the name of any man's wife whom you wished to bed. But no matter.

My mornings and early afternoons, in those days, were spent with Old Hooshmand. A terrible tyrant was Old Hooshmand, but a sound historian and in his time quite the best man in Persia on matters Egyptian. The Middle Kingdom in particular. But, dear me, what a martinet he was! Two young students, Medes I think, retaliated and cut off his beard while he slept. But he is long dead and warrants no calumny.

My late afternoons, then, were spent in Melchior's astronomy lessons, and oftentimes the practical observations stretched on long into the night. That is always the way with astronomy, of course. It is a bad subject, if you object to working after dark. But, on those many nights when we students were released early, I stayed on anyway, particularly after the old man pulled me aside and asked for my help. You can scarcely imagine how it flattered me.

He was somewhere around seventy-five years old even then, nearly the age that I am now. I had helped him roll up the astronomical charts and put them away after a lecture, when, while we were both alone, he asked if I might assist him with a report that he had to prepare for the temple elders. It was a matter of routine, of course, and he was not the only astronomer with such appointed tasks, for every few days the temple elders and soothsayers would call for star charts, so that they could cast their predictions and craft their policies. Now and then the old man would suggest, only to close confidants of course, that the elders were so incompetent in astronomy that they might better spend their time eviscerating chickens or examining their own stools. But that is neither here nor there.

I said that I was eager to assist him, but frankly wondered why he had not chosen a better student or at least one who aspired to be an astronomer.

"Because," he said rather bluntly, "for some strange reason I believe that I can trust you to keep your mouth shut." I was taken aback, until he explained, with some reluctance, that his powers of sight had begun to diminish and thus he could not see the stars as well as before. I was to be his spotter, then, leaving to him the more important tasks of recording the heavenly bodies on the charts and making enough interpretations, as he explained, to allow the temple elders to still get it all wrong.

So most nights found me on the roof of his tower with the old man beside me, his charts spread over his knees and a small, clay oil lamp on a bronze stand at his elbow. It was not as bad as you might imagine, with me gaping slack-jawed into the night sky or anything like it. I knew the major constellations and their appointed paths. The old man and I would refer to his charts and then I would check the various positions in the sky. Back and forth, like that, the work would soon enough be completed. If there were comets, and I was there to see them, it was simple enough to indicate their paths, and then he would sketch them onto the charts that he kept for such events.

I did not do it for any single reason. Surely I lacked enough silver to habituate the wine-shops with my classmates each night and, frankly, I tired of their prattle. But, no, it was not that entirely. Neither was it all flattery, for he was unconsciously parsimonious in his praise like many other aristocrats, and even then I was not an easy victim of flattery.

From the beginning I liked the company of the old man. I much preferred his conversation to the endless and tiresome student chatter of who was courting which barmaid and who had won money gaming and who was too drunk to sit exams. Of course I am certain that you never talk of such things with your student friends nowadays—it must be all Plato, Greek verse and Sarvastivadan ethics. No talk of women or anything like that, eh? You can stop shuffling your feet, for I was once a student too.

Most of our time together then was spent on the rooftop working. But, when we had finished and he had descended to the upper room, where the light was better, we had time to talk, while he would commit to vellum the night's observations. And I returned night after night. I would help him grind and then mix the sticks of dried ink, if need be, and then watch across the low table, as he peered at his notes and, always with the cheapest of brushes, limned the information in his rather antique calligraphic hand.

It doubtless made me a better historian, although it was not a consideration then. From Melchior, I, a foreigner, learnt the workings of the Iranian state better than any ambassador ever could and I gained a perspective that is now all but lost to the living. For he was an *Achaemenid*, you see, at least on his mother's side. He was both *Achaemenid* and some Greek, because Alexander's people intermarried. His father was a Magian, not only a priest but also of the original tribe of priests. Once, you know, that tribe monopolised the priesthood, but that is long since no more.

He took great pride in being an *Achaemenid*, of course. But it was not that he saw himself primarily as a Graeco-Persian aristocrat, but rather that he felt himself part of a great tradition that was clearly dying. So much so that as a young man he went about clean-shaven in the old Hellenic style. It was only when he was ordained that he grew his beard at the insistence of his father.

When Melchior was young, the present dynasty of upstart kings and the nomadic savages who enforce their wishes was fewer than nine decades old, and many of the ancient ways survived: more so, certainly, than they do now. They must have been grand days, when the legacy of the *Unani* coursed strong. There was still Greek theatre, when he was a boy, and provincial games not limited to the two nomadic so-called arts of riding and archery. There were public debates and instruction in rhetoric. There were saints and seers who lived in caves and who conversed with the gods, and in those days the gods of Greece ruled happily and easily alongside the one god of Persia. The Parthians had not waged war on Persia's Hellenic culture, as they seem so determined to do now.

They were "times of honest inquiry and honest faith," he so many times remarked. He insisted that the twin traditions of the empire resembled a good marriage in terms of how they complemented one another. The Persian religion, with its ironclad sense of personal responsibility, fitted perfectly with the Greek respect for rigorous thought. Alas, it was not to remain so, and our parvenu leaders brought with them their less enlightened ways. He found it an amusing paradox, he used to say, that from such open spaces came such closed minds.

He bore it well, the decline of the old ways, and I initially thought it because the surviving *Achaemenidae* had little left but their dignity and thus embraced it all the more. That was true, of course. But the old man was an optimist. "Empires come and go," he used to say. "Our enemy's empire is cruel and has not long to live, and our empire, too, is increasingly cruel and thus may not outlast our enemies. But nothing is lost, as long as there are teachers, and beside them students who themselves become teachers in turn." I am still not certain that he was right, but, as I grow older, I more and more wish it were so.

Thus, curiously, as his spotter I was granted an honour that I did not deserve. I suppose that, in a purely technical sense, I was the first to see the Sign.

Many assume that it was the old man, and, of course, I never contradicted them, because he was somewhat vain about his eye-sight. But in reality I saw it first and then told him. In principle that should give me the first and full credit for the discovery, except that it made no great impression on me at all. I did not know enough. Observation is pointless without education; show a miracle to a mule and it will only try to eat it. Whatever I saw was meaningless without my teacher's knowledge. In reality, then, I beheld the Sign, but the old man truly saw it first.

It was in the month of November. Either that or quite late in October, for it was very long ago. We were watching some activity in the constellation Leo that the old man thought worthy of interest. As you ought to know, if you keep up with your astronomy lessons, Leo is the constellation of kings. Within this, Jupiter, the planet of righteousness, drew closer and closer to conjunction with Regulus, the star of kingship.

The old man explained carefully that the star of kingship, within the greater constellation of kingship, was about to join the planet of righteousness. Moreover, and only a month before, Jupiter had converged with Venus, the Mother planet, again in Leo. And indeed earlier that summer Jupiter and Venus had drawn so close together that they appeared to become a single planet. To me this was mere movement, but to the learned it meant more.

Suddenly the Heavenly Bodies were all there above us, performing a court dance beyond my comprehension: indications of earth and righteousness and kingship all intertwined within the celestial royal palace. The old man thought it most propitious.

"I am not certain what is happening up there," he said, "but the portent is considerable. Indeed," he added dryly, "once they see our reports, the temple elders will probably decide to give the emperor a bath."

So we continued working by night, the old man and I, and Bilquis would come quietly up the steps and pass a tray of food silently through the hatch so as not to disturb our work.

It was on that singular night, and of this I am quite certain, that I described the positions of Jupiter and Regulus, pointing to their respective places on the stellar map. It was a warm night and still. Far in the distance we could hear a donkey braying, but otherwise all was silent apart from the cicadas performing one of their last concerts.

"There and there," I said, pointing to the map and describing the whereabouts of the star and the planet, "in a sort of a triangle with that small star above and just underneath the star below." For that was the way in which we worked. But the old man looked up at me in confusion.

"Again?" he asked, bending down to scrutinise his charts.

I pointed once more to where Jupiter and Regulus could be found. "See the star at the bottom?" I replied. "They are about the breadth of your hand up from that and maybe a finger's width below the star above them."

"Where?" he demanded.

"Just up from that one," I sighed, squinting at the map, for his oil lamp was not very bright, "then below, well, you do not have it so put one in here." I marked the place with my finger.

"There?" he asked. I said yes. He looked into the skies and strained, but most of the stars were too faint for his old eyes. "Follow me," he declared abruptly, standing and gathering up the hem of his cloak and clambering swiftly but stiffly down the steps from the roof to the top room. I followed him down, and he pulled half a dozen scrolls from their shelves and opened them on his low table, one atop another.

"Here? The upper star! Is it here?" he demanded pointing to Leo. I looked and shook my head. There the map was blank. He flung it into the corner and pointed to the next one, covering a smaller area but in greater detail. "And here?" he asked. "Or here? Or here?" He continued until the charts lay all in a heap in the corner. I looked at him in confusion.

He returned a stare that was both puzzled and transfixed, as though he beheld an apparition instead of his assistant. Finally he spoke: "The stars, dear boy, do not sprout up like cabbages. Even small stars. Let us try this again."

And once more he collected the charts, and we studied them in the top room and later on the roof, until he was convinced that the heavens had indeed revealed something utterly new. Its position and date was duly marked on every chart, and it was nearly dawn when we concluded. It was a new star, recorded for the first time.

He asked if I had seen the small new star on the previous night, and I said no; at least I had no recollection of ever having seen it before. "Despite your uncertain memory, I am very grateful," he said. "A man could live one hundred lifetimes and never behold a new star, much less a new star so bright and in so propitious a spot. Of course I would have missed it without you." I felt proud.

A faint eastern glow signalled the coming sunrise, and some miles away a cock crowed. Elsewhere a dog barked, for some farmer had likely risen early to milk his cows. These were small, distant noises that paradoxically made the dawn seem all the more silent, and the two of us watched the stars dissolve into daylight. By then I had the feeling that something momentous had occurred.

He rose and yawned, stretching his stiff joints. Then he chuckled and said: "With your attention to detail, it is good that you chose to specialise in history. It is a safe career for the slipshod. Historical figures, being conveniently dead, never complain about sloppy methodology." He laughed and clapped me on the shoulder, bade me goodnight, and then retired to his rooms. I went home to bed.

I came early on the next night, and we sat on the roof, nervously eating pomegranates and spitting the seeds into the garden below, waiting for dark and far too excited to speak. Of course the new star came again. And over three nights it became quite clear, even to me, that the star was moving further and further, night by night, pulling our attention along behind it, moving straight into conjunction with Jupiter and Regulus within the House of Leo. It appeared to have been born for a purpose. Oh, and the sun was in Virgo, the importance of which will later become obvious, and it was moving with Saturn, which is the planet of the *Yehud*, the Jews.

After making our observations over each of those first few nights, the old man dashed like a schoolboy down the steps to mark up his maps. I took to going down ahead of him for fear that he would fall in his haste. Frequently, as stars threatened to collide overhead, we came close to having our own collision there on the roof, as we scrambled through the hatch.

Once the most recent position of the new star had been recorded on the celestial charts, usually at the cost of copious ink stains, the old man would attempt in vain to wipe clean his hands before unrolling the terrestrial maps of the world over which the small new star shone.

"Dead west, or close enough to it," he said, setting down the callipers. "Somewhere between here and Araby or, who knows, further still. My guess is Judea. But it may yet move in another direction. New stars may make up their own rules, for all we know." He poured us each a cup of buttermilk and fresh herbs from the red earthenware pitcher and slumped back in his chair, for once again it was nearly dawn.

Needless to say, I was skilled neither in the arts of divination nor in the sciences of observation, but I was young and energetic and impatient then and doubtless pestered him with my questions. What could be foretold, I demanded. A movement of a great empire? The birth of a monarch? A change in the fortunes of man or merely a change in the weather? I was desperate to know what I had helped to discover.

"There is no doubt but that it heralds something important," the old man said at length, "but what I cannot yet say." He took another sip of buttermilk, then shot me a sideways glance, an odd one. "I do know one thing," he added, smiling, "and it chills me to the very marrow. Indeed, the thought is so potentially grim that I wonder if I dare tell someone of your relative youth and inexperience. The horror may indeed prove too great." His eyes opened wide like those of an owl, and I trembled.

I begged him to share the secret, swearing that I was sufficiently resilient to cope with anything.

"Very well," he said at length, hauling himself stiffly off his cushion and smoothing down the front of his ink-stained robe. "Because of this astounding event, I am forced to take the horrifying step of visiting Bahram, the High Priest, a dim and dismal creature to be avoided at all costs. And because you first saw the star," he added feigning malice, "you must come with me." I grinned, for although I had never seen the High Priest, I had heard much from the old man. Meeting such an official would be a rare opportunity.

"But that must wait until tomorrow. Can you stop by after breakfast," he asked, "then we can walk there together?" I readily agreed. Before I went home to bed, I stopped at the house of Hassan the copyist, woke him, and asked that he hurriedly prepare clean versions of our charts for our audience with the High Priest. I could hear his wife complaining upstairs, but Melchior had brought much custom to him and to his father before him, so the artisan readily obliged us and went clumsily about the darkened house lighting his lamps, having promised to work through the few remaining hours of night and into the morning.

On the next morning, the old man and I walked together to the Great Temple, down through the bazaar, and under my arm I carried his precious charts neatly rolled and tied with green ribbands. The world seemed a different and magical place that morning, but for the life of me I could not understand why everyone else went about his business as normal. I felt as though the town should have changed colours, or businessmen should have begun giving away their wares for free, or perhaps everyone ought to have broken into song, for something strange and new had come, born unexpected over these few nights. Instead they merely peered and poked and haggled, bought and sold, jostled, joked or complained according to their natures, blithely unaware of the great, mysterious secret that I shared with the old man.

"What do we tell the High Priest?" I asked him, as we walked. He swung his stick as though he did not need one, striding like a youth. He wore his finest robe, a pale blue one with silver thread embroidered on the collar, with the nap of the velvet artfully trimmed into tiny squares throughout. Moreover, he was in a rare mood.

"First and foremost," he said, "we need to inform him of the new star. He is, after all, the High Priest, and duty requires it. Next, and only if he asks, I will suggest some plausible interpretations. Last, if there is any possibility at all, we will seek permission to...*investigate*." He put particular emphasis on the last word, raised his eyebrows, and gave a knowing smile, as though we were schoolboys and the investigation was some great adventure of which we must not tell our parents.

"What sort of investigation?" I asked, but he winked at me and laid a long bony finger aside his nose, denoting a secret.

Although it was early, there was already a substantial crowd in the temple courtyard outside of the Palace of Elders. Many were afflicted, proffering bandaged limbs or waving sticks in hope of alms, but others had any number of requests pertaining to rites or to ordination, or to decrees or to annulments, seeking for their sons appointments to a seminary or to any number of religious sinecures. The old man moved through the throng, until he reached the limestone steps on which stood four temple police in leather armour, intentionally blocking the door. Their presence was relatively new, as was their armour. It had been no more than a few months since they had arrived and set themselves before the great door, jostling and searching, pushing and insulting virtually anyone who dared try to enter. Many legitimate visitors stayed away. And some said that the guards, who were normally satisfied brandishing their authority, now increasingly demanded bribes as well.

The captain, a burly man with a large facial scar, looked the old man up and down with quiet insolence. "And what about you, then?" he demanded. He had imperial markings on his sleeves to show that the local constabulary had no authority over him.

Melchior smiled and, with a small wave of his hand, completed a courtly bow that had apparently not been seen in a provincial capital for a generation or more. The captain stared.

Then the old man thrice thumped his staff on the pavement and declared in a booming voice: "I am the Lord Melchior of the House of Demetrius; Professor of Astronomy; Advisor Plenipotentiary to his Excellency the Satrap; and Astronomer Royal, Second Class, to his Exalted Highness, the Emperor Phraates the Fourth. And who," he asked, shifting to dulcet tones with a polite nod of his head, "might I have the honour of addressing?" He spoke in the very loftiest Persian.

The three guards stared, first at the old man and then at their captain, who himself stood transfixed. Melchior might just as well have driven down from the clouds in a gilded chariot.

"Very well," Melchior announced dryly. "I see that I shall have to present my particulars. We must be so very full of distinguished visitors at the palace today. Lord Caspar of Nagarahara," he instructed me, and I nearly choked on hearing of my promotion, "please produce our documents and show them to our martial friend here." I began to unroll the maps, but by then the Parthian captain realised that, by being troublesome, he had much to risk but little to gain, whoever we visitors might be. He stepped aside, grunted, and waved us through. Melchior thanked him graciously.

"I hope that you do not mind being temporarily ennobled," he said to me, "but I have been eager to try this, and today there is a new captain of the guard," the old man confessed, as we entered the building and climbed the stairs. He smiled a guilty smile: "I am not particularly proud of it, but otherwise the permissions take up half the day. Mind you, it always helps to threaten them with the charts, because none of them can read, poor fellows, and they are too proud to let their underlings know it."

We turned left at the top of the stairs, for the old man knew the way, and we reached the great double doors that led to the offices of the High Priest. The handles and hinges were cast of heavy bronze, and the woodwork was deeply carved with peacocks. A middle-aged merchant sat on a long bench waiting and sweating under his most formal velvet robes, and we took our places alongside him. It was dark and still in the hallway, and no one spoke.

At length a gangly and spotty young man, dressed all in black, emerged through the doors, tapped the merchant on the shoulder and led him inside, closing the doors silently behind them. Within moments, however, the same young man re-emerged and approached us. His footfalls were so quiet, that he might well have worn cloth soles on his court slippers. He seemed a twitchy fellow, probably the secretary to the High Priest, and he fidgeted with his hands as he spoke. But his eyes, colder than the dark hall, betrayed no nervousness.

"Your name, my lord?" he asked Melchior, stooping slightly.

"The same as it was last time, young Keshvari. And the time before," Melchior replied brusquely. He sighed, but then forced a half smile. "Lord Melchior, the astronomer," he added unnecessarily.

"But His Excellency does not expect you," said the secretary in a pretentious whisper.

"It is a matter of some urgency," the old man answered in normal tones. "His Excellency will understand." The young man sniffed disparagingly, then once more slipped behind the heavy doors. Like so many secretaries to powerful men, Keshvari made the most of his power as door-keeper.

"Who?" I began to ask in a hushed voice, but the old man put a finger to his lips to silence me and then made a circular motion suggesting that someone might be listening nearby.

Within moments, the merchant was hustled out through the double doors, and Keshvari beckoned, inviting us inside. I had expected to see an ordinary office, perhaps a grand one befitting a High Priest, but I was not prepared for what we found.

It was, as well you might expect, a sumptuously appointed room although much too dark and close, indeed stultifying, since all the curtains were drawn. The walls displayed long looking-glasses of the most expensive sort, but they had begun to deteriorate, and patches of silvery decay blotted parts of the reflections. The two central pillars, as well as the ceiling, were hung in stiff painted leather, elaborately worked in the manner of manuscripts with interwoven vines and flowers and acanthus leaves. The floors were strewn with fine carpets several layers deep, many of them silk. But the cushions and low tables were unused and dusty and mostly stacked in a corner, while in the centre of the room stood an enormous canopied bed hung with musty, wine-red, velvet brocade curtains, and all of the dark woodwork of the four posts and the headboard and footboard was deeply carved with monsters lurking in thickly interwoven vines. Inside the bed, beneath what appeared to be a vast weight of blankets, lay a small shrivelled man.

"Closer," croaked the figure in the bed, beckoning faintly with a pallid and emaciated hand. We approached him with the secretary close behind us, still fidgeting. I began to notice a dreadful stench emanating from beneath the bedclothes and I tried to draw breaths as shallow as possible. But Melchior rather cavalierly tossed his cap and his stick onto the very foot of the High Priest's bed and, sweeping back his cloak, knelt on the floor and clasped his hands at the bedside.

"God's blessing, Excellency," said Melchior, and the High Priest stretched out his hand, until it rested on the crown of the old man's head.

"God's blessing, Melchior," gasped the High Priest.

Melchior rose to his feet, brushing the dust from the knees of his trousers. "And so how is it today, Bahram?" he asked. "Are you getting any better, or are the palace quacks still making it worse?" Scandalised, the secretary averted his eyes, but the High Priest took no notice.

"The latter, as you suggest," the High Priest replied. "My disease and my doctors are in a race to finish me off, and I know not who will win. However, it will not be me; that I can assure you. Why have you come?"

"Duty," said Melchior, "otherwise I would not have disturbed you. Frankly you ought to sleep and let young Keshvari and the leech-handlers deal with your supplicants." He strode to the window, jerked wide a pair of curtains and threw open a window. Melchior sneezed in the billowing cloud of dust he had caused. "Fresh air and sunshine will do more than any doctor," he said brusquely, and a shaft of light cut through the gloom, illuminating the dying man and revealing a thousand golden motes of dust that whirled like tiny planets. The secretary stared in mute horror, but the High Priest smiled faintly.

Melchior returned to the bedside. "Oh, and this is my colleague and former student, Caspar," he said, and I blushed. "Maps please," he added, extending his arm. I passed them across.

He untied the green ribbands and spread the charts across the bed, almost under the chin of the High Priest. "I will spare you the lengthy description and go straight to the facts," Melchior explained. He pointed: "See here... and here. All in Leo, you will notice. And keep an eye on Saturn."

The High Priest pulled himself up in his bed, and the secretary rushed around Melchior to pack pillows behind the invalid. The High Priest stared hard at the vellum sheets, wheezing softly. "What does it mean?" he asked at length. Melchior shot me a knowing glance before trying to explain as diplomatically as possible.

"The planet of righteousness, Jupiter, suddenly moves into

conjunction with the star of kingship, Regulus, and all within the greater house of kingship, Leo, but beside Saturn indicating the Jews. That much Your Excellency already knows, of course," he said diplomatically. "Then, three nights ago, from out of nowhere comes a completely new star, born for the occasion, as it were, joining in conjunction with both Regulus and Jupiter. That, of course, you can read from the map." The High Priest nodded unconvincingly.

Melchior waited for a comment, as long as he dared. Finally he drew a deep breath and continued. "We are most honoured that you ask for our interpretation. Obviously your own will be shrewder. But it looks to my colleague and me as though something of immense importance has either happened or is soon about to happen. I am guessing here, but it might be as vast as a kingdom or even greater. Perhaps an empire. Who is to know without a little," and here he paused, "*investigation*." Once more he put added emphasis on the last word, and, while the High Priest studied the map, and the secretary studied the High Priest, Melchior gave me a surreptitious wink.

"An omen of importance, eh?" wheezed the High Priest. "Of the utmost importance would you say?"

"I would," answered Melchior. The High Priest was silent for a long while, and his eyes slowly closed, until they had shut completely. I wondered if he had fallen asleep, and half almost expected him to snore. But suddenly one eye jerked open wide, and he pulled himself up higher in his bed.

"Might there be a mistake?" he asked. Melchior shook his head no. "Too bad," said the High Priest. "Others will see this star. As powerful as we are, we cannot hide the Heavens. People will think that it heralds the birth of Mithras. And this is a decidedly inopportune time for his arrival. Not that I think he is coming any time soon, mind you."

Melchior's brow furrowed. "Why? Many of our countrymen might welcome a heavenly saviour," he replied, damping his irony as much as he could. The secretary watched him as a mongoose eyes a snake.

From somewhere off behind the drapery that enshrouded the bed, an old crone shuffled into the room, bearing a cheap pottery plate containing a piece of horsemeat about the size of one's hand. The meat appeared to be fresh, and the dish was so full of blood that some slipped over the edge and spilt onto the carpets. She pressed towards me, and I stepped back, until I saw the large glass jar on a small table near my elbow. It was full of leeches, kept convenient for the palace physicians. She lifted the glass lid and dropped the horsemeat in with a plop, smearing dry her bloody fingers on her homespun woollen gown. The water grew pink, as, frenzied, the blind worms attached themselves to the dead flesh and began to suck out the blood, their tails writhing, as their black bodies fattened.

The High Priest gave a long rasping cough, wiped his pale lips and propped himself on one elbow. "This is not easy to say, and I demand confidentiality," he began, "but the emperor has fallen ill. Perhaps dangerously ill. He is, in fact, in a coma."

Melchior interrupted him: "Poison, no doubt, and the courtiers suspect his wife, of course." Keshvari's eyes bulged. "And, if she is successful, it would put her son Phraataces on the throne rather than the rightful heir. Thus far it is obvious."

"How... how..." gasped the High Priest.

"I do not live under a shrub, Bahram," Melchior said brusquely, as he paced beside the bed. "When a healthy man falls into an unexplainable coma, especially when he is an emperor, the astute suspect poison. Moreover, the Empress Musa has reason aplenty to want her son on the throne rather than the young heirs, whom she so conveniently packed off to Rome seven years ago as hostages of her countryman, the Emperor Augustus."

"Guests, my lord! Guests of Augustus and not his hostages!" the secretary objected. Melchior looked at him dismissively, as if he were a barking dog.

"She was an Italian concubine given by the Roman dictator as a plaything," he lectured, as though back in the classroom. "She bore our own emperor his third son, whom she keeps beside her in the palace, tied to her apron strings. The lad is, not to put too fine a point on it, a great sissy. The two older boys, the heirs, she packed off to Rome, the land of her fathers and our enemies. If anything happens to the princes and to her dear husband in a poisoned coma, then her son becomes emperor. It sounds straightforward enough to me."

"The older boys are the guests of Rome," Keshvari insisted.

"Very well, they may be guests," snapped Melchior, "but, were I such a guest, I would want someone to taste my food beforehand, and I would ask you to do it." The secretary's hand began to tremble, but he otherwise betrayed no emotion.

"Enough!" cried the High Priest in a thin voice. "I hope that the rest of the empire is slower to make the connection." He coughed for almost a minute, then, for a similar period, he rested to regain his strength. "As you must know," he continued, "a new star is meant to herald the birth of Mithras, who is supposed to arrive when empires crumble, when families turn against one another, when wars are rife and leaders weak."

"His timing sounds perfect," Melchior observed, as the secretary glared.

"Too perfect," admitted the High Priest. "None of these problems are, given present circumstances, appropriate topics for public discussion. Certainly not now."

Melchior answered quickly. "It will strengthen the hand of the insurgents in Khorasan and threaten the state," he continued, "unless the star signifies something else altogether. The matter needs research. We have little experience in observing new stars."

"And what else might it signify, then?" demanded the High Priest. "I have little time, and the emperor has less. What can be learnt now?"

"In the West lie the Roman tyrants and their empire, Bahram.

What looks to be a prophecy intended for us may be meant for them or even someone else. We need research." The High Priest thought for a while and, as he did, he seemed to sink lower beneath his blankets. He said nothing, for he was not a man who had come to power by taking risks. Melchior smiled: "Unless you want us to ask the court sooth-sayers. They could cut up some chickens and make a diagnosis."

The secretary interrupted. "Lord Melchior, you realise that anything to do with Rome falls outside of the temple and under a separate jurisdiction. This is not a matter of doctrine, but rather one of national security. You know that, and as a priest yourself you ought to show more propriety and respect."

Melchior spun on his heels. "More respect?" he demanded. "For the state security services?" He turned back to the High Priest: "Everything in this empire seems to be run by the secret police these days. Are they now responsible for the coming of Mithras? How about keeping the sacred flame? Bahram, without exception, the most brainless students I ever met, the slack-jawed, the mouth-breathers, all became police of one kind or another. I would not have thought that, unassisted, the state security services could fry an egg."

The High Priest waved a hand weakly over his bed covers. "Melchior! Melchior!" he said. "Leave it to me. I will seek permission. Leave it in my hands."

Flashing a smile at me, Melchior dropped to one knee, and again the High Priest lay a hand on my teacher's head. "God's blessing, Melchior," wheezed the old man.

"Long life to Your Excellency," replied Melchior. Then he grabbed his cap and backed away from the bed. "And kick a few doctors and bureaucrats down the stairs, Bahram. It will make you feel much younger." The High Priest chortled, until he was again racked by coughing.

As we withdrew, I watched the thin-lipped secretary studying Melchior, and his eyes neither blinked nor revealed the slightest trace of emotion.

Chapter Three

IT IS AN HISTORICAL POINT that you would be wise not to ignore. East of here and almost a century ago, the Kushans swept down into Hindustan from Cathay, you know, not because they were victorious warlords laying waste to all before them, but because they themselves had been beaten badly by the Huns and cast out from their own vast pastures. Behind each invading army, it seems, lurks a larger and more hostile force pushing them forward.

Far to the southeast, the flatland historians of Hindustan are, then, rather like half-blind men watching children play with marbles: they see movement a few inches from their noses, but have no idea of the forces at work beyond their view, not even an inkling of the far-off larger marbles careering into the smaller ones, which in turn strike and drive closer the ones smaller still. Thus the Huns propelled the Kushans, and what moved the Huns, alas, we know not. I have always suspected the imperial armies of Cathay.

Of course, I did not know that principle then, for, in much the same manner, Melchior and I were moved by forces so immense that, even now, I cannot fully comprehend them. Not that it would have mattered, I suppose. Given a second chance, the old man and I, we would doubtless have done the same all over again. The opportunities were too vast and our curiosity too intense.

And so, where was I? It was after our return from the expedition and after his arrest. At the cost of a few pieces of silver, I paid several visits to the old man in his cell. Did I tell you that before? Of course I did. Do help yourself to the buttermilk and the oranges.

I left the gaol where I had seen Melchior, and I blinked under the bright morning sun. There was one thing I wanted to do more than any other, and that was to find Balthazar, which was of course impossible. My need for him was not political. Of course Balthazar knew less about the workings of the temple court than an eagle knows of baking cakes. From a distant African kingdom on the Erythraean Sea, he was much more foreign here than ever was I.

But Balthazar was a warrior king, as big as a door and stronger than a wall, a great, black, merry warrior king, as happy in a battle as in a wine shop. Indeed, he was as capable of drinking in battle as battling in a tavern, and I have been with him in both. Wherever he went, he left behind him a great wake of enthusiasm. He made anyone who was fortunate enough to meet him feel as mighty as a god and maybe as reckless. That gift was precisely what I needed more than anything else.

Besides, the old man loved him like a son, you see. And what an unlikely pair they made: a joyful giant full of drink and war and poetry, and an aristocratic don, pale and frail, but with much quiet insight. A young Dionysus and an old Apollo, together they combined the best attributes of man, and each instinctively knew the greatness of the other.

Upon our return from the journey, we parted on the road, we did. So Balthazar had gone far beyond my reach in those dark days. And it was not until only eight or ten years ago that I received word from him. It took about three years for his letter to arrive and perhaps five successive caravans to deliver it. I still have it somewhere, just as it came, in its own fitted case of red Morocco leather, written on creamy, thick vellum illuminated with all the colours of a summer's day. It looks like a letter from paradise. He said that he had given up trying and had thus assigned the Grand Vizier to count his great-grandchildren, bless him. But that is another matter.

I returned to the tower that morning, after I had first seen the old man in gaol. I needed to conduct some delicate business, but then was not the time to exclude Bilquis, lest she felt even more neglected. I recounted my conversation with the old man to her, we spoke of strategies, and Bilquis confirmed my own suspicion that, since Bahram had died, speaking to his replacement, Keshvari, would be a mistake.

Keshvari was only the acting High Priest. After Bahram had died, the elders could not agree on a successor, and so Keshvari's appointment was temporary. He was a clever man and ambitious and definitely not to be trusted. Melchior and I had seen that side of him before, when we visited Bahram in his chamber. Now in a position of temporary power, Keshvari doubtless thought that securing Melchior's execution, especially with himself as prosecutor, would increase his advantage as an incumbent over the other aspirants to the High Priesthood. The state was already beginning to stir up hatred against foreigners and against the Old Ones, the Hellenes, such as my teacher. So, more than wasting our time, talking to Keshvari would have been reckless or even dangerous.

But we went to the Great Temple nonetheless, because Bilquis knew that there we could find Qazi Kamran. The temple grounds were unusually crowded that day, with vast numbers of people all dressed in white. From the look of it, some large family had arrived for one *Zardasht* ceremony or another. The bazaar-wallahs, the vendors, must have been alerted for there were more of them than usual, hawking strings of jasmine blossoms, vials of rose-water and saffron for the rice, bowls of almonds and pine-nuts, apricot kernels and fat green raisins.

We made our way through the crowd, and Bilquis was correct. One of the vendors of sacred strings and amulets, clustered tight outside the great iron-shod door, said that Qazi Kamran was indeed inside. Even were there room to spare inside the temple, I could not have entered, of course, because I am not *Zardasht*; not born into the religion, for such is the tradition and such is the law. But Bilquis was, and was quite devout as well. So, despite some difficulty owing to the throng, she slipped inside to pray and to wait. That was important, because there are several exits from the Great Temple, and, if Kamran chose to leave by another route, we might have missed him, and meeting him later would have presented a problem. He was not merely an ordinary *qazi*, but rather the Chief Justice and a priest as well, thus not an easy man to meet on short notice.

I could hear the ceremony quite clearly through the *jali*, the pierced and carved marble screen. A child was being bound with the *kushti*, the sacred thread, and I could hear the voice of Kamran reverberate through the temple in a deep and sonorous baritone. The seventy-two threads stand for the seventy-two books of the *Yasna*, he intoned. The twelve threads in each strand symbolise the months of the year, the six tassels the great festivals, the hollow inside the thread the space between this world and the next, and so on.

The temple was lit by small hanging lamps, but chiefly by the great fire sacred to *Ahura Mazda,* the creator and One True God. Non-believers are forbidden to see the flames, of course, but through the screen I watched the reflected firelight flicker and dance up the dark walls inside. Given the atmosphere, and given that Kamran sounded pretty much like God anyway, the child doubtless stood paralysed by the great solemnity of it all. But his or her parents and grandparents surely stood alongside, reassuring and beaming with pride, as people do.

Once bound by the thread, the child becomes an adult, say the *Zardasht*, and henceforth its each and every moral choice is but another single vote in the long, long election determining whether the universe and its successors will be ruled by good or by evil. Every human action, whether premeditated or spontaneous, is a vote for God or a vote for the devil that can never be rescinded. So a light string becomes a heavy moral burden.

Finally, it ended. From where I stood outside, the crowd thickened and the celebrants emerged from the temple, as, from the fringes, some threw jasmine blossoms presumably onto the child somewhere in the midst of the throng. Then they began to move up one of the narrow side-streets to do what all good *Zardasht* do at such times, namely, spend the next two days eating and laughing and playing with their children.

Finally Bilquis emerged with the *qazi*, still in his white clothes, but he had shed his gloves. I had seen him before, of course, but assumed that he would not know me. However, he did and, as I bowed to kiss his hands, he pulled me into an embrace, as though I were an equal. He led us up an alley alongside and through a small iron gate into the temple gardens. He knew why we had come and knew that his own offices or, worse, a local wineshop would be much too public for what we had come to discuss.

Kamran was a man of about sixty, more than a decade younger than Melchior, and I wondered if he had been one of the old man's students. I fervently hoped so, for it was a near certainty that he would sit on the tribunal and pass judgement.

He was a small man with a very shiny, bald head, hooded eyes, and delicate hands, like those of a child's doll, with which he gesticulated constantly. He bade us to sit under a beautiful old *chinar* tree, then fussed, realising that he was still dressed in liturgical white. He did not know whether to sit and dirty his clothes or stand and look officious. He dithered, until Bilquis spread her shawl on the grass, then he gratefully plopped himself down like a large frog, smiled, then said nothing and did nothing apart from blink a great deal. He seemed friendly enough, but it was disconcerting.

Bilquis and I waited for each other to speak, but finally I took a deep breath and began. "*Qazi-sahib, Ustad-sahib, khal-e-shoma khubast*," I started in my most formal manner. He raised a hand to halt me.

"*Ustad* Melchior is well-known to me. His father and my grandfather were classmates," interrupted the judge. "His family is above reproach. He has been one of the empire's finest astronomers and he fought well at Carrhae. He is loved by his students and respected by his peers. Indeed, had this not happened, he might well have been sent to the capital for special honours. But, alas, it is not to be. Even as little as three weeks ago, I warned him, but he would not listen."

"*Qazi-sahib*," I began hesitantly, "what he saw, what we each saw, and what he said..." But he raised his hand again, interrupting.

"Caspar-*jan*," he interjected using the term of affection, "Melchior is a priest, even as I am a priest. He has drunk the sacred *Haoma* and prepared it with his own hands. And he is no ordinary priest. His first fire, they say, was kindled from the Farnbhag flame in Kabul. He is a magus of the finest lineage and order."

"Cannot a priest speak his mind?" I asked. Kamran ignored my question.

"Were he simply another old man," he continued, "I would throw the charges into the river and be done with them. I would declare him senile, award him a state pension for services to education, and pack him off to some nice tower, where he could gaze heavenwards and babble to his heart's content. But I cannot. He is too big to let slip through a loophole, and, believe me, I know every one. And he has helped me not one bit."

"What law, religious or secular," I began, evenly as I do when I first grow angry, "makes it a crime to describe what one has seen?"

"Forgive me, Caspar-*jan*," he answered dismissing me, "but you are an honoured guest in these lands. It is a technical matter, and you are not *Zardasht*, you are neither born a follower of the Prophet Zarathustra nor a reader of the *Avesta*."

"But I know your ways and respect them," I continued. *"Ahura Mazda*, the One God, is the Embodiment of Truth. Just as *Angra Mainyu* is the Marshal of Daemons, the Polluter, and the Father of Lies. Then in whose service does one speak the truth? Obviously that of God." My charge was uananswerable, but Bilquis interrupted, and Qazi Kamran looked surprised.

"Each morning, *Ustad-jan*, when I go to the local temple and approach the sacred fire," she murmured. "I put ash on my forehead and pray that, like the flame, 'I lead the light of righteousness and knowledge before others.' Have I learnt the words properly?"

The judge looked down and rubbed his eyes. "Yes, sister," he said, "as you know perfectly well, you have learnt the prayer correctly."

"Then has not my uncle done," she asked, "what every day we pray to do?"

The judge sighed deeply and then asked: "What is to be done, my friends, when the truth contradicts the truth? The holy books are true. Melchior swore to that, when in his sacred initiation he stood beneath the *dar-i-Mithr*, the portico of Mithras. Does he now say that the self-same truth is false?"

"Of course not," answered Bilquis indignantly.

"And yet he claims to have seen another truth. A different and conflicting truth," the judge explained. "The birth of Mithras will be heralded by a star. And we know that he will be of a virgin born. But on a mountaintop, not in some cheap hostelry in a far-off, western *Yehudi* village. And in a cave rather than in some... some device for feeding livestock. At no time does Melchior even begin to mention the dogs or the snake of prophecy, just sheep and shepherds or something. It is all very exasperating, as well you can imagine."

I simply shook my head. I am not of the faith, so not all of the detail made sense. Along the expedition, we had espied several dogs, I am fairly certain, but I cannot recall seeing more than a single snake during the entire journey, and it looked far from sacred to me. I think that a camel had trodden upon it. So I thought it best to keep quiet.

The judge sighed once more, but his hands kept making circles and arabesques in the air. "So what is there to do?" he asked. "Even now he could apologise and say that he was mistaken. Heat stroke or something. Within a moment, I would summon our weasel of an acting High Priest and send him scurrying back to the sanctuary, where he could cause little harm. But," he sighed a third time, "I think it highly unlikely. Melchior is an *Achaemenid* of the old school, and, for all their deeper sort of wisdom, they never managed to move with the times."

"Do you mean lie?" I started to ask, but Bilquis jabbed me in the ribs before I could finish.

"*Ustad-jan*, my uncle believes what he saw," she whispered fervently. I had never before thought it possible to mix strategy and sincerity, but she did.

Yet the judge turned not to her, but to me. "If he has lied, then it is a crime. And lying about great matters is a great crime." I started to object, but he stopped me by once more raising his hand.

He paused and looked up into the vast rafters of the *chinar* tree. "But if he has not lied, and I believe that he has not lied, then he has broken his vows, and that is a crime no less serious. If what he claims to have seen is true, then he must deny the truth of the scripture. He cannot have it both ways."

He sighed deeply. "Of course I will listen to the evidence, as will the other two judges, and we will confer and I will do my best to ensure that all is weighed on merit alone. But," he added, "it is likely to come down to one thing or the other, and I cannot tell you how deeply that grieves me. Once we ignored issues such as these. But now times are different. The world has become less forgiving."

He stared down at his hands, and the conversation stilled, and we grew silent in thought. Bilquis looked as though she might burst into tears. Sensing that, no doubt, Qazi Kamran stood up and led me down to the foot of the garden. He pointed to the last few stragglers dressed in white, carrying platters of food and *amphorae* of wine to the family celebration up the way. The party must have been near, for we could hear the musicians tuning their drums, while the breeze bore the faint aroma of charcoal smoke and kebabs on the grill.

"Do you know the other title of Mithras?" he asked. I shook my head. "He is the Bearer of the Contract," he explained. "And the meaning here is that the truth is a contract and that the contract is the truth. If you were Melchior's student, then you are bright enough to understand." I remained silent.

"As children of *Ahura Mazda*, Himself the Great Truth, we must keep our word, for that is part of our contract with God," he continued. "Mithras is the agent of God, if you will, who tells each of us to always tell the truth in our every dealing with one another. But we priests have another holy obligation of our own."

"It is not an easy assignment," he continued. "Being a priest requires us to preserve the rituals that give people strength, a ritualised truth in which they root their very lives. It is the truth of ritual, when grandparents watch the small ones bound by the sacred thread, generation upon generation. Continuity is often their only source of strength. So if ever we must choose between two truths, is not one kinder than another?"

"Even if one truth is not the truth?" I asked. He winced and made small frustrated fists of his hands, but then he smiled ruefully.

"Is not one kinder than another?" he repeated.

"Is something true, because it is merely kind? I have met some charitable liars in my time," I nearly shouted.

"You may not believe me, but I admire you. You *Paktues* are wonderfully direct," he said, referring to our own people by the Greek name for us. "If we Persians are quill pens, you are mallets: hard-headed as the shoals of Hell, perhaps, but blunt and decent. No, you misunderstand. More often than not in life there are two conflicting truths. Or call them two imperfect truths, or even two half-truths, if you insist. But they are all that we know, until God Himself gives us clarification. Until then, they sometimes collide. And, in such a case, the first responsibility of the leaders is to the needs of the led. Anything else would be cruel. Not to mention violating the sacred contract between Heaven and Earth."

I was unsure of how to think or even of how to feel, but he put his hand on my shoulder. "When the court convenes," he said, "whether my court in a few days' time or, for that matter, in the final court in the Far Heavens beside the House of Song, follow your conscience. Meanwhile," he added, "pray to your gods, and I will pray to mine." He clasped my hand, smiled kindly, and trundled up the hill to the Great Temple, leaving me to collect Bilquis and find our way back home.

We took the quicker path to the tower. Along we went through the Street of the Bootmakers into the Street of the Saddlers and up along the Glassblowers Bazaar, where Bilquis paused to admire some cobalt blue goblets newly arrived from Herat. She had been silent all along, and, although she held the glasses up to the light and weighed them in her hand and spoke of prices with the stall-keeper, her mind was somewhere else.

"So Qazi Kamran will sit on the tribunal," she said to me after some time. "That is valuable information."

I agreed. I was dismayed that he had not been one of the old man's students, but it could not be helped. However, I said that I was gladdened to learn of his distaste for the High Priest. That might be worked to our advantage.

"I do not like Kamran," she declared. "I neither like him nor trust him. You will note that, apart from once, he neither spoke to me nor answered my questions. He spoke only to you. I know not whether his problem lies with women, with my forbearers, or with Melchior as my uncle."

"Perhaps he never had an intelligent daughter," I suggested, knowing that my answer was insufficient.

"Or his daughters an intelligent father!" she snapped. "Anyway I do not trust him."

I admitted that few people reached such an exalted position as Chief Justice without some measure of guile, but that he seemed as straightforward as we had any right to expect under such circumstances. She wanted to know what the *qazi* and I had talked about at the foot of the garden. After I told her, oddly, she seemed to doubt him more. Like many women, she viewed the world in terms of personal loyalty, which after all may be the best way in which to see it. Men often tend to think of controversy in abstract, as a battle of conflicting principles. But principles are easily betrayed, while people are betrayed only at much higher cost. But my thoughts were interrupted by Jamil, a small boy who dashed through the crowded bazaar and straight into us, jabbering and pointing.

"*Caspar-jan! Harakat, harakat! Bibi-jan! Bibi Bilquis, harakat!*" he sputtered, urging us both to come quickly and pointing up the lane toward the tower. Jamil was the young neighbour whom the old man had hired to tend the gate, brew hot mint or hot lemon, and help Bilquis in the kitchen. He was small for a boy of ten, highly animated, and, as far as I could determine, perpetually covered in a thin veneer of dirt.

What is it, we asked. "Your guests, *sahib!* They have been waiting!" he exclaimed. "There is no bread! They have nothing to drink! But they are waiting!" Despite his ragamuffin demeanour, he was a well-mannered lad, a typical Persian concerned that our guests might be neglected and not suitably refreshed.

Surprised, for we expected no visitors, I asked him who had come, but he was too distracted to answer. I gave him a few coins to buy bread, fresh herbs, and fruit and buttermilk for whatever guests there might be, and he swooped like a swallow into the nearest alleyway.

Bilquis and I quickened our pace through the shoppers and pushcarts and made our way to the tower. In the narrow lane beside the high mud wall were tethered at least a dozen horses bedecked with kilim bags and saddle-cushions of nomadic carpeting. As we neared the tiny garden, we saw a small crowd of neighbours by the gate, but beyond, in a tight circle, under the grape arbour, sat grim-faced, bearded men in bare feet, dusty homespun trousers and long sleeved, multi-coloured, striped cloaks.

Beneath the cherry tree, a pile of short swords, in braided leather scabbards, was stacked atop a small mountain of their heavy leather boots shod with iron nails. By their trousers they resembled Persians, but the sky-blue turbans worn by the majority identified them all as *Yehud*, the Jews of the *serai*. The smallest and burliest of them, their leader, rose to greet me, and his comrades followed him solemnly to their feet. But before I could reach them, our neighbours swarmed about me.

"We have heard," cried the fruit-seller from the corner shop, "that the police have taken the professor! What can we do?" He clasped my right hand in both of his, and, for a moment, it seemed as if he would not let go. One of the neighbours, an old crone named Anahita, tugged at my sleeve.

"You were not here," she explained, "so I brought some milk for your guests." She glanced at the drovers nervously and then whispered: "Are you sure that they are not dangerous?"

The twins from the sawmill, strapping red-haired giants, waved to me from the back of the crowd, over the heads of the local children and their parents. As we slowly moved forward, each neighbour had a word of condolence or support for the old man. Some were rigid with anger. Bilquis and I tried to say a few words of hope and thanks to each, as we pushed through the small mob and made our way toward the back of the garden.

As I reached the visitors, Daoud pulled his dagger from his cummerbund, dramatically hurled it to the ground, and then opened his arms to embrace me.

"*Shalom!*" he declared in his own language, wrapping his arms about my waist and twice kissing my cheek, "*Shalom aleichem,*

Caspaaar!" He always pronounced my name with an excess of vowels, and he smelled, as he always did, of horsehair and saddle soap and campfire smoke. "Sit, brother!" he commanded, as though the garden were his.

I could not contain my delight in seeing him and apologised for our lack of hospitality. "So?" he asked, raising both hands and one eyebrow, "are you becoming a Persian? Big mistake!" He laughed: "Always so many rules! Who is the host? Who is the guest? Who cares, I say! You have no time to cook, so my men have gone to the bazaar. They will return with food. So sit, Caspaaar!"

He rose briefly to his feet again, when he saw Bilquis. He bowed, addressed her as his sister, and then crowded over to make a place for her beside him on the thick grass. I started to explain what had happened, but he stopped me.

"As well you know from before, brother, all news comes first through the serai," he said, stroking his thick black beard. He was correct, and it bordered on the uncanny. Outside the edge of the city, within the vast walls that sheltered the caravans, the drovers, and their cargoes, one could learn almost anything, from the price of fresh limes to what the emperor ate for lunch.

It was kind of them to come, and I told them so. Yet it was not surprising; Daoud and his men had saved our lives before and thus felt responsibility for Melchior, as well as affection.

Several of his companions spoke in Aramaic, until Daoud signalled for quiet. "Why, Caspaaar? Why?" he demanded. "An old man! A good man too!" The others nodded. I explained as best I could about the aftermath of our journey and how Melchior spoke to students of what we saw. Daoud said nothing, but shook his head and scowled darkly. Then he offered us gold, in case we needed it for food or debts or the old man's defence. It was no hollow promise, for Daoud was a wealthy and generous man, but Bilquis thanked him and demurred, insisting that we would come to him, were we ever in need.

We were interrupted, then, by a loud cry from just over the

wall, and several of Daoud's men leapt to their feet and reached for their swords. But there was no need. "The food," Daoud murmured with a nod of insignificance.

A dozen more drovers crushed through the gate, bearing great bundles over their heads, which they and our neighbours, by now far less worried, began to unpack and spread across the grass. Soon enough, the small garden was overflowing, not only with people, but with steamed legs of lamb and earthenware pots of yoghurt, hillocks of hot flatbread and bowls of onions, bales of tarragon and mint to be eaten raw and fresh, and altogether far too much fruit to fit onto every platter that the old man had ever owned. Pomegranates and pears, oranges and apples and apricots, melons of all shapes and colours and sizes, and more than a bushel of green grapes were piled atop a horse-blanket, until it resembled a cornucopia. Neighbours feasted and helped themselves, cheek by jowl with the drovers, and even one or two local toddlers wandered about, slathered in grease, wielding bigger hunks meat than ever could they eat.

Finally, young Jamil and more neighbour children arrived, some carrying kettles of boiling water and others juggling tall stacks of earthenware cups borrowed from most of the surrounding houses. Jamil had, I gathered, returned with hot lemon for ten guests, but had been wholly overwhelmed. Bilquis asked him to set aside enough food for Melchior's evening meal, and out of what were rapidly becoming scraps he amassed a small feast, wrapped in a series of head-cloths and shawls, which he set aside for later delivery.

"Melchior may wonder why we celebrate his arrest," I joked, for the old man ate simply even at the best of times. But Bilquis scowled at me. Soon we were all enervated and overfed. Daoud leaned across to the blanket laden with fruit, picked up an apricot, and set it before her.

"Eat!" he commanded, smiling broadly. She thanked him, murmured "no," and set it aside. He put another before her and, now laughing, said: "Eat! If you do not keep strong, how do you defeat your enemies, girl?" She smiled faintly and unconvincingly, turning her head away. Daoud paid it no mind. With his dagger, he slashed two great hunks from a melon and he looked at her for a moment, then shrugged and tossed the second slice to me.

"So what shall we do?" he asked after a while, picking his teeth, but politely covering his mouth with one hand. He leaned toward me, pushed his dagger across the blanket, until the handle touched my knee, and said: "I have twenty men here. How many do we need?" The neighbours shifted restlessly about us. The eyes of their young men brightened, but their parents looked fearful at such talk of sedition.

"It is not so difficult," he mused. "We have dealt with Roman centurions before, so your temple guards will not present a challenge. All enemies have similar throats."

"This is enough!" Bilquis announced loudly.

Daoud ignored her. "You have seen the road to my village. Neither Romans nor Persians dare to come near it. There is plenty of room, and you are all welcome there. Now," he said, turning to details, "I have always preferred doing this sort of work by night. Let us take thirty men to be on the safe side. Ten men with swords can remain with the horses; the others will carry ropes and daggers. Oh, we will need a small boy or a whore—I have a small phial of Syrian poison for the guardroom jug."

Bilquis rose to her feet. "Commander, or whatever you call yourself these days," she said to Daoud, "you are my friend, you are my uncle's friend, and thus you are always welcome here. Moreover, we are grateful for your generosity. But now, Caspar and I must bring food to my uncle in the prison. Thank you for your visit." Her message to go was not lost on our guest.

Daoud paused for a moment, and his eyes narrowed in thought. He looked at her and then at me, and then motioned to his men to rise. As they pulled on their boots, strapped on their swords, and left the garden, some of the older neighbours sighed with relief, picking up their kettles and their platters.

Daoud embraced me at the gate. "This is no matter for women. We are ready, Caspaaar!" he said with a shrug behind him towards Bilquis. "*Yehud*, Scyths, Syrians, Qashkai, Balouch, Turkomen, the whole *serai* will come if I ask them. Most will come for free. They are not fond of the police. Not these police. Not any police." I thanked him and pledged to remember his offer. He mounted his horse and from the far corner looked back over his shoulder and waved to me, as his men rode back to the *serai*.

When I returned to the garden, Bilquis had packed some left-over food into her shawl and strode past me to the gate.

"I am going to see my uncle," she said, tossing her head. "Is it too much to ask that you do nothing to have us arrested and killed while I am gone?" I admitted that Daoud and his companions were unlikely guests in the house of an astronomer, but, invited or uninvited, guests remain guests. Moreover, they had saved our lives during the expedition.

"You brought them here," she objected, throwing down her bundle. "You promised me that you would not and then you brought them here anyway." I protested that I had done nothing of the sort. Moreover, when would I have even had the time to invite them?

"They are your friends. It was even your expedition that brought this upon the head of my uncle," she said furiously. "And now, the police will be back, because you have brought these bandits here. What will the *qazi* think when he is told of this? How will Keshvari play it to his advantage?" She began to weep. "You are a fool, and a dangerous fool," she cried, sweeping up her bundle and striding away.

I said nothing, you see, because she was so devoted to the old man. Those times must have been harder on her than on any of us, even than on Melchior in a way. After all, it is easier to be a victim than to love one, and Bilquis was always driven by her heart.

This was a memory that seemed to trouble him, and for a time Caspar gazed long and silently out the western window into the darkness, and I waited quietly on my cushion, unwilling to disturb his thoughts. A few moments later, I noticed that he had drifted into sleep. I gently pulled up the pashmina shawl that had slipped down his chest and left the room quietly.

Chapter Four

YOU ARE QUITE RIGHT and you are well prepared this time. The Emperor Phraates never emerged from his poisoned coma. He died eight months later, after what must have been a determined struggle on the part of his nurses to coax food and water down his gullet. His elder boys died in Rome soon thereafter, swiftly and conveniently of some unidentifiable disease, likely an iron blade. Thus, shortly after our journey, Musa's own son, the half-Roman Phraataces, ascended the throne and married his own mother. Yes, you heard me correctly. Musa and Phraataces, mother and son, wife and husband, became the joint-rulers of Persia. If you talk to the old people here they are still scandalised by it.

Two years afterwards, Phraataces was himself poisoned, and Musa vanished suddenly, as if she were a *djinn*. Some say that she was smuggled back to Rome in a silk-trade caravan. Others said that she had been spirited away to Armenia, which that foolhardy Phraates had given back to the Romans. But I suspect that she could be found easily enough, if one cared to excavate the palace wells and sift through the bones at the bottom. Enough of this. We are from a different place and to some extent a better one.

But we knew none of it, Melchior and I, when we left the palace of the elders on that crisp sunny morning so very long ago.

"He is not the brightest planet in the firmament, old Bahram," Melchior mused as we strolled down the hill through the bazaar. "We were once students together, so I could observe him close up. Astronomy is not one of his subjects, to put it mildly. I sometimes wonder what is."

"Will we earn approval to investigate the new star?" I asked the old man as we walked.

"Not from Bahram!" Melchior replied. "He is old and distracted by dying. He will forget. Or Keshvari will frighten him or else destroy the orders after Bahram signs them. We need support and we need to take it from somewhere else. We need information as well."

"Where will we get it?" I asked.

"From the *serai*," he answered, and at the time I thought it rather cryptic. There were no astronomers in that place, and indeed no people of learning. At least that is what I thought, when I was so young as to believe that all learning came from scholars and their lectures and their scrolls.

We walked down through the bazaar, past the cheaper wine shops and the dirtier taverns there just inside the western gate, even past the few orchards and fields which in those days still separated the town from the fortifications that contained the caravans. The town has long since burst its former boundaries, of course, but *serais* were often originally built outside of the city walls, for they contained many armed strangers who were always feared by the rulers and often wisely so.

The *serai* was built of mud-brick and smaller than it is now, but even then it seemed enormous; everything is more impressive when you are young. A platoon of scowling Parthian infantrymen patrolled the parapets high above us, looking down on the people below in more ways than one. Outside of the enormous wooden doors, a unit of light cavalry practiced their archery from horseback, galloping back and forth and shooting arrows into straw targets set atop a dunghill beside the mud wall. Our city did not contain heavy cavalry then; we were too small to warrant a full contingent of troops.

Inside was a pandemonium of commerce, much as it is now. But there were then not so many caravans from Cathay, it seemed, and to me the caravans looked more exotic than ever they do today. That may be because I have since spent more time travelling in caravans than ever I would wish upon an enemy.

But then it was different and, for me, exotic. Dromedaries, horses, mules, and donkeys packed the vast courtyard amid bales of silk wrapped in skin or jute, crates of pottery and glass packed with straw, *amphorae* of wine, casks of spices, bottles of strange scent, and all manner of wonders. It smelled of dung and camp-fire smoke, of horses' sweat and leather and cinnamon bark.

A fight had broken out amongst some of the drovers, I recall, because men from somewhere to the east had slaughtered a dog for their lunch. Some people do that, you know. Most of the others thought it disgusting, and so they pushed and puffed and postured, until they all grew tired or until something else drew their attention. As you grow older and travel further, you will note that every region has its dietary prohibitions, and each thinks the other is odd or disgusting, but neither one makes more sense than the other. Or so it seems to me.

But much of the charm of the *serai* was its wonderful diversity. You could smell the food and see faces and costumes and products from almost everywhere on earth there in one vast arena: Armenians and *Yehud* and Beddou nomads cheek by jowl with Azeris and Turkomen and Hindustani, Baltis, and Thibetans. And, of course, there were Gandharans from home. It was then that I realised why the old man would have our investigation begin in the *serai*, for almost at our doorstep stood the world remade in miniature. Such is the magic of trade.

In less educated lands, people believe that life is best if they hoard silver or gold and consume only what they make; thus imported goods are taxed grievously. Such thinking is a province of the ignorant, for our ordinary things are luxuries in distant lands, and what is commonplace elsewhere may be a treasure to me. Better we trade freely and profit from one another's strengths. But such is a modern notion born in an age of travel and learning, so it was not so much a consideration at the time.

"But whom shall we ask? Where shall we begin?" I wondered aloud as we entered the gate of the *serai*. The old man sat himself down on a wooden box in the shade of a thatched awning and motioned that I join him.

"There is more to investigation than asking questions," my teacher explained, "and sometimes asking questions is the very worst strategy. This is one of those times." I was confused.

"If we start by asking questions, then to whom shall we speak?" he queried, rhetorically of course. "These people are here to buy and sell," he continued with a gesture. "So they may give us an answer which they think will lead them to a bargain. Or they may be helpful people who will craft an answer in measure with what we wish to hear. Or they may be vain and will thus invent a reply that makes them appear to be well informed. Asking questions can be a mistake, unless you have a clear and firm idea of what to ask, how to phrase it, and whom to approach. So for a moment we will sit."

And for a moment we sat, or maybe longer. A small boy appeared beside the old man, stuck out a grubby hand, and mumbled a request for *baksheesh*. I started to wave him away, but Melchior reached into his cloak and gave him a coin. The boy retreated a few paces and stared into his palm.

"Another thing," asked the old man eventually, "how do we look?"

I studied him and then myself. "Fine?" I asked, feeling foolish for I knew that my answer was insufficient.

"Precisely. Fine is the right word," Melchior replied. "We look like people who have just come from the Temple of Elders. We do not look like anyone who works here or anyone who comes here. They are dressed in skins and homespun, we in fine cloth. If they assume that we are important people, that will influence their answers. If we dress as they do, we will not fool them, and they will assume that we are spies or, at the very least, people attempting to appear as what we are not. That too will influence their answers."

"Thus they might, for example, think that we seek political intelligence, whereupon they will almost certainly mislead us for their own profit. Moreover," he added, "if they think that we are from the government, they will assume that we are arrogant and rich and stupid and thus try, sensibly enough, to separate us from our purses. I have no objection to that. The only right of the poor in this land is to outfox the rich, and no one is richer than the state. But that does not serve our immediate purpose."

The small boy watched from nearby, built up his courage, and once more drew closer. I could see him clutch a silver piece. "You did not give him coppers?" I asked, astonished by my teacher's generosity. The old man ignored me and focused his attention on the boy, who grew steadily bolder.

"Sahib?" the boy asked hesitantly, "What do you seek, *sahib*? Do you need *shamshir*? My uncle has watered steel swords from Damascus. *Abrashom* for the women, *sahib*? Buy our Cathay silk, and the Roman ladies will be forced to wear wool." Slowly picking up the pace and grinning with newfound confidence, the boy doubtless mimicked the patter of his father and his uncles in the bazaar. "Mirrors from Iskandria where the best ones are made, *sahib*, and *kohl* from Hindustan, to make your lover's eyes as black as obsidian. Rich Khorasani carpets in the colours of the evening sky and Roman glass that sparkles like a river."

"Come here, boy," urged Melchior, and, when the lad drew closer still, in one swift movement he caught the boy's hand and held him fast. The lad struggled and tried to pull away, but soon realised that the old man meant him no harm. Melchior opened wide his eyes and spoke in a deep whisper.

"I have those, boy," he hissed. "I've all of those and more besides! I live in a house of mirrors, boy, and my swords are forged of moonlight and all my carpets fly!" The child stared back in amazement.

"My horses are of silver made, their eyes of iridescent glass, their saddles silk that shimmers like the August sun," he gasped.

"They feast in ivory stables on Afghaun apricots and sweet Armenian wine, and they speak to me in poetry, for they know no other tongue." The boy was transfixed.

"So none of your mundane wares are that which I seek, boy," he continued. "My grooms are paid in emeralds and my sweepers in pearls. A prince's ransom is but dust to me." He pointed a long bony finger: "No, find me a star, boy, for I wish… to buy… a star!" And, as he spoke, he drew out the final word, until it seemed itself to stretch all the way to the very heavens and come back to earth again.

"Size is no matter, for I shall keep it in a velvet box," he explained, "and nothing but a new star will do, for the old ones grow dirty and lose their shine. Find me a new star, boy, and you will earn your commission on the sale." To prove his point, he held up another shiny piece of Parthian silver.

He let go the boy's hand, and the child nearly toppled over backwards in his haste to pull away. For a moment, he looked as though he might burst into tears, but soon enough he erupted into giggles and ran off through the *serai* to tell his playmates of the strange old man who shopped for stars.

"Watch," my teacher commanded me, "if you can watch without being seen to watch." From the corner of my eye, I saw the boy chatter to his friends and point toward us, as they collapsed in laughter. Next he told two burly men loading a dromedary, and they looked at us and shook their heads, cuffed him gently for the interruption, and pushed him on his way. Group by group, he worked his way through the vast *serai*, doubtless telling all who would listen to his tale about the wealthy old madman in the corner.

"Someone will know why we have come," the old man explained in an undertone, "and then he will find us." Only a few moments later the boy spoke to a man sewing a saddle, and from halfway across the *serai* I could feel the fellow's sudden, piercing gaze. He set down his needle and bronze palm-guard and slowly wiped his hands on his leather apron, never looking away from us. And then he came toward us warily, almost as a cat stalks her prey. Melchior watched him calmly, but I felt a shiver of excitement.

The man stopped before Melchior and looked him over. "You have seen it, then?" he asked softly. He smelled of sweat and leather and beeswax, and his forearms were knots of muscle. The old man nodded. The craftsman added: "You look like no Parthian that I have known."

"My family is named Demetrios," my teacher answered.

"One of the old ones, then," he muttered. He pulled up an empty crate and sat beside us. "Forgive me for not bowing, my lord," he said in an undertone, "but this is not the place. So, if people pass by, I will quote you a price on mending your saddles. It is safer that way." The old man nodded once more.

"You have seen it then? The new star?" the saddler asked.

"Yes, we have," Melchior replied. "And we know not what to make of it, so we felt that inquiries were in order." The man looked puzzled.

"It is Mithras, of course," said the man in hushed tones, astonished by our apparent ignorance. "The star of Mithras! Surely you know that! It means that somewhere a virgin has bathed in a lake and was there impregnated by the seed that the Prophet Zarathustra promised. Her baby will be Mithras incarnate. Now, finally, the changes come!" Striking his fist into his other hand, he added fervently: "And by the heavens they are long overdue. Once I thought that the priests lied, but now no more!"

The old man stared at him for a moment. "And what else do people say?" he asked. "That the sacred lake is found perhaps in Khorasan, where the rebels lie in wait?" The man watched silently. Melchior added reassuringly: "I am not a Parthian, you know, and I am not averse to change."

"I... I would not know," said the man haltingly. "I am a saddler, not a scholar, sir. Perhaps you should find an astronomer then." He had no idea that he spoke to the greatest astronomer in many days' march.

"Doubtless that is good advice," Melchior replied politely. "Thank you." The blacksmith stood, took a small step backward, and made a tiny, almost invisible bow. Then he returned to his work with some hesitation, looking at us every so often over his shoulder.

"Too cautious but not cautious enough," the old man said in a low voice. "Had we been state informants, the palace torturers would be hard at work on him this night. And no doubt he would babble then, bargaining for death, and lead them to his rebel friends, as well as anyone else whose name he could recall."

We waited a while longer, but no one else approached us, and even the small boy seemed to have forgotten the market for stars, playing with other children in the fragrant straw beneath the horses and camels.

I went to buy us food, and, as I waited my turn beside the copper cauldron full of spinach, one of the old cooks gave me a toothless grin and demanded: "D'ye want rice or bread with the *sabzi*, dear? Or would you rather have a nice piece of the moon? Fresh out of stars we are!" She cackled, and everyone around us chuckled too. I smiled sheepishly, as she filled the earthenware bowls with her wooden ladle and threw in a few homemade pickles for free. "Don't fret," she added softly, touching a finger to her greasy locks, "my old father went soft in the melon as well. Just love 'em and remember 'em for what they were. That's what I say."

We ate our lunch in silence, and I returned the bowls to the crone. The old man rose and picked up his stick and declared: "That is enough, I suppose. We did not come here to learn that Persian rebels have seen the star. That much I had already deduced easily enough. There was something else I wanted, but perhaps it is not to be."

I gathered our few things and followed him toward the gates of the *serai*, which were crowded with dromedaries festooned with bells and balls of coloured yarn. We stepped aside to let the beasts pass, and the camel-driver paused and tucked his switch beneath his arm.

"I have a star," he murmured so softly that he could scarcely be heard, "but it is not for sale." I smirked and started to walk past, but the old man caught my arm.

"And why can it not be sold?" the old man asked. When I saw the eyes of the drover, I knew that he was not mocking us. Melchior had noticed it sooner.

"It belongs to a king," the man replied carefully.

"And where, pray tell, lives this king?" asked Melchior.

"The king shall be born in the west," he answered.

"And where doth his kingdom lie?" asked Melchior. He phrased his questions in a slightly antique way, as though they were part of some strange litany.

"His kingdom is above us and below us, and he governs all that lies between," said the man. I remember it, as if it were yesterday, but it was very long ago.

"I should like to talk with you about this king," said the old man softly.

"And I with you, my lord, and my master would as well," the man answered. "But not here and not now. The tales best heard are told after dark."

Keeping an eye on the Parthian guards beside the doors to the *serai,* he whispered a few words in the old man's ear. Then immediately he roared to his beasts, which roared back and cursed at him in the way that dromedaries do. Then, flicking them with his switch, he drove them through the enormous wooden gates and out onto the dusty road beyond.

We went home. Between then and nightfall I must have asked a hundred questions of the old man, but he had no answers and made few speculations. I returned to my room to collect my cloak, then joined him at the tower, before we made our rendezvous with the drover.

I started for the door of the tower, when the old man paused.

"Caspar," he said, "leave the dagger here." Although surprised, I could not argue with him, so I pulled it from my cummerbund and laid it heavily upon the table.

"How did you know that I had one?" I asked him.

"Because we are bound for a bad place and because I too was once as young as you," he replied, adding, "take one of my sticks if you must."

Although it had begun to go dark, we were still perhaps two hours before curfew. Nonetheless, we worked our way down through the city, along the deserted residential streets rather than through the main bazaars. The lanes were dark, but within the flat-fronted mud houses and from inside the leafy, walled gardens, lights burned brightly, as families gathered and ate their evening meal together and talked away the problems of the day.

"If ever you find yourself heading into trouble in a strange place," the old man cautioned, as we wended our way down the hill, "carry no arms. There you will always be someone's guest, and it is upon his honour to protect you. Knowing that, few enemies are likely to pick a fight and risk battling your host and his clan."

Beneath us, further down the hill towards the city gates, the rooftops were all domed and made of mud: buildings of the poor who could not afford wooden beams brought at great expense from the distant mountains of the north. Thin plumes of smoke rose from many cook-fires, but seemed to vanish in the darkening sky, where they could still be smelled but no longer seen.

"Weapons are for the home," the old man continued, "for your own territory, where it is your responsibility to protect your family and your guests. Besides," he added, "if you are on strange ground and find yourself forced to fight alongside your hosts, they will inevitably have weapons to share." I later found him to be correct more than once.

Our contact had named a wine shop near the city's western

gate, not far from the *serai* that lay beyond the walls. The city gates had been closed and locked at dusk, of course, but the soldiers guarding them loafed or slept or threw dice nearby. They paid scant attention to the drinkers and gamblers and their women, the touts who stood in the crossroads and the footpads who lurked in the alleyways. A man shifted unsteadily in the street beside a half-shuttered house, shouting his protests at some lover, and for his troubles she leaned from an upper window and emptied an earthenware pot of ale over him. At least I thought it was ale once upon a time because of the colour.

We came in time to the wine shop, which was pulled down a few years later: a dirty place stained inside and out from the smoke of an unventilated oven, a *tandoor*, as we call it, or what Persians call a *tanoor*. Long ago, there were many of them, but now they have chimneys to carry off the smoke. The door was so low that visitors had to stoop down to pass through it. It was small by design, so that anyone already inside has a tactical advantage, able to strike down an intruder or policeman, before he could stand erect and draw his sword or knife. It was a place much frequented by travellers and drovers from the *serai*.

Inside, it was smoky from the *tandoor* baking bread, so at first I thought that I could hardly breathe. Once my eyes stopped watering, I saw that the tavern was crowded with rough-hewn men at rough-hewn tables. The room had been full of their noise, but, as we entered, they set down their clay pots of wine and grew silent, wondering who we strangers might be.

Our drover sat in the back. He sent two of his companions scurrying away, as he beckoned us toward him, but kept one other man beside him, a hard-eyed man, small and dark. We sat down, while at tables nearby the drinkers began again to talk in low voices, watching us all the while. The old man and I shared a long bench with our backs to the door across the table from our hosts, who called to the woman and asked her to bring us wine. It was from Shiraz, clear and better than I had expected from such a place. It made sense upon reflection, for these were travellers who would know good food and drink better than the people settled in villages and towns.

The man whom we had met in the *serai* appeared to work for the other one beside him, who was small and dark and middle-aged, but well-muscled beneath his rough-woven cloak. His hands were gnarled and scarred far more than his years might suggest, perhaps from the rigours of mounting caravans. He looked at us and smiled, using his lips but not his eyes.

"It is safer here," he whispered. "The *serai* has enemies for the likes of you and me."

The old man smiled back, and his lively blue eyes made him seem far less careful than I already knew him to be. "What enemies do you think that I might have?" he asked in an innocent tone.

"They are there. In the *serai*, my lord," our host continued evenly, narrowing his eyes as he spoke, "They are in the bazaar. They are within the Palace of Elders for all I know. But they are not here. Not in this tavern. I promise you that. You see, I have already bet my life on it." Then he laughed.

A large, drunken man rose from another table, staggered, but swiftly regained his balance and began to approach us, calling our host by the name Daoud. Our host snarled at him in a language that I had not heard before and waved him away. The man retreated to his companions and to their wine-pots.

"The star," asked the old man gently.

"Is not for sale," said our host, as though completing a sentence which they had rehearsed. "It cannot be owned by any man."

"Because it is too far?" Melchior asked.

"It is not too far," our host replied, "And I can take you there. I can take you, if the right people approve. But it is not for sale."

"What sort of man owns stars?" my teacher asked.

"No man. No ordinary man," replied the drover, tilting his head, "We call him *messiah*." Melchior simply nodded.

The small man's name was Daoud, as we suspected. And he was a *Yehud*, a Jew with family nearby and more in Jerusalem. And so, by fits and starts, the old man asked satisfactory questions and provided satisfactory answers, and so our host told us what he knew of the star.

Far, far away west, in some Roman province named Judea, which the *Yehud* called their ancestral home, a king was to be born unto a very old royal family, which, I gathered, had been moribund for some considerable time. For a long time since, they had been oppressed by their enemies, who seemed to be numerous; most recently by the Romans who, of course, are the enemies of all free men. The birth of this king had been foretold by one or two of their prophets and gave them hope, which served them well through at least two Roman invasions of Jerusalem, their capital city. Now this great leader appeared to be born beneath a new and special star. He would, said Daoud, set things right.

The old man was silent for a while, and the two watched him without displaying emotion. Finally the drover spoke. "He comes for all the Jews," he murmured.

"Do you know Zeno?" asked Melchior. Daoud said that he did not, noting that the name sounded neither Persian nor Roman nor *Yehud*.

"*Unani*, a Greek. A Hellene," the old man explained. "A philosopher. He said that the gods of the Greeks resemble Greeks, while Ethiopian gods have black skins—and presumably the gods of donkeys bray and the gods of scorpions have six legs."

Daoud smiled and refused to take offence. "A good man respects another's gods," he countered, "and my God is the enemy of Rome. So he is a friend of the Persians."

Melchior nodded. "Our Persian troops have marched into Jerusalem in defence of your princely family, the Maccabees. My father was one of those troopers," he added.

"We never forget a friend," Daoud answered.

"Then we have need to see this king," said the old man. "But we must get there first."

"How many voyagers?" asked Daoud.

"Two," said Melchior.

"The tyrant Augustus and his puppet Herod will send thousands in search of my king," said Daoud, speaking slowly to emphasise his point. "All that the Persian emperor will send to save us is two?"

"Two," repeated the old man, "myself and my student. That is all. That is all for now." Daoud furrowed his brow, until he heard the old man's emphasis on the last sentence, which signified opportunities later.

"I will think and then speak to our leader," our host explained. "Do not try to find us. I will find you." The old man bowed with a gesture unfamiliar to me, a hand touched gently across the breast, one that I later recognised among the Gentile peoples and *Yehud*. We gathered our sticks and our cloaks and went out into the night.

I waited until we passed the guardhouses and the gate and entered the empty streets through which we had come, for there we would not be overheard. "He believes that we are spies for the emperor, bringing help against Rome," I whispered.

Melchior looked at me and smiled faintly. "Are you certain that we are not?" he asked.

Despite my being both intrigued and confused, I asked him no more. These were dangerous matters, far beyond anything I had even considered.

chapter five

THREE TIMES, OVER THREE DAYS, we returned to the palace of the High Priest, Bahram, and thrice the guards refused to let us enter. They were polite, uncommonly polite, indeed, which suggested that they were under special orders. And each time they took pains to explain that the High Priest was too unwell to receive visitors. I would have believed them, had Melchior not asked to see the secretary. Keshvari, we were told, had given orders not to be disturbed.

"It is a game," Melchior explained. "Keshvari was meant to send our request to the emperor's security service, but I'll wager that he has taken our charts to his own astrologers in the hope that he can learn something to use to his own advantage. If they could provide him with a good enough interpretation of what our star portends, he would get his audience with the emperor himself, awake or comatose. Keshvari is gambling that I will not barge into the palace, and for the moment he is correct."

"Why? Because we want to take our time?" I asked. I did not know if my teacher had a strategy, much less how it might unfold.

"Because we are being followed," Melchior said in an undertone, and I started to turn. "Don't look back, man!" he croaked softly but urgently. "Keep your eyes straight ahead!" We quickened our pace ever so slightly, and it was an almost irresistible strain not to turn around and try to see who was following us. Apparently, from the way that the old man spoke, our follower was not too close.

"I first saw him about ten minutes after we left the tower, and I thought he would leave when we reached the palace," he explained in a near whisper. "He's dressed like a labourer, but he walks bow-legged like a Parthian cavalryman. He's almost certainly from some part of the government, but probably not an assassin. Even the government isn't stupid enough to hire cavalrymen as assassins. The cavalry is all sabres and swagger and saddle soap. Most of them, anyway."

"Why would anyone want to assassinate…" I began, but he interrupted.

"I said he was not an assassin. I will explain it all later," he said, with his unusually long legs striding forward. For an old man, he was extraordinarily quick, when he chose to be.

The streets of the bazaar grew narrower and more crowded. Twice Melchior stopped to examine a piece of fruit from one of the barrows and stole a glimpse behind him. It was clear from his expression that we had not yet lost our tracker.

"When we come upon a yellow door up ahead on the left, be quick, as you follow me through it, and mind your head." It was a low door, painted many times over in a dirty lead yellow, and no sooner had we hopped over the threshold than Melchior slammed it shut and secured it with its heavy wooden bar. It was a place that I had never seen before, but must have passed a thousand times. Inside was a mud-walled courtyard of considerable antiquity, and a blue-tiled fountain played in the centre. Around it, in the dust, sat perhaps a hundred children, quietly studying their small blackboards, on which were written their lessons. They were learning the Persian alphabet. The teacher, a tall cheerful-looking man in his fifties, approached Melchior with his arms spread.

"*Ustad-jan!*" he called in delight, using the most affectionate form for a teacher. "After so many invitations, you have finally come back. This is good! This is very good!"

Melchior embraced him, but was quick to interrupt with

swift introductions: "Hasham, this is my student Caspar. Caspar, Hasham is the best of teachers, and I wish I could say that he learnt it all from being my student, but he knew it already." Hasham blushed, but Melchior continued quickly. "Hasham, I am being followed."

"By whom?" the teacher demanded.

"We do not know. But whoever it is will not be dangerous," said the old man. "But keep him busy. And kindly show us to the back door."

Hasham broke into a broad smile, and his eyes continued to dance. He pointed us towards the back, and, as we crossed the courtyard, we heard pounding on the door behind us. Hasham ignored the banging and addressed the children.

"We are going to play a game," he explained quite soberly, and the children listened. "This man, about to come through the door, is pretending to be *Angra Mainyu*, the Father of Lies. Do you understand?" The youngsters all nodded eagerly, for they liked games and all Zoroastrian children know of the horrible Father of Lies. Hasham looked across the courtyard and gestured that his assistant should open the door. "So when he enters, everyone should get up, rush to the doorway, and make as much noise as possible to scare him away."

And by then we were into the alleyway behind the school. For a considerable time we could hear, far behind us, gales of high-pitched laughter and shouting. "Hasham was the greatest sportsman and scholar of his generation," said Melchior, betraying a hint of pride, "and a handsome boy too. The girls could never keep their eyes off of him. And all he ever wanted to do is teach. He's poor as a mouse and happy as a songbird. They tell me that his three children have become teachers too."

Within minutes more, we found ourselves coming up to the gates of Melchior's tower. I was still flushed with the excitement of being followed and, better yet, of having evaded the spy.

"You started to tell me…" I began, when I realised that Melchior had stopped stock still in front of his compound. He lifted one hand to silence me, as he looked all the way down to the far end of his street, where two cavalrymen waited on horseback, armed with bows and lances, half hidden in the shadows of a great *pipal* tree. Yet, even at some distance, you could see the sunlight glinting off the steel rings of their chain-mail armour and the polished domes of their spiked helmets. This was not how they dressed ordinarily here in the town.

Then Melchior nodded toward the door of his compound, which swung on its hinges, half open. Someone had been there or was waiting there still.

There was no point in trying to go back the way that we had come, not with the cavalrymen so close. Melchior eased me aside gently and walked through the door into his garden, and I followed behind him. Two more soldiers stood inside the gate. They were part of some special detachment that I had never seen before, dressed in black and armed with expensive razor-sharp scimitars of Damascus steel. The ends of their turbans were wound across their faces, revealing little more than their eyes.

Melchior ignored them and walked among the beds of roses and between the sticks and strings supporting the hollyhocks on toward the back of his garden, where another old man leaned heavily on a pair of fancy canes with chased silver handles. He was more or less of Melchior's age and equally tall, but even more gaunt, and, like his guards, dressed all in black with the addition of an expensive woollen cloak. He was blind in one eye, which had corrugated and clouded over unpleasantly. It was doubtless from a sabre wound of some kind, for an old pink scar ran deep from the corner of the eye down his cheek and disappeared somewhere beneath his collar.

"I should have known that you'd keep an orderly garden," said the man. "It complements an orderly mind. Now offer me a cushion, old friend. These knee joints of mine are almost worn through with age."

"You won't be here long enough," said Melchior, his eyes flashing angrily. "State your business, Sattar, although I probably know it already."

I had never, before or afterwards, seen the old man refuse hospitality to anyone. However, even Melchior must have thought the better of his obvious displeasure and he made a gesture to the houseboy, who came out of hiding and brought us cushions. The man called Sattar leaned heavily on his sticks and lowered himself down gratefully.

"Caspar here is my student," Melchior explained, eyeing the visitor as though he were a cobra. "He is instrumental in my investigation, in my research. But of course I bear full responsibility for anything involving the state."

Sattar fixed me in his gaze, took off one black glove, and leant over as far as he could to touch my hand. "When we were healthy young lads like you, this gallant fellow Melchior saved my life. And I've tried to return the favour ever since, but he has never given me the chance."

"We all read the holy books, Sattar, and you owe me nothing. Every action is a vote for good or evil," said Melchior tersely. "I only did my duty."

The visitor ignored him and spoke to me. "Imagine. A cavalry commander rescued by an infantry officer. Unheard of. But of course that is what happened. It was the second day at Carrhae. Some say the worst day. I was riding out of that copse on the lip of the ridge just before noon. There must have been eight Romans who had broken away from the Fifth Legion. They came out of nowhere, surrounding my mount and me. This man was unstoppable. He killed the lot of them. Relentlessly, one after the other."

"There were only seven, Sattar. You killed one, I killed three, and the other three ran off to be killed elsewhere. We have been through this before."

"Such bravery!" added Sattar.

"It was nearly fifty years ago," said Melchior pointedly. "And some of us stopped killing when the war ended."

Sattar kept ignoring him. "And, ever since, I have asked myself, why was a great soldier like this wasted in the infantry. The infantry! He was a natural cavalry officer, and his pedigree was not what anyone would expect to find in the infantry. Melchior, your infantry colleagues, foot-soldiers, were mostly shoemakers' sons, weren't they?"

Melchior's eyes narrowed, and his voice grew reedy. "I was invited to join the cavalry, Sattar. But I told them that I was allergic to horse manure. I think I still am."

"I was so very grateful to your professor here, that I asked him to come and work for me in government," Sattar told me. "Time and again. But he would never accept my offer. So much talent wasted! An intelligent mind born for, well, born for intelligence. A loss for a noble service. A tragedy for the state," complained the visitor.

Melchior broke into an ironic smile: "As I told you before, Sattar, every act is a vote for good or a vote for evil. We just work for different candidates, that is all."

The visitor's expression soured. He folded his hands in his lap and sighed. "Very well. You never change, do you? But you know why I am here. Most people who matter have seen the star, and, if they missed it, they have seen your charts."

"I am surprised," said Melchior. "I would have thought that Keshvari was unwilling to share anything so valuable."

"He hasn't shared anything with anyone apart from a few idiot astrologers," Sattar explained. "But our people work for him too, not that he knows it. So we see whatever he sees. And we have people among the astrologers, of course."

"And your opinion is?" asked Melchior.

"Fascinating," said the spymaster.

"So you think it is Mithras, do you? Sent from Heaven to save us from the misrule of a comatose emperor and the bloodthirsty men surrounding him?"

Sattar chuckled coolly. "Stop the games. I am interested in what the *Yehud* think. And, once I know what the *Yehud* think, I want to know what the Romans think. This is no surprise to someone like you, Melchior. If the Jews believe that they have a new star or a new king, will they revolt against Rome? If indeed they revolt, how will Rome react? In order to suppress Judea, will she rush her legions down from Palmyra and leave it free for the taking? If not, will they send us back our captive princes from Rome in return for our promises of good behaviour?"

"And if there is a revolt, which way will the *Yehudi* king jump?" added Melchior.

"If you mean Herod, then of course," said Sattar. "The Egyptians listen to him. Always have. And there is no love lost in Alexandria for the tyrant Augustus. So we, meaning the state, find your star most interesting."

"What do the palace experts think?" Melchior asked.

"No doubt they will get around to it, amid charming off warts and predicting the weather," drawled Sattar. "I deal directly with General Rostam Shah up in the capital and, when need be, the emperor himself."

"When His Highness is *compos mentis*," added Melchior.

The spymaster scowled. "We act in the emperor's best interest regardless."

Melchior rose to his feet and instinctively brushed his robe, as though it had been soiled by something. "Thank you for your thoughts, Sattar," he said brusquely. "Shall we set another place for supper?"

"No, thank you," replied the spymaster, who knew that it was no invitation. I rose and gave my hand to the guest. He struggled to his feet painfully and then leant heavily on his sticks. Slowly he began to hobble back through the rows of flowers to the gate. Midway, he turned to face Melchior. His smile had long since gone, and he eyed him coldly.

"Still the same. Still the same. But, when you return, professor, if you return alive, you will give me the full report," he snapped, gesturing with his stick. "In this life, that is the only thing that we both know for certain."

Then, turning on his heels, still hunched over his canes, he slowly limped through the remainder of the garden without ever looking back. His bodyguards fell in behind him and pulled shut the gate. In the distance, we heard the cavalry mounts whinnying and the clatter of their hooves.

Melchior had a faraway look in his eyes, and he remained motionless for some time. Finally, he appeared to snap himself back into the present moment and he laid an arm on my shoulder as we walked back to his tower.

"Well, Caspar," he said with a wry smile, "we have our permission."

Chapter Six

FOR SOME REASON, it was incredibly noisy in the *serai* that afternoon. Even after all these years, just thinking about it makes my skull nearly split. I mean it is always noisy in a *serai*, except for a brief period at night, when the men and animals are asleep. But this time was noisier than most, and it was the one time when we needed some quiet.

We had been summoned by Daoud, the old man and I, so we had gone as swiftly as possible to the *serai*, where we were shown upstairs to one of the upper storerooms, where we could meet in private. Of course, Daoud's people wanted us hustled out of sight as quickly as possible. It did no one any good to see us two scholars mingling with the rest. That would have raised more suspicions.

But I think that someone's consignment of metal pots had been damaged in transit, and so it seemed that everyone in the *serai* had a hammer and was busily whacking away at those damned pots, pounding out the dents. It was sheer cacophony and absolutely deafening.

Daoud perched on the windowsill, leaned forward, and said something to us. We sat on sacks of wheat, not but a few feet away, and still we could not hear a word. He appeared to shout his answer. We shook our heads and craned forwards. Daoud shouted once more, and once more again, but on this final time, for some reason, the hammering stopped, and his voice seemed to echo around the entire *serai*.

"JERUSALEM! WE LEAVE AT DAWN," shouted Daoud

who, realising that he was overheard, dropped his voice to a whisper: "And don't tell anyone!"

"They might have worked it out already," said Melchior dryly, and Daoud's men laughed. Daoud smiled and shrugged helplessly.

"I am glad that your leader gave permission," I said, and Daoud looked puzzled. "You said you had to ask your leader. When we met in the wine shop," I explained.

Daoud took a moment to remember the conversation. "That was what we call an excuse," he replied. "I had to ask myself, since I am the leader. I work for myself, so I love my boss. And so I asked myself nicely, and I considered my request, and I gave myself permission. Now remember, do not be late. We leave just before daybreak." He finished his message nearly shouting, as the hammering had started once more.

"Do we need our own weapons?" Melchior asked, as loud as he could.

"I tell everybody the same thing," Daoud shouted back, smiling. "Bring brains, professor. I can always use more brains! Weapons I got!"

We left the *serai* and walked back home, as twilight began to settle over the town. It was always the prettiest part of the day, when the last, long shafts of sunlight seemed to hug the surface of the earth, slicing sideways through every leaf and blade of grass, making them glow twice as green as ever. Some women had made the day's last trip to the well, and their hips swayed gently, and their strong tanned arms clutched their earthenware pots. From the rooftops and front gardens, the smoke from cookfires had begun to trickle upwards into the sky. Cows stopped foraging and began to think about wending their way home to comfort and safety. It was a time of day when everything seemed at peace.

Indeed, I was just about to say something very similar to Melchior, as we entered the beginning of town, the part filled with cheap hostels and wine shops, when we rounded a corner just in time to hear an enormous crash and see someone go hurtling past us in mid-air, accompanied by bits of the wooden door through which he had just been propelled. He hit the dusty street very hard indeed. From inside the building there was an almighty roar, as another man flew out into the street and landed nearly on top of his predecessor.

Then what stepped into the doorway might have been a door itself. It was an enormous and heavily muscled man. His skin was as dark as burnished *sheesham* wood, and he filled the shattered doorway completely, except for what appeared to be two or three smaller, normal-sized men hanging on his arms and shoulders and neck. With two enormous giant-steps he was through the door, over the threshold, and into the street, with the three men still hanging onto him, flailing and kicking with all their might.

He began to pluck them off, one by one, as a normal man might brush off crumbs. However, the two whom he had hurtled through the door had regained their senses and went at him from the front, while what looked like three more started to come through the door behind him. The odds against him stood at eight to one and rising. One of those coming through the door reached into his filthy cummerbund and removed a slim dagger.

That was it. Without asking permission, I reached over and took Melchior's stick almost instinctively. Then I waded into the fray. Whoever the visitor was, he was a visitor. And he was badly outnumbered.

I was rather stronger then, as well as hot-headed, and I swung that piece of wood like a war-club. I picked my first target and made contact with the back of his skull. If the man with the dagger ever awoke again, it would not have been for many days to come. The second one took two hard blows before he let go of his victim and sank to the ground. One took a swing at me and missed, but, before I could do anything, the enormous man raised a fist the size of a leg of lamb and brought it down on my attacker's cranium. His eyes crossed reassuringly, as he sank to the ground. But there was another coming up on my left.

Eventually I looked around and saw that no one was conscious save me, the enormous African, and of course Melchior, who sat on a nearby step laughing.

"What is so funny?" I demanded.

"Poor fellows never stood a chance," said the old man. "I didn't even have time to make any bets."

The middle-aged giant seemed undamaged, except that his clothes had been nearly torn to shreds. He pulled a loose sleeve up over his shoulder in a failed attempt to restore his dignity.

"I owe you a great debt, young sir," he said in a deep, rolling voice, using an old-fashioned form of Persian. "Indeed, you and your distinguished companion should feast at my table without a moment's delay." I demurred. We needed no reward. Protecting visitors, I explained, is one of the most rudimentary elements of hospitality in Persia and in my own homeland as well.

The man looked rueful: "I said 'should' rather than 'will.' That little altercation involved a large gambling debt caused by their, shall we say, *unusual* way of throwing dice. So at the moment I am somewhat shy of resources…"

Melchior interrupted him, saying, "Come home, visitor, and you shall dine with us!" And thus we met Balthazar, the third voyager and a king without a kingdom, or so he was back then. Even to the very end of his life, Melchior idolised him. And Balthazar thought the same of Melchior. Two men were never so different and yet never so appreciative of one another's virtues.

As we set out towards the tower, Balthazar made a request. "I need to see Yasmine before we go to supper," he said. "She is staying not far from here, and she will be sick with worry otherwise. To be so loved, and by such a beauty, should make any man behave responsibly… if only once!" He grinned mischievously, and of course we agreed, as it did not appear to be far out of the way. And, as we walked, he told us his story.

He was a king of course, a real king from a genuine kingdom somewhere to the south of Araby, beyond the land of the Yemenis and somewhere on down along the sunlit shore of Africa. It was a kingdom rich in spices and scents, and even when you were several days away from it in a boat, if the winds were right, you could still sniff its perfumed coast. It was a kingdom rich in iron, which in turn they traded to the peoples of the African interior for gold and rare woods and beautiful stones and elegant cloth made of pounded bark. These in turn they sold for great fortunes to the captains of *dhows* ploughing the coastline to the markets of the Orient and trading even with Rome itself.

And it was a kingdom of great antiquity, as old perhaps as even Persia, Balthazar explained. The land had once been ruled by a queen who had married the wisest man on earth, Suleiman, the king of Judea, about one thousand years before. Melchior said he had heard of this land called Sheba, and it was said to be everything that Balthazar claimed.

"But due to some difficulties which I would rather not explain, my kingdom is forfeit," Balthazar said. "And so, for the present, at least, my own true love, Yasmine, and I have given up our distant homes to wander the much larger kingdom of Almighty God, going wherever we desire, staying no longer than we wish, sampling every pleasure on offer. And some that are not." And with that he laughed, hard enough and loud enough, said Melchior later, that it nearly shook the fruit from the trees.

"Your queen, or your princess, must be very special indeed," I suggested. After all, a life of endless travel suits few men and even fewer women. Balthazar broke into a broader grin, and his eyes narrowed in appreciation.

"Yasmine is a perfumed bath, she is warm milk on a cold desert night," he began. "Her eyes shine like African malachite, and her breath is as sweet as the dates grown in Paradise. Her disposition is as pure as the meat of a coconut, and she loves me more than breath and life. But we are not married, you see. We are of different religions."

81

He turned into an alleyway, where a tethered camel began to bray and stamp its hoof.

"Yasmine! My sweet!" exclaimed the king, and, reaching into one of his surviving pockets, he produced a piece of *gur*, a kind of brown raw sugar much loved by camels and by people too. Yasmine moved her head past the sugar and tried to bite his arm, but Balthazar jerked out of her way.

"She has something of a temper," he explained, "but all beauties do. I think she is a little irritated that I left her alone for so long." She lunged at him again, but he deftly popped the sugar into her mouth, and it surprised her enough that she stopped trying to bite him. He moved around her side to inspect the saddlebags. Satisfied, he untied her reins and began to lead her out of the alleyway.

"Like all of the best camels, she comes from the Sudan," he explained. "They are renowned for their speed, for their endurance, for their load-bearing capacity, and for their lovely dispositions. Sudanese camels are said to have the gentlest, kindest, and sweetest... AGH!" he shouted. Yasmine had bitten him on the shoulder. He turned around and raised his hand to swat her on the nose, but Yasmine reared her head back and bared her long teeth.

"Bad camel! Shame on you!" he complained to no avail. As he shifted his hand to slap her, she kept checkmating his moves with her sharp incisors and her long neck. The monarch soon realised that this would take more effort that it was worth, looked to see that he was not bleeding, and continued on his way.

"She is really a splendid beast," he muttered, half in explanation to us and half to convince himself. "Profoundly good natured on most days."

Balthazar was right about Yasmine's strength, for, once we reached the tower, an amazing assortment of bundles were removed from her various panniers and saddlebags. She was tethered beside the garden rain barrel, with clean water to drink, fresh leafy greens to eat, and a soft patch of grass on which to sleep when the need overcame her.

Once indoors, the houseboy ferried copious quantities of hot water and towels into the spare room in which they lodged Balthazar, while Melchior began explaining to Bilquis how it happened that an African monarch had come to stay at their tumble-down tower and how, early the next morning, Melchior and I would sneak off across half the known world, following an unidentified star into the lands of our enemies, leading us to the birth of a Jewish prophet or possibly Mithras.

I took this splendid opportunity to go home and pack for my journey and, as I left, even halfway down the street, I could hear Balthazar singing, presumably in the bath. He had a fine and resonant voice that could demonstrably pierce a mud-brick wall at least eighteen inches thick.

At the boarding house, I explained to my fellow students that there had been an illness in my family and that I would be gone for some weeks or longer. It was a lie, but a harmless one, and it sufficed, although I felt dishonest when the housekeeper gave me a box of her sweet carrot *halwa* to carry home to my kinfolk. I left some money for the rent whilst I would be away and tucked my few spare scrolls and belongings under my bed. I did not have to wonder about what sort of clothes one wore to meet a newborn *Yehudi* king—among students in my day, there was no choice of wardrobe at all, only clothes. I put mine into a small straw bag along with a blank scroll, a pen, and a travelling inkpot. I presumed that I could find extra supplies of ink along the way.

I returned to the tower, where pandemonium had apparently broken out. The houseboy sat in the garden and suggested that I might join him there rather than go inside, where it was far less quiet. From what he relayed, poor Melchior's desire to keep order exceeded even his own considerable powers. Balthazar had suddenly declared his plans to join the caravan at dawn, since he had already made up his mind to head westward. But, considerate as he was, he would not follow us further than Jerusalem, since he did not want to interfere with our mission.

Meanwhile Bilquis announced that she would accompany us on the journey, a notion that was simply preposterous. There were women attached to caravans now and then, but they were of a decidedly different sort. Then, making matters worse, Balthazar had apparently encouraged her, and so Melchior was fuming. I briefly considered spending the night in the garden with the houseboy and Yasmine the camel, but duty seemed to demand something more.

"Ah! Caspar! I was waiting for you," thundered Balthazar, as I crept up the steps. I looked quickly around the room. Balthazar was stretched out on a pile of cushions with the wine jug at his elbow. He wore a voluminous crimson jerkin of some fine and light woven material embroidered with golden threads. It made him look utterly comfortable, and yet as regal as it was possible to look, in the old man's bare rooms. Bilquis stood near the back, periodically tapping her foot angrily, looking likely to burst into tears. Melchior, who appeared to have acquired a headache and had gone into temporary retreat, was trying to decide which star charts to pack into a long leather valise.

"Saturn?" he asked half to himself. "Will anyone have charts of the House of Saturn? Oh, dear me." But no one paid much attention.

"Did you know," Balthazar continued in a portentous tone, "that this woman's name is Bilquis?" I said that I did, since I had been coming to this tower for nearly three years. "Of course you have," the king apologised, and then he supressed a hiccough. "How silly of me! Some kind and generous person has served me too much wine. I meant, did you know that she is named after my illus... my illus... my ancestor, the Queen of Sheba? Queen Bilquis who married King Suleiman?" I said I did not, but Bilquis interrupted.

"And she was not a consort of any king of Sheba, Uncle Melchior, she was a ruler in her own right. And she chose her own husband and she travelled all the way to Judea more than a thousand years ago, which is much farther than from here to Jerusalem. Isn't that what you told me, King Balthazar?"

Melchior looked very subdued indeed. "More wine, Your Highness?" he asked ironically.

"Yes, please!" the king replied enthusiastically, reaching for the earthenware pitcher. His was neither the personality, nor this the time of night, for subtlety or self-restraint.

"Well," she demanded of Balthazar, "is it farther or is it not?"

Balthazar shot a glimpse at Melchior, who glowered at him. The king grimaced guiltily. "I shall have to consult with my camel," he muttered. "Perhaps I ought to do it now." Somewhat unsteadily he rose to his feet and slowly tottered down the stairs and into the garden, where he could relieve himself.

"Enough. I won't hear any more of it," said Melchior softly. Bilquis started to stamp her foot again, but stopped. She could see that her uncle was serious.

"But, Uncle…" she began.

"There are certain standards," he continued. "I promised your mother before she died. Would you make a liar of me?"

"No, Uncle," said Bilquis softly.

"Then I consider the matter settled. But I am sorry," said the old man. Bilquis made a soft choking noise, as though she was starting to cry, and, with her hands covering her face, she fled down the stairs into the night.

Melchior gave up trying to select star charts and tied shut his old leather bag. "Remember this conversation, if you are ever tempted to have any daughters," he said. He picked up the wine jug and Balthazar's cup and set them on the wooden chest, so that they would not be trodden upon in the night.

"I asked Balthazar if he had some gold for the journey," said Melchior. "And he said that he could lend me a few staters which he keeps hidden in his saddlebags. And I have a few coins of my own."

"That is good," I said, having given no thought to how we might finance our journey. Melchior took something from a leather purse and threw it to me, and it sparkled as it whirled through the air across the room. I caught it in my hand and saw that it was a small Parthian gold coin.

"When we get to the *serai* tomorrow, before the caravan departs," he said, "I want you to buy some frankincense and some myrrh. And mind the change. We have a long way to go and we haven't many of these."

Chapter Seven

THERE IS LITTLE POINT in recounting much of what happened as we left the tower early that chill morning. We departed an hour or so before dawn, and Bilquis came out of her room just long enough to bid us farewell, but she let the houseboy see us out. No doubt she was still hurt and angry at being left behind.

We walked towards the edge of the city, and, as we neared the western gate, we began to hear the cacophony off in the distance. Then, when we reached the *serai*, I had never seen so many camels. There must have been more than five hundred of them, each braying, stomping, or snorting, either complaining about its load or about how heavy it feared that its load might be.

We were to travel in a caravan of considerable size, especially coming from a smaller city such as ours. But Daoud was a skilled businessman and, of course, well-known and respected by the traders and so he attracted a lot of custom.

I think the only nationality not represented there were the Hans from Cathay, for, of course, they were banned from coming so far west, for fear that they would meet the Romans and steal our trade in Cathay silks, for which we were the middleman. A few Hans had tried to sneak through some years before, but they had been apprehended and lost their heads long before they reached Persia's easternmost border. Our neighbours to the east, the Kushans, also took a cut from the silk trade, and in this case took a cut from the necks of the competition.

But here in the *serai*, and spilling far out through the gates and into the fallow land and the road surrounding the compound, was a jumble of people and boxes and parcels and hampers and things wrapped in old carpets or cheap cloth or sewn into leather. People wrapped packages in twine and rope, dragging them across the dusty ground and hoisting them onto the backs of their pack animals. Everywhere was the keen of camels and everywhere was the babble of twenty different tongues. It was, Melchior observed once more, a kind of symphony of commerce.

I turned to look for my teacher and found him headed toward Balthazar, who appeared to be deep in discussion.

"Did Daoud tell you to give us this one? Did he tell you specifically?" Balthazar asked one of the workers in the caravan, a Turkoman from the far north. The man shrugged amiably. It was apparently his job merely to find camels for those who needed them, although most people brought their own.

Balthazar scowled. "Daoud most certainly did not choose it. You did!" insisted the king. He turned to Melchior: "Look at this and give me your express opinion as a scholar, soldier, and man of the world." He seized one of the beast's legs and lifted it back, until we could see the bottom of its hoof. "Look at how it walks, and how it wears down the pads here. The wear is asymmetrical, because this poor creature has an uneven gait," he continued. "This camel is arthritic. It will be down with knee trouble before our second week out." He turned to Melchior, asking, "What do you think?"

He might as well have asked the astronomer what angels eat for breakfast or how sea-serpents reproduce. Melchior knew almost nothing about camels, apart from riding on them and occasionally eating part of one at a wedding or similar occasion.

"Splendid!" said Balthazar, obviously pleased. "Then I can teach you on this trip. It is useful information, and people tell me that I am a gifted teacher." He turned back to the small Turkoman: "Now, my good fellow, let us go off and find Daoud-*khan* and see about getting us some healthier animals." The Turkoman looked resigned to giving us better camels, and, from the little I knew so far of Balthazar's good-hearted but relentless determination, that was a wise decision. I could see Daoud in the distance, surrounded by his caravaneers and customers, counting pack animals and negotiating the fees.

But I had been given my own assignment. After looking around the *serai* and talking to a few tradesmen, I took Melchior aside and explained that this was the wrong end of the caravan trail for those who hoped to buy frankincense. Since it came from somewhere deep in the deserts of Araby, it would be cheaper to the west, where we were heading— Jerusalem, perhaps. Melchior instructed me to buy a small amount anyway and to get the most fragrant kind possible, even if all we could afford was a small handful. He would tell me no more, and I found this purchase most perplexing.

Preparations were delayed when about forty policemen, all heavily armed, marched into the *serai*, demanding to see Daoud. They were misshapen men for the most part, and their patched and worn uniforms were a mix of cast-offs from the army and the cheapest materials available in the bazaar. Their motley assortment of rusty billhooks and hangers, daggers and staves and pikestaffs further displayed their intentions. But they were even more trouble than they appeared to be, for our masters had seen fit to pay them not even enough for food, expecting them to make up the difference by what they stole from the public. The state itself would never see a tenth of what they took, and, whenever a hard-working person attempts to provide some valuable service, the police interpose themselves and demand a share.

For this reason everything came to a standstill. As if by magic, the place went silent, so silent that we could hear birdsong in the distance. I suppose that what I really heard was the stultifying effect of the state on commerce anywhere. Some of the policemen sauntered through the crowd, poking people and animals and packages with their sticks, attempting to peek into the parcels being bound and loaded atop the camels. But tradesmen hurriedly pulled blankets or cloths over their goods to hide them from the greedy eyes of the government. The police pushed the limits of their authority as far as they could, while their victims tried to retain their privacy, their goods, and their tempers.

Daoud ran quickly from the far end of the compound, out of breath from haste. The longer that the police stayed in the *serai*, the more trouble and expense they would incur. Daoud was accompanied by twenty more men than the police had on hand. The entire *serai* took his side in these matters, not just his own men, and at least sixty glowered and bristled with swords and hatchets and axes and knives.

The chief of the police contingent was a man whose name I have forgotten, but he came from Rayy, a small man with a pinched face. When he demanded that Daoud accompany him back into town, ostensibly to inspect licenses and paperwork, some of the caravaneers started to brandish their weapons, but Daoud stopped them with a glance. They finally agreed that the police chief and Daoud would meet alone in the upper store-room, where we had been with the caravaneers the day before. And so upstairs they went to determine what bribes Daoud would need to pay, in order that our thieving masters would let him go about his business.

Shortly thereafter, Melchior pointed to a corner where one of Sattar's troopers watched us from a nearby stall. He was dressed in ordinary clothes rather than his black uniform, but I recognised him as one of the men in the old man's garden. "Nowadays," Melchior said under his breath as we walked to the far end of the bazaar, "we practically need a state to protect us from the state we already have."

And so the caravan set forth only about an hour late, and thus the morning sun was just beginning to peek over the small-est houses to the east, when we struggled onto our camels and lurched forward and then back, as the beasts rose clumsily to their feet.

I was, and indeed still am, much more accustomed to riding horses, as you must be. And so, although that was not my first time on a camel by any means, I have always found them to be pleasant beasts on which to ride. Their pace and their motion are stately, and the saddle is sumptuously soft, and the view from on high is unexcelled. Climbing aboard the animal is another matter entirely, but we accomplished it without breaking our necks and so we set forth.

After Balthazar had spoken to Daoud about the lame mount, Melchior had been given a splendid, spotless white camel as a replacement. It was not young, but, as Melchior said, neither was its rider. Her name was *Shireen,* or Sweet. Still, she seemed to be more grand than anything else, and her glance was perhaps the most imperious of all the camels in all the caravan. She was a snooty, old dowager of a camel. The old man said that, on our return, he hoped to enter her into a sneering competition with Keshvari, the High Priest's personal secretary, and thus win enough to pay for the trip. He added that it would be a pity, however, if the camel taught the acting High Priest how to spit—yet another anti-social habit was hardly what the young man needed.

Melchior had brought his best blue velvet cloak, in which he would have looked splendid atop the camel. But he had that wrapped carefully in his bags to protect it and wore instead a long, rough, hooded over-garment of hand-woven wool, much mended from the look of it. It was the colour of the desert and perhaps half as old as the desert too. On top of his head and beneath the hood, he wore the ancient traditional Persian cap, which rose to a point that tilted over to one side. It is what the Greeks call a Phrygian cap. That, like his best cloak, was made out of pale blue velvet and delicately embroidered in silver thread. I think that, if you wanted to see one nowadays, you would need to go to find the bas-reliefs on the road to Persepolis. Such hats have not been worn in years, especially since so many of our traditions have been suppressed by our Parthian masters.

Balthazar rode, of course, on his beloved Yasmine, who seemed to be in no better spirits than the day before, hissing at the other camels and occasionally biting one or another of them on the hindquarters. She would suddenly straighten her neck with the speed and accuracy of a serpent and then sink her long front teeth into the rump of a perfectly innocent passing camel. The bitten animal would shriek and lurch about to defend itself, nearly hurling its cargo to the ground in the process and usually frightening the daylights out of whoever was unlucky enough to be in the saddle. Since there was little that he could do, Balthazar made much light and cheer of this, but the people whose camels were bitten shot him angry glances, and each time the king winced in embarrassment.

Balthazar wore his voluminous, long, crimson shirt with a design picked out in gold thread or gold printing—I forget which, as it was so long ago. And, on the first day, at least, he wore a pair of bronze *bazuband*, cast in some complex African pattern that reached from his wrists nearly up to his elbows, as a swordsman or an archer might wear, or perhaps a warrior king. As we rode, near the back of the caravan, I thought that we made a handsome sight, going forth on a secret mission of immense importance, perched high on our elegant beasts and feeling, for all of the world, like three kings instead of merely one.

Beside us, on swift, small, racing camels, were two groups of a dozen archers each, hired by Daoud to provide security against bandits, who were always a threat then and now. And in addition there were perhaps thirty of his men, including cooks and camel-boys, as well as their wives and camp followers. Then the caravan itself was comprised of perhaps one hundred merchants and, of course, the three of us.

We came to learn a lot about the commercial travellers from the near month in which we spent on the caravan to Jerusalem, but we learnt even more from Daoud. And, whenever he had time to spare, he would pull out from the great moving queue and wait on the side of the path, letting its members pass him, until we, in the rear, came up to him. Then we four would drop behind just a little farther, out of an earshot of our travelling companions, and there we would continue to follow our caravan and talk of many things.

According to Daoud, one traveller from the Levant, an unassuming man who seemed more like a schoolteacher than a trader, carried three bolts of silk worth nearly as much as the High Priest's palace. Three bolts. They were hidden somewhere among his belongings, perhaps wrapped in leather and stuffed beneath his camels' saddles. Such was the price fetched in Rome by the very finest silks of Cathay.

"The Roman appetite for silk is big, too big," said Daoud, who had a small black racing camel that looked unimpressive, although she was supposedly, apart from cheetahs, the fastest living creature between Mashad and Damascus.

"They say that six months ago," he continued, "right on the floor of the Senate, the tyrant Augustus counted the Roman gold, Roman *aureae*, heading east from their empire to pay for silk. A sum worth kingdoms, the emperor complained. Romans are crazy. Why do they need silk for that kind of money? The desert people, the *Beddou*, say that God gives nuts to those with no teeth."

Indeed it was beginning to prove a Roman weakness that may yet—perhaps in your lifetime, God willing—bring an end to their wretched empire and their attempts to dominate their neighbours. Not the trade, which is good for everyone, but rather the Roman dependency on luxuries. Can you imagine a woman wearing a dress worth as much as a farm or the contents of a wardrobe worth a palace? Such is Roman culture nowadays, and so I suspect that we shall be here long after their empire is gone.

"In this caravan," said Daoud, "there are more goods worth more money than I'd care to guess." And so it is in almost all caravans, I learnt on that trip. But Melchior summed it up nicely.

"It's no different than life," he said. "The most valuable things, things you'd never dream of seeing or opportunities that you'd give anything to take, are always within an arm's reach, tucked into a place were you'd never bother to look. And not only the material ones."

"And hopefully," added the cynical Daoud, "they are hidden in places where the bandits and the customs agents won't think to look either." This, he continued, is why caravans need to take so many precautions.

"We needed to leave the *serai* at dawn, because that is tradition, and we would not want anyone to suspect us of changing plans," he explained. "But of course that is exactly what we will do. Change plans." He said that we would halt by a small streambed in the late afternoon, rest for a few hours, and then travel throughout the night. It would be cooler, he acknowledged, but also more difficult for bandits.

"It is quieter at night," said Balthazar, "and hence harder for bandits to attack us with any element of surprise." He had a lot of experience travelling in caravans, from Africa to the Orient, and in time that knowledge would serve us well.

"And also, if we keep up the pace through Syria," Daoud concluded, "we may slip past sleeping Roman customs agents, and that is always worth a bonus to a clever businessman such as me." He laughed, and, with a flick of his reins, his camel responded instantly and shot forward, almost leaving him behind in mid air. And we saw him thrown far back in his saddle, grinning broadly, his feet splayed out in front of him, hurtling up the long, long length of the caravan that was his great responsibility. As he flew forward, he flung his free arm up into the air in pure exuberance, clutched the reins with the other, and called out to his camel in some secret, joyous language that only the two could understand: "Ah! Cha-cha! Cha-cha!"

We camped beside a small stream, as Daoud predicted, and the caravaneers and their women prepared us a rich, sweet brew of herbs laced with thick camel's milk. Even though it was only early afternoon, we had been travelling since dawn, and at that point I had not built up my stamina for the hard life of the caravan. The little sounds of the stream were hypnotic too.

And so I drifted off to sleep, while Balthazar told one of his astonishing tales to Melchior and Daoud, as the fire crackled. Hours later, as we awoke to the first planets appearing on the twilight horizon, I recalled nothing much about it, for it was like so many of the king's wondrous stories. But in broad daylight I remember more and more faces of those who came to stare at this strange black king, but who then stayed and listened to his marvellous tales. He spoke of a land far to the east, where ants were the size of dogs and they mined gold from deep in the earth. Or perhaps that was only what I dreamt that he had said.

The caravaneers awakened us hours later, again with cups of this same thick, sweet, and invigorating herbal drink. It cut through the chill instantly. Some of our companions were already aboard their camels, and others were performing last minute adjustments, tightening cinches or fastening bridles. Daoud mounted up and headed toward the start of the caravan, saying that he still had to collect fees from some of the travellers, us included, but in our case it could wait until we were unpacked and settled down for the day in about twelve hours' time.

And so we set off through the night, with the only sounds being the faint whistle of the desert wind and the soft noises of a caravan on the move, the jingle and slap and clank of camels and cargo. We left almost no trace behind us in the sand, as we wended our way across the desert, just as caravans have done ten thousand times in nearly as many years.

We said almost nothing on those long nocturnal journeys. On the first few nights, I suppose, we chatted as we rode along. And, of course, so did the others up ahead, for we could hear bits of their conversations blown back to us on the desert wind. They spoke of the things of which all commercial travellers speak: of families left behind, of great bargains missed, of hope for riches. But, within a few days, they too fell silent, at least while we travelled by night. Even King Balthazar, who was an inexhaustible supply of wit and laughter and tales of adventure, grew reflective during these long rides, coming to life again only when we dismounted and approached the campfires of morning.

"In times like these, the very best times," the old man said, "people fill up with emptiness," but back then I was not so certain of what he meant.

We had been allowed but a few hours of sleep that afternoon and evening, there by the stream. And the camels, refreshed by the spring water, appeared to have stored up days of energy that we lacked. And so we stopped to rest, as the night sky grew pink from the coming dawn.

It did not take very long for some of the caravaneers and camp followers to bring us plates of some sort of stew. I believe that they had ridden ahead and started fires before we arrived, because it was ready so soon after we made camp. I took my water bottle and began to wash my hands, but Balthazar stopped me. He took me aside to where the sand was untrampled and showed me how to scrub my hands in the clean sand without wasting any water. By the time that we attacked the stew a few moments later, I don't believe that any of us even tasted it, since we wolfed it down so quickly.

Daoud approached us with one of his assistants, walking in the loosely jointed manner of people who have just spent hours on camelback.

"Delicious," said Balthazar to Daoud, speaking with his mouth half full, "is it goat meat or mutton or camel? Or something else?"

Daoud smiled. "Yes," he answered ambiguously, and we all laughed. He flung himself down beside us and spoke in a low voice: "Our spotters say that we are being followed. We don't know how many. We only see what we think are scouts for a larger party. But it could mean nothing." Melchior nodded.

"They tell me you were at Carrhae," he said to the old man. Melchior nodded again. The long night had left him with little inclination to talk.

"Then you won't be frightened by a few bandits," said Daoud.

"Not with a good man in charge," said Balthazar. Daoud smiled, acknowledging the compliment, but all of us knew that it meant little more than good wishes. Even in that vast and inhospitable desert, there was nothing more lethal than bandits.

"Next, my favourite part of the journey," said Daoud, taking a small leather bag from inside his shirt and hefting it in his fingers. "We have how many passengers who have not yet paid their fares?" he asked. Beside him, one of his deputies answered with noticeable hesitation. He said four.

We looked puzzled. "Me, my student, and of course His Royal Highness," clarified Melchior pointing to Balthazar. Daoud furrowed his brow and again looked at his deputy, who held up four fingers.

Daoud hesitated oddly, and then shook his head. "Well, perhaps we can work out a discounted rate. Shall we make a small reduction for each? Added up, it would come to…" But Melchior interrupted.

"How many passengers?" the old man asked Daoud's deputy. In a low voice the man answered four. Melchior addressed Daoud: "I asked about you before we chose to come. Everyone in the bazaar says that you are the most honest caravaneer between here and the sea," he said. Daoud fidgeted and began to look as though he were guilty of something.

The caravan leader stared at his hands for a moment, thinking. "Look," he said, speaking a little too rapidly, "no one ever called me greedy. And your mission means much to me. Call it three passengers. Leave it at that." Daoud rose to his feet and turned to go. "Have a good sleep, everyone." Then he spoke to his assistant: "Three. That's it. Three."

Melchior, sitting down, caught the leg of Daoud's assistant. "No nonsense, now," he demanded, "who is the fourth passenger whom you wanted to charge us for?" Even though Daoud was facing away from us, we could see him cringe.

"Come on man, out with it!" urged the old man, gripping the assistant's trouser leg like a vise.

Daoud stood stock still, his shoulders hunched high. "That woman. Your servant or relative or something," his assistant answered Melchior. "The woman Bilquis."

Chapter Eight

HAD THE CARAVAN not already been travelling for the better part of three days, and were there not a danger from bandits, Melchior would have sent her back home or even ended the expedition then and there. He was furious at her disobedience that bordered on treachery. Bilquis was always a headstrong girl, and at that young age people sometimes fail to think of how their actions might inconvenience others.

We waited for her to be brought from the women's camp, where she had made herself nearly invisible among the other women, and Melchior grew angrier the more that he thought of it.

"There is nothing you can do," said Balthazar. "If you send her back, even if you find a spare animal for her to ride and someone to escort her back to the city, you put them at deadly risk from bandits."

"I swear," the old man began to complain, "that I have never seen such blind selfishness."

"But, friend," said Balthazar, interrupting him, "there is nothing else to do. Nothing at all." Melchior thought for a moment and then nodded.

Bilquis joined us, looking around guiltily and hoping to gauge our reactions. She had worn a shabby, old cloak since she left the tower, the more to blend in with the women of the caravan. She fidgeted for a moment and then, reluctantly, told us what had happened.

She had simply followed behind us and attached herself to

the women in the caravan—the cooks and cleaners who were the wives and sweethearts of the caravaneers, and the few prostitutes who serviced the businessmen so far from home. When Daoud's men inquired, she merely explained that she was here to care for Melchior and the rest of us. It was common for important travellers to be accompanied by their servants. In the rush to organise the caravan and set off, none of the organisers bothered to ask us until, of course, it was too late.

Melchior controlled his tongue admirably. He sat the poor creature down in the sand beside him and told her most of why we travelled so far, sparing none of the risks. She and her selfishness, he said, had brought us no advantages, but had compounded our difficulties—and it would be hard to tell how much, until, perhaps, it was too late.

"And when we finally meet this newborn king of the Jews," Melchior complained, "what are his regents going to think of Persians, if we are the sort of people who take our nieces travelling in caravans with scullery maids and loose women? For all I know, the infant king's ministers and attendants and advisers and palace guards may take one look and send us packing before we are even granted an audience. We may not even get beyond the gates of this newborn king's palace. The entire trip will have been in vain because of your selfish mistake."

She was quiet for some time and then apologised. "I am sorry," she said softly, wiping away a tear. "I merely wanted to look after you."

"I have my student to look after me," snapped Melchior, turning away. She gave me a look of resentment, as she rose to her feet.

"I will go back to the women's quarters now," she said. "They will be packing the dinner things, I imagine."

"You will stay with us here," said Melchior with a note of resignation. "Better we talk amongst family than talk amongst strangers. Bring your belongings. And tell Daoud's people that I shall pay for four. See if he has another good camel. If he hasn't, you had better ride with me."

Her eyes brightened, and then Balthazar rose to his feet. "And I shall need your assistance, Bilquis," he added, taking her hand. "If Caspar is to look after Melchior, and I am to look after Caspar and Melchior, then who is to look after me? I am a king," he declared in his booming voice, "and so I am extremely fragile." The burly monarch was ever the diplomat, and Bilquis hugged him. Even Melchior shook his head and smiled at the thought of Balthazar's supposed fragility. But the old man could see the purpose of the king's diplomacy, since there was nothing more to be gained by being angry with his niece.

The caravan began to come awake in the mid-afternoon, a lazy time that I always enjoyed, for it was still too hot to move far, but there were yet a few hours until the darkness would overtake us and we would begin to travel again. Most of the commercial travellers still wallowed and snored, wrapped in their shawls or stretched out on their rugs and mats. A few studied their accounts or said their various prayers, and in the women's camp cauldrons were boiling with water for hot drinks, and preparations were being made for the evening meal. But, at that time of day, the most interesting part of the caravan was where the caravaneers made camp.

After dozens or even hundreds of journeys across the desert, they had learnt to exist with little sleep. And there was always a great deal to do which could not be done on the back of a camel. So, in these late afternoons, the caravaneers used the time to repair the tack and saddles, wax the leather, sharpen tools and weapons, and to perform light veterinary tasks, such as removing pebbles from the soft pads of the camels' feet. Surrounded by hundreds of miles of silent desert, adjacent to almost one hundred sleeping travellers, was this small, outdoor, portable workshop with men cutting and stitching and making and mending and preparing for the long night ahead.

Melchior was always an early riser and he had found Daoud. They were sitting beside one of the drovers, who was tempering a buckle on the white coals of a fire that another kept hot by pumping a leather bellows. Melchior held a short sword, presumably belonging to one of the drovers, and sketched lines into the dust at their feet.

"Our camp was here," he explained, "and so we dug the trench along two sides. About five feet deep, no more than that. The Roman 3rd Legion came just before dawn. A few fell into the ditch. Others, marching behind, turned left, which let them meet our cavalry head on, while exposing their right flank to our archers."

One of the caravaneers used tongs to lift the buckle off the flat stone that was his makeshift anvil, and he dropped it into a small leather container of water, which hissed and boiled for some time. Water was a precious commodity in a caravan, and so they conserved it.

"It is a good strategy, but not for me. We never have enough time and manpower to dig a latrine, much less a trench," Daoud continued. "You had young soldiers in the 14th Foot. My customers are rich merchants, so fat that they can hardly climb onto their camels. I would need to hire bandits to dig the trench to protect me from the bandits."

Daoud told me that they had spotted more scouts, and by now his caravan guards were certain that bandits were watching us. Villagers would not so often send people to spy on us from hillsides, and anyway there were no villages for quite some distance.

It would remain to be seen whether we would be attacked, Daoud explained, or whether they would wait for a target less protected. Sometimes, he said, he had travelled for two weeks, knowing that he was watched every day, but at the end the bandits vanished into the deserts without attacking. One could never know if they decided that his caravans were too well protected or if something more promising appeared in another direction or indeed if there was any reason at all.

Running caravans was a dangerous business, he explained, and hence the great profitability for those who survived. He said he had once come across one that did not. It was about two days west of Ctesiphon. "Maybe four hundred camels, judging from the skeletons," he recalled, "and maybe a hundred and fifty people, so about the size of this caravan. And not a survivor was left; just sand blowing over scraps of sun-bleached cloth, over white bone and hanks of hair. And not bit of cargo. Neither a fistful of spikenard, nor a jar of aloes, nor a tiny piece of camphire remained. All gone. Stolen, carried off far away and sold. All that remained was the desert and the dead and the sound of the wind, never stopping. Like a memorial, I suppose. Singing a dirge to its paying customers, its permanent guests. Singing softly. Forever."

Melchior set the short sword down on the ground beside one of the caravaneers. "All we can do is remain alert," he said to Daoud.

"Working in the desert is an education," Daoud answered. "It teaches us patience. We have to always be ready. But before anything can happen, God has to make up His mind."

When we returned to our campsite, Daoud's men had found a young camel for Bilquis, and she had named it Sahar, or Morning. If it had another name before, the beast revealed nothing about it. Balthazar was teaching her how to check the bridle and reins and saddle and stirrups. Bilquis had travelled this far in the caravan only riding behind one of the other women; she had never ridden a camel by herself.

"Once I am finished teaching you about camels," Balthazar explained, "you shall never be happy until you make your uncle buy you at least five of them. You will insist that they come to live with you in your small garden. And you yourself will ensure they are the first creatures that you greet every morning and the last friends to whom you bid farewell before you go to bed at night.

They have all the personality that people have, but they never borrow money or gossip maliciously."

It was clear that Bilquis was enjoying herself immensely. Balthazar made the appropriate clicking noise, and Sahar dutifully sank to her knees, first dropping her forelegs then her hind legs, until her body rested flat on the sand and Bilquis could scramble up into the saddle.

"You can put your foot on her neck, right there, and lift yourself," Balthazar explained. "She will not mind. Unless you are fat like me." Bilquis giggled, and Balthazar grasped her ankle and moved her foot onto the appropriate place on Sahar's neck, then pushed Bilquis upwards. Once she was securely seated, he walked around to the front and scratched Sahar's nose on that place where camels are always so grateful to be scratched. Then he gave her a swift kiss and made the other clicking noise that tells camels to rise. And so Sahar rose first from her hind legs, pitching Bilquis far forward, then from her forelegs, throwing Bilquis back in the other direction. Bilquis held tight to the reins, but more importantly gripped the saddle and the thick carpet on which she sat.

"There," said Balthazar, looking up at her. "Now all we need to learn is stop, go, right, left, and the other command."

"What other command?" she asked.

"Sometimes," he whispered in a conspiratorial tone, "if they are Sudanese camels, such as Sahar most certainly is, and if you know the right command and they feel so inclined, they will fly through the air."

Bilquis's camel never learnt to fly, or, if it did, it remained a secret from all of us. But Bilquis learnt to ride her well, and over the days to come she became quite expert in handling these mercurial beasts. She had a strange way with them for some reason, even Balthazar's camel. Yasmine may have had a well-rounded personality but all she exhibited was irritation and venom. Or so I thought, until about midway through the journey.

I had shared with my companions the box of carrot *halwa* given me by my housekeeper before we departed. Bilquis asked for a second small piece, which she fed to Yasmine, and thereafter the camel would not stay away from her. Unless she was well tethered, Yasmine would pull up the wooden stakes and follow her about—and indeed this happened for days on end—making moon-eyes and what Bilquis supposed to be affectionate little noises.

We were all astounded, believing that there was no record of anyone ever having fed *halwa* to a camel before. We had seen Yasmine given a piece of *gur* just before she bit Balthazar when we first met him, but this carrot confection seemed to transform the animal.

"Obviously! It is a well-known fact," Balthazar declared, "that the grandest beast in the Great Pushkar Camel Fair is always fed *halwa* from the hand of the sultan and no one else. Indeed, if the camel should bite him, the sultan is beheaded at once, since it signifies that the royal family has lost the favour of Almighty God Himself."

"Balthazar," said Melchior, shaking his head and chuckling, "I have never heard such tommyrot in all my life. And there is no sultan of Pushkar. He is a maharajah. And bitten by a camel? And then beheaded? Oh, dear me!"

"Well," said the king, doing a poor job of pouting, "we can spend all day arguing technicalities, but the fact is that all camels adore *halwa*."

And on that matter he was correct of course. Over days, as Bilquis kept feeding sweets to Yasmine, even Daoud noticed the difference; perhaps because fewer of his customers complained that they or their mounts had been bitten by Balthazar's savage beast. A complete transformation appeared to have come over Yasmine, and she became as sweet-tempered as Sahar.

"It makes sense," said Bilquis in a way that of course made no sense at all, "people adore *halwa* so why shouldn't camels?" That did neither explain the transformation nor such a long-lasting change from a single sweet or two. But, whenever I took out the box, Bilquis acquired more *halwa* to feed to her admirer.

It must have been several days later. I am not sure how many, for, as I said, it was all many years ago. We awoke in the late afternoon as always, and when I set off in search of a hot drink, Balthazar was well into a game of dice with some of the merchants. He smiled, as a bearded businessman from Latakia scrutinised his roll.

"I am not sure," mumbled the trader.

"You are a silk merchant, a taker of risks, a natural gambler," encouraged the monarch. "I am a mere government employee, although I suppose that, being king, it means that I own the government." The merchant smiled, but remained unconvinced.

"Now let me make this more interesting," Balthazar continued. "I see your ten pieces of gold and raise you a ruby." The other players laughed in approval. I was surprised at the enormity of the stakes, and other passers-by paused to listen. But before I could peer over Balthazar's shoulder, he picked something off the blanket and flung it to me.

"We're playing for sweets. Have a gold piece," he offered before returning to the game. "Now you have one ruby and nine pieces of gold, since Caspar has eaten one." The merchants and the spectators laughed.

It took me little time to find the camp followers and the makeshift kitchen that contained their samovars, but service was slow, for there were many other travellers newly awakened and in need of refreshment. When my turn came, I brought a second cup for Balthazar, but his game had ended, the businessmen had gone off, and the king looked troubled, as Melchior sat beside him. It had been a dream, he said, or a piece of a recurring dream.

"It was a beautiful woman with black streaming hair," the king explained, "and she had great rings under her eyes, as though she had been weeping."

"What more do you remember?" the old man asked.

"Blood," said Balthazar. "There was much blood. Too much blood."

"Anything more?" my teacher asked. The king shook his head a little too violently, as if the memory disturbed him.

"What do you think that it means?" asked Melchior.

Balthazar cocked his head to one side. "Indigestion," he laughed, but insincerely. "Another cup of this noxious brew before bedtime and I would have seen much worse. Probably your emperor without his trousers on. I don't put much stock in these things," he added.

"I am not certain," said Melchior softly. "My own experience, untested though it may be, is that dreams sometimes bring us useful messages."

"These are not areas that I wish to explore," murmured Balthazar.

It was one or two days later, as we rode across the desert, that Melchior asked him why he had left Sheba. It was a question that none of us had dared to ask.

"Because, officially, I am a dead man," said Balthazar smiling wistfully. "I was young, very young, when my father died, and so the kingdom was ruled by my uncles acting as regents. It is a common enough practice everywhere. And I suspected nothing until I was in my teens and set off to study in Alexandria, for there were good teachers there then and now. But the ship was scuttled off the coast. Some of my own guards plotted to kill me, but I had overheard them whispering in the night and so I slipped into the water unseen. They sank the ship and rowed away in a small boat, while I swam to shore and made my way to Sanaa, where I had elderly relatives who kindly schooled and supported me thereafter."

"I gathered from travellers, who had later visited Sheba, that my treacherous guards had lied to my uncles, telling them that I had been murdered as planned. So the regents declared that I was dead and they continued to rule. Even the old generals and administrators who had been friends of my father seemed to support them. It is always so in small kingdoms, and I have travelled ever since," he said. "There is much to see in this fine world."

"Have you ever thought of going back to reclaim your throne?" asked the old man.

"Sometimes," said Balthazar. "But then I think of what it might make me become. I might be transformed into one of my own uncles. Think of it. I would eat the same food and breathe the same air. I would hear the same complaints and listen to the same conspiracies and adjudicate the same petty rivalries and poisonous grievances. I might well come to see my opinions as wisdom, my rule as just, my presence as indispensable. Enough so, perhaps, to commit murder. Over time I might become what they became. And no kingdom is worth that."

"Are you certain that is what would happen?" asked Bilquis.

"We have a saying," he answered. "A diet of meat makes a lion; feed him on grass and he becomes a cow. Slowly I would become what the kingdom makes its kings to be. Isn't it so, Melchior?"

"The court might change you," the old man answered, "unless you change it first. You could, you know. How did your father rule?" Balthazar said nothing more that evening.

When we finished that night's travels and began to make camp, Daoud rode his camel into our midst. All of the usual traces of merriment were gone from his face.

"Drink hot lemon to keep awake. I've told the cooks to make it sweet and keep it coming until nightfall or we run out of supplies, whichever comes first. And if you have anything valuable, get it off your mounts and put your bags somewhere in the middle of the camp. Put them with my things if you like."

"Is it…" I started to ask but he finished the sentence for me.

"I have no idea what will happen," he said, "but we are being watched, and the enemy is close. Our scouts have seen signs in the desert, and they think that, if we are to be attacked, it will be today. Otherwise we get too close to the Roman outposts and the next big oasis. Once we're within reach of help their chances diminish."

It was not much later that some of Daoud's archers rode up beside us. They explained that we were to move our camels into a larger defensive ring formed with the rest of the caravan and put ourselves into the middle, where we would be safe. Balthazar approached their captain.

"We are not all tradesmen, captain," he said. "We can fight but we need weapons."

"Agreed," said the officer. "Can any of you use a bow?"

Melchior raised his hand reluctantly. "I could fifty years ago. But the Romans who would have vouched for me are all dead." The archers chuckled approvingly.

The officer replied, "Very well, everyone gets short swords, and this one gets a bow as well. Over to the tent, as fast as you can. The man with the eye-patch will give you your positions along the camel barricade, and I want you to stay there. If you have to piss, stand there and piss. And if anything comes in from outside, just kill it and tell me later."

Melchior followed the rest of us, but he was stopped by the officer: "Catch me a couple more of those Roman eagles, and we'll cook them for supper." He had recognised, by the old man's age and by the reference to Rome, that Melchior had fought at Carrhae. He saluted as the old man passed.

Bilquis was sent to the women, who were collecting as much water as possible and shredding cloth for bandages. We were given our weapons; cheap and heavy short swords they were. In addition, Melchior was given a bow, and much to his delight he found that he was still strong enough to use it. He propped one end against his foot and pulled the other end back in a single neat motion, catching the bowstring in the nock, made of cows-horn, at the very end of the bow. Then he took the strung bow in his left hand and with the first fingers of his right hand drew the bowstring back plenty far enough to hold and shoot an arrow.

"Better than men half your age," said officer. "You must have practised on those two-legged targets who spoke Latin." The old man smiled.

Two or three of the merchants had found flat stones on which they honed the double edges of their swords, suggesting that some of the businessmen had once been soldiers too. The edges were blunt, one complained, and the short swords were of cheap manufacture, so they would never hold a sharp edge for very long. One of the archers smiled: "They won't need an edge for long. We only get one chance to use them," he answered.

Some of the more nervous passengers scribbled notes to loved ones or wrote wills, having paid little thought to who would deliver their messages if we were overrun by bandits. Their letters would simply bleach beside their bones.

But, for the most part, we did what people have done in wars since the very dawn of time. We did nothing. We waited, straining our eyes in the bright sunlight, scrutinising the horizon for any signs of motion, baking in the desert heat, and watching the occasional carrion-eating bird circle hopefully overhead, as minutes turned slowly into hours.

Balthazar gave me a lesson in the use of short swords. "Keep your body low and keep working the point upwards," he explained. "Then swing fast in a semi-circle and, if you miss his leg tendons, cut upwards again. Watch me. Hold tight onto your buckler and keep that left elbow close to your body. Then punch it towards his face and disorient him. Put your shoulder into it and use your weight to push it forward, and then cut upward again with the sword." He had learnt some unusual and useful skills in his long travels, and he was lithe despite his size.

The camels were tethered a circle, pegged down as tightly as possible to keep them from moving. They formed a sort of living barricade, and, from the worried noises they made, they seemed to know it. The archers, Daoud's caravaneers, and those others of us capable of handling weapons stood immediately behind the camels and manned the outer periphery. Behind us, in another much smaller circle, were piled all the packages and bundles that had been loaded onto the camels during our voyage. Inside that ring, huddled behind the packages, were the women and those businessmen who were either too weak or too ill, or mostly too frightened, to fight.

Daoud moved around the outer ring, giving advice and encouragement.

"What happens next?" I asked him. I think that everyone he spoke to, apart from his mercenaries, asked him the same question.

"We will stay here until nightfall, if need be. And if we have not been attacked by then," Daoud continued, "we will push ahead as quickly as we can. We are at slightly greater risk while on the move, but they are at even greater risk attacking in the dark over uncertain terrain. That much we know."

Melchior and I sat on some wooden chests and waited, as everyone waited. I realised that everything we did we might be doing for the last time. It made all things seem important. But then there was little to do but think and talk, and maybe learn.

Our earlier conversation with Balthazar had disturbed me. "Are we really so malleable that we become whatever we do? Does every action change us so much?" I asked Melchior. He thought for a while.

"Our Zoroastrian friends say that every moral act helps determine the fate of the universe," the old man answered. "But does repetitive action change us forever? Perhaps people are malleable like gold, not inflexible like iron. This is why religions try to instil positive habits through meditation or prayer.

"Commit enough acts of robbery, and something usually changes and one becomes a robber. Similarly, with sufficient prayer, you could become a saint. Plenty of people do." We watched a small dust-devil form in the desert and then vanish as quickly as it had come. "In my case," the old man added, "it may just be possible to avoid becoming a fool despite a lifetime working with High Priests and elders." His eyes twinkled merrily, and we both continued to watch the desert.

It was maybe forty minutes later that we saw the plume of dust rising over to the west of us. It looked large, and when the bandits rode into view, my heart sank. There were a lot of them, and they were on horseback. That meant that they were very well-organised indeed, for horses can move much faster than camels, but travel less far. So the bandits needed to know precisely where we were, and they needed to have a good place to water their animals, within perhaps no more than four hours of the attack.

It was when they gathered, about five hundred yards to the west, that Melchior began to look for Daoud. "They have the sun at their backs," said Melchior. "Look at them." Daoud had been at the end of the circle nearest to the attackers, and he came back at a trot.

"Look where they are," insisted Melchior, pointing. "They are going to make one pass, firing two volleys. Then they will ride off and regroup, giving us a half hour or maybe more. Do you think that they know we have archers?"

"What makes you ask this?" Daoud asked.

"Answer me!" Melchior insisted. "There is little time. Do you think they will have seen our archers?"

"I cannot imagine why," Daoud replied.

"Then tell your men to hide their bows and tell everyone to fling himself onto the ground when the bandits ride past," said the old man.

Daoud shook his head violently. "This makes no sense at all," he complained. Melchior put an arm over Daoud's shoulder and led him to the other end of the barricade, whispering intently.

We squinted into the sun as best we could. There could have

been a hundred or more bandit horsemen. It was hard to tell. They grouped themselves into some sort of line or similar formation, but it was difficult to see from far away. Eventually one of the caravaneers, a Kazakh, taught us the old Central Asian trick of pressing gently on the outer edge of each eye, changing the shape of the eyeball and improving one's long-distance vision.

The bandit horde became just a little clearer. One or two dispatch riders apparently brought the bandits more instructions, for we could see the little plumes of dust, as they rode from the far distance up to where the band had gathered. The wind had stopped, and all had grown still, and so the distant trails of dust hung in the still desert air, as though they had been painted over the flat, featureless horizon.

Then Daoud called for attention. "If the bandits start to attack, you will all wait until I give the signal, then drop onto the ground and stay there. Archers, put down your bows and nobody touch them until I give the order." Daoud's archers looked sceptical, but no one complained. They were professionals.

"You had better be right," said Daoud to Melchior in an undertone.

"I hope that their scouts haven't seen our archers," said Melchior, "but I am fairly satisfied otherwise."

We waited for another twenty minutes, but then suddenly we saw the western horizon start to fill with roiling clouds of dust, and even before we noticed that the line of bandits had grown closer, we began to hear the pounding of hundreds of hooves, rumbling like thunder from a distant storm.

Two or three of the businessmen went very pale and seemed as though they were about to throw themselves onto the ground prematurely, but, when they looked into the faces of the disciplined archers and caravaneers beside them, they thought better of it and remained standing, clasping their hands behind their backs to keep from trembling visibly.

The roar grew louder, and the horde grew closer, and then

they turned as if they were a single living organism instead of dozens of individual men and mounts. Like the head of a serpent, the far end of the line moved faster than the rest, and the others swung in behind them. In one swift manoeuvre they shifted, so that rather than make contact with our barricade as a wide line of cavalry perhaps fifty horsemen abreast, they came at us head-on and single-file, in a line one hundred horsemen long.

This left them presenting a much smaller target to us defenders. Since every horseman rode directly behind his predecessor, we could shoot at no more than one man at a time. And it meant that, when they passed us, a hundred would have a chance to pick us off, single file, one after another. I began to wonder if Melchior had miscalculated. This first pass may have been our only chance to use our archers to advantage.

Closer still they came, and louder grew the pounding of hooves, until it seemed as though they were right on top of us. Finally, Daoud gave the signal, and we fell to the ground, listening to the arrows whistle overhead. Not all of them missed of course, and the barrage seemed to continue for many long minutes amid the roar of wounded camels and the pounding of horses' hooves and even the screams and whoops of the bandits, as they rode past. It must have taken a minute or but little longer, although it seemed like an eternity. As I stood up, I could see the last few horsemen turned and firing back at us. Just as Melchior had predicted, they had each fired twice: once head on, as they attacked, and then again over the haunches of their horses, as they galloped away to safety.

Daoud and Melchior appeared to have stood stock-still and watched the entire attack, although I am sure that they must have taken cover somehow. Daoud looked astonished and impressed.

"You are right," he shouted over the din. "Absolutely right. It couldn't be anything else. Amazing."

"Did you see their feet? Did you?" insisted Melchior rather triumphantly. "They had rope stirrups. I knew it."

The captain of the archers approached them: "There will be lots of meat for dinner, sir. We have at least four camels mortally wounded and another fifteen that might be able to walk if we don't make them carry a load. Two more of those attacks, sir, and we'll need the bandits to carry our cargo for us."

"Captain, those men are Parthian regular cavalry," said Daoud. "Imperial horsemen. Nomads from the northern provinces. Rope stirrups."

The officer nodded, uncertainly. "That's the only cavalry on earth that fights bareback," Daoud continued. "And did you see those Parthian shots after the attack—backwards and over the horse's flank? A classic manoeuvre. And who else could ever execute a trained attack-turn like that? Bandits can barely show up for battle at the same time, much less wheel on a sword-point. Lord Melchior is right."

The archer shook his head. "You must be correct, sir, but how did Lord Melchior predict it?"

"I watched them fall into attack formation with the sun at their backs," the old man replied. "It made me remember something. I'd seen them do that before. I had been offered a commission in the cavalry, you know." The officer nodded, impressed.

I wondered, as I suppose everyone did, why government cavalry would attack trade caravans. Balthazar suggested that loot might be a sufficient answer. Indeed, as we stood there in the desert, there was no point even trying to guess whether it was a rogue unit or if they operated with any official approval and, if so, from what level.

"Captain," said Daoud, "get the women and the caravaneers to tend the camels as well as possible. If any camel is mortally wounded, cut its throat, but leave it where it lies. They make good barricades dead or alive. Then bring the businessmen here." The archer saluted.

"These traders are not going to like this, you realise," said Melchior, and Daoud rolled his eyes.

The screaming of the camels was a terrifying sound to hear, and we thought it would never stop. The death cries of the mortally injured beasts were less disheartening than the screams of terror from the other animals who smelled the blood of their companions and feared for the worst. Bilquis came past, half drenched in blood, but carrying a large bundle of clean bandages.

"Save some bandages for us as well. It's not over yet," said Daoud, stalking off in pursuit of the archers.

"We've had to kill four of the camels," Bilquis explained. "Another dozen are badly wounded; the rest we are patching up. And Balthazar, I am not sure about poor Yasmine. It was two arrows. I am really not sure if she will..." She was unable to finish her sentence and began to sob.

After a moment, Balthazar lifted her chin with his finger and looked in her wet red eyes. "We say our prayers and we keep working," he explained gently. "That is what we do. Do you understand?" Hugging him closer, she nodded her head.

The sun continued to beat down unmercifully, and some of the camp followers lugged their heavy water skins around the circle. No one wanted to ask how much water was left. Perhaps it did not matter, and I had a feeling that, soon enough, we would either be free and on our way, or never in need of refreshment again.

Melchior kept staring into the desert and he finally spoke. "They smell plunder and they are not going to wait all day," he explained. "My guess is that we have twenty minutes for certain and maybe nothing more. Of course they might give up and go away, but that is pretty unlikely, in so much as we didn't defend ourselves. We look like an easy target."

"So what is our plan?" asked Balthazar.

"Know thine enemy," said Melchior. He was interrupted by a roar of protest from the businessmen, objecting to Daoud. They clustered around the caravaneer and were nearly incandescent with rage.

"We paid you to defend our property, not to give it away," shouted one.

"Let your archers start defending us. Then, if enough of them die, we can parley," said another.

Daoud raised his hands for silence. "I will say this once more. Only once more. Everything bulky goes into a pile outside the circle beyond the camels. The archers will show you where. Then everything small and valuable goes here inside the circle with us. You have five minutes. Oh, and one more thing. Six minutes from now, if there is anything bulky inside the circle, my men will take it away from you and put it outside the circle for the bandits—whether or not you've hidden your silks inside the bundles. Is that clear?"

It was clear, but unpopular, and the businessmen roared their objections and shook their fists.

"Do you know what I paid for those aspalathus branches? All the way from Bengal," complained a fat man, trembling in anger.

"And if we are lucky, you will get it all back," answered Daoud. "And if we are not lucky, believe me, you are not going to need any of this." The crowd shouted furiously. The caravaneer turned to his guards: "Captain," Daoud said, and a dozen of them drew their short swords and glowered at the traders, one of whom strode forward and shook his finger beneath the captain's nose. He was an Armenian, with a rainbow-striped cummerbund tight around his paunch.

"So what will you do? Order your men to kill us all?" he mocked, motioning for the crowd to press forward, but no one did.

Daoud spoke softly, with his hands still at his sides. "No, I think that I will kill you myself," he said. The crowd fell silent, and the humiliated merchant slunk back into their midst. "You now have four minutes," added Daoud, and he walked through the archers back to the barricades.

Soon enough, with a lot of complaining, but little more trouble than that, the businessmen sorted through their belongings and created a mountain of bundles about one hundred yards from the barricade. In it were medicinal plants and bedding and the less expensive bolts of cloth and *amphorae* of wine and the juice of aloes—the bulkier and cheaper items that Daoud had instructed them to collect.

"The nomads think that we are poorly armed," Melchior explained. "They are also greedy men. We are gambling that they will let their guard slip when they see the chance for booty." Balthazar nodded.

And so it came to pass. About two hours before dark, they came again, and, as before, we watched them press into formation, begin to move, then perform their wheeling manoeuvre and come at us single file. But this time, instead of firing arrows, the head of the line paused when he reached the mountain of bundles stacked at what appeared to be a safe hundred yards from our encampment. One by one, somewhere between a third and a half of them dismounted and began to search through the pile, looking for the most valuable items and the most portable ones. They believed, Daoud said later, that they could always choose to ride into our camp and butcher us for the rest of our belongings if what we offered them was insufficient.

We had staked our lives on whether the bandits had seen our archers, and this was proof that they had not. When Daoud gave the order, groups of our mercenaries rose into the air, as their camels lurched to their feet. All of the archers began firing, from camelback in a horned formation branching out on either side of our encampment. Their small racing camels began to trot forward, encircling and enclosing the enemy, drawing the horns together, as the archers pumped one deadly volley after another into the bandit horde.

Our archers, coming at them from two directions of attack, prevented the standing nomads from taking cover behind their horses and regrouping. Instead, as the two pincers of mounted archers moved forward, the nomads began to find themselves flanked from the better portion of both sides. It was then that Daoud called in the infantry, comprised of the rest of us charging up the middle; "an army of caravaneers and kings," as Balthazar later described us.

After the first dozen volleys of our arrows, perhaps half of the bandits remained on horseback, but, as the horses panicked and jostled back and forth, the mounted bandits blocked one another's line of sight. But of course our archers could hit them from two directions at once, and so perhaps twenty more bandits went down in the first five minutes, and, when they hit the ground, our swordsmen had arrived in time to make fast work of them.

Again we had only about thirty-five infantrymen, led by Melchior, who had dropped his bow and drawn a short sword. Balthazar started by bringing up the rear, but he rapidly strode ahead of the rest of us, waving his sword over his head and roaring like a forest fire. I would have loved to know what the Parthian bandits made of him. They had probably never been attacked by an African giant before, and not many them had the chance to reflect on it afterward.

I soon lost track of him in the throng, and so my only clear memory of him in the fighting was as we approached the bandits. A lancer had dismounted and came at Balthazar with his spear, which was considerably longer than Balthazar's sword and his sword-arm combined. For even a large man, this was an unpleasant dilemma. But Balthazar, typically, had a unique response. He hurled down his sword, grabbed the lance, snapped the shaft in half over one knee, and ran the point back through his attacker. The bandit looked rather surprised as he fell.

Daoud clutched a dagger in his left hand—a tactic of the professional fighters in the Roman coliseum, he later explained. So while he parried with his sword, right-handed in single broad strokes, the smaller and sharper weapon came up repeatedly, two or three times in quick succession. He very quickly cut his way into the bandit force, moving ahead so fast that we were afraid that we would lose him in the hostile throng.

Altogether, the degree to which the nomads got in their own way, and our surprise counterattack, made our relatively small numbers an advantage. We lost perhaps six of our people altogether, about four archers and perhaps two caravaneers. I think we slew forty or fifty bandits, and another fifty rode away, but we had no time for an accurate count, because no sooner had the mounted bandits ridden off than Daoud gave the command to reload our camels and prepare to break camp.

A merchant asked if we could pause to bury our dead, but Daoud refused. "There is no time," he said, "and the desert is full of ghosts; they will not be lonely here." Quite wisely, he wanted to put as much distance as possible between us and whatever brigands might be still capable of attack.

Balthazar had taken an arrow to the shoulder, but, once it had been removed, Melchior licked the blade and pronounced that it was not the poisoned kind. Bilquis treated the wound with salve and bound it up with clean bandages.

"You see?" said Balthazar through clenched teeth. "We kings are extremely fragile. I shall need to be mollycoddled for an entire year at least. Fed by hand, most likely."

"Lean forward," said Bilquis, who had become quite adept at applying bandages.

The king winced, but continued. "Fed exclusively on rice pudding with coconut and things like that. Dried fruit too, but only the most expensive and exotic kind. And fanned by beautiful ladies working in shifts around the clock."

Bilquis's camel, Sahar, survived unscathed, and so we helped Balthazar aboard her, while Bilquis and I shared my camel. The wounded Yasmine limped along behind, complaining louder than anyone, but spared from carrying anything heavier than a few light bundles of clothes and bedding.

"You, my sweet, will need to dine on carrot *halwa* until you are completely cured," Balthazar called out to Yasmine behind him. "And we will find some handsome young men to give you pedicures. There is nothing after *halwa*," he said to Bilquis and me, "that makes camels feel more loved than a good pedicure." Whether Yasmine understood him or not, she stopped complaining, and we moved into the desert at a reassuring pace.

We were glad to leave, and I think that all of us felt lucky to survive. We were all strangely exhilarated as a result of surviving the attack and overcoming the marauders. It was not until the next morning that the exhaustion became apparent. But, as we rode, even Melchior was uncommonly talkative, for he normally travelled in silence, lost to reflection.

"Until Caspar and I saw a newborn star," the old man told us, "the most remarkable thing that I ever beheld was on that final morning on the fields of Carrhae."

It was of especial interest to me, because while we all knew that he had participated in the battle and had apparently served with distinction, he never spoke of it to me or to the other students or even to Bilquis. She believed, as a woman would, that there was some painful memory still too tender to permit discussion, even after fifty years. Instead I remain convinced that Melchior, like many old people who remained mentally active, preferred the present and the future to reminiscing about the past. He would discuss anything, if it helped solve a problem or clarify a thought, but he never dwelt in the past for its own sake.

"Like today, we feared the worst, but we stood up against the legions," the old man recalled. "The Romans marched forward with their shields interlocked, in that famous manoeuvre that the Romans call the *testudo*, a hollow square of spears bristling like a porcupine. In many another country, youths like us lined up against them, and it was the last sight that they ever saw."

"We sent our Parthian cavalry around both sides in our normal horned pincer formation, with the infantrymen coming up the centre and the archers behind. We were badly outnumbered, but there was little else to do. We had tired the enemy by retreating and making them follow, and by grinding them down with cavalry skirmishes that hit them and ran off again. But the odds were hardly in our favour."

"So our generals gave the command, and the trumpeters gave their call to charge. They used the old copper trumpets then, the backward-facing kind introduced by Alexander. We were a splendid army in those days," he said. "And we were prepared to die if need be."

"But then something odd started in the Roman ranks, and their phalanx began to buckle and fold before our eyes. I could see them, because I was in the forefront with my men. The Romans panicked," he recalled. "They looked Heavenwards in sheer terror. Some dropped their spears where they stood. Others turned to run, but there were tight lines of others pushing from behind, confounding their retreat. Here and there a deadly breach appeared in the line of defence formed by their shields."

"But mostly I remember a kind of scream," he said, "but it was not really a scream. To say that is to insult them, which they do not deserve. It was a rush of wind, a gasp of horror made simultaneously by perhaps ten thousand of the empire's most seasoned troops. And then it was effectively over. They broke and ran. Our cavalrymen came from behind and sometimes picked them right up into the air on the points of their lances. Our archers shot high over their heads, so the arrows rained down on those leading the retreat. Those Romans at the fore dropped down, shot through with arrows. A few paces behind, their frantic comrades tried to climb over the dead and the wounded, but as often as not they fell among them, to be trampled by those even further behind. It was a disaster."

"By the end of the day," Melchior concluded, "our gruff, old emperor, Orodes, owned an entire flock of bronze eagles on their once-proud standards. As well as ten or twenty thousand Roman dead and as many enslaved, and the same number run off into the desert to die of drought and madness. And he owned the severed head and the hands of that old, egotistical imbecile Crassus, who destroyed himself and an entire army, simply in order to come better than third among the empire's triumvirs. They say that old Orodes wept at the horrible waste of Roman youth."

For a long time, nothing was said, until Balthazar asked why the Roman troops had broken ranks. Melchior smiled quizzically.

"We asked some of the captives," he recalled. "And they told us of a miracle. Over the heads of our advancing army, there descended from Heaven itself shafts and spear-points of lightning that thrust at their eyes and jabbed at their armour. The lightning bolts came in a hundred colours, they said, and from each bolt there came smaller ones, like reflections that seemed to dance over their heads and taunt them. They had never beheld such things. Some believed that the gods had turned against them, or that the one god of us Persians was stronger than all the gods of Rome. Others thought that we had some secret art, a new weapon like Greek Fire. Mostly, however, they did not spend a lot of time thinking. They ran and they died."

"Did you work out what they saw?" asked Bilquis.

"Why, of course!" Melchior replied. "It took us all of a minute to realise what they were describing. It was silk. They had never seen silk before, only linen or wool. We had our long standards, and from them we unfurled long regimental banners of silk with different colours for different parts of our force. Ours, for the infantry, were scarlet, and they were beautiful and quite expensive too. Then, as now, they had to be imported from Cathay, you know."

"But it was the first time that these people from the West had ever seen silk. As we unfurled our banners, the silk danced on the air and shimmered above their heads and sparkled in the morning sunlight. And the Romans were mystified and frightened, and they drew the wrong conclusions and died for their error. I have always found that interesting, and sometimes educational," he added.

"Now, of course," said Bilquis, "the Romans cannot get enough of it."

"And it enriches every caravan and bazaar between Aleppo and the courts of the Eastern Khans," added Balthazar.

"Quite true," said the old man. "But is also makes me think of those bandits. They thought that they saw something that they recognised, but instead they were looking at something else; in this case, a trap. Caspar, what is the lesson here?"

I asked: "Will this question be on tomorrow's exam?" And Melchior laughed along with the rest of us.

"Secretly," he answered, "I am hoping to learn something. And you are plenty perceptive enough to teach." Flattered and proud, I thought hard. In the distance we heard the jackals bark.

"The question is: what will we see when we reach the court of the newborn king?" I said. "And will we let our preconceptions affect our observations?"

"Spoken like a true man of science," said Melchior. "We don't know what sorts of facts we are searching for, but if we miss the main point, as the legions misunderstood our silken banners, then we might well have overlooked the greatest event of an epoch, not just of our own short lives."

"We need," said Balthazar, "to be on our guard."

"And by virtue of your being a monarch," the old man added, "your eyes may see things that the rest of us miss." Although it was quite dark, I could almost feel King Balthazar smile with pleasure.

I firmly believe that the old man never intentionally flattered anyone throughout his life, but he did see virtues and possibilities that the rest of us missed. As a result, he made everyone see his own value and individual gifts.

And so we rode. And, that night, the desert sky seemed darker and clearer and more silent than ever before, and best of all was our star, shining new in its heaven, unsoiled by life or death, drawing us on to challenges more exciting and more important still.

Chapter Nine

WE WERE HAUNTED NO MORE by bandits on that journey, but there were other spectres to deal with, some made of mind and some of matter. At least that was what the anchorite told us, when we passed him on the road. Such people exist, you know, and usually in places where no one goes. That is, I gather, the point of it all. But I suppose this makes no sense to you, and there is no reason why it should.

By the way, the hot mint is delicious, and you should try some.

We travelled well enough thereafter, still moving by night and resting by day. Bilquis had befriended the women in the camp, and they prepared various unguents and salves, which they applied to Balthazar's wound. The oldest of the women, who seemed to have no obvious menfolk among the caravaneers, knew the desert plants and she concocted most of the remedies that they applied to Balthazar, usually under duress, for most of them stank appallingly.

If you did not make the mistake of standing downwind, it was amusing to watch him make faces, trying to turn away from the disgusting smell, as they applied various concoctions to his shoulder. In his intentionally entertaining manner, he complained vociferously and accused the gaggle of women of everything from incompetence to witchcraft. I am by no means certain that the oldest crone was unfamiliar with the latter. She answered him well, however, and told Bilquis to apply her remedy sparingly, since there were at least twelve wounded camels waiting in the queue for the same treatment, and her four-legged patients were far better mannered.

And so the African monarch grew stronger, and his wound healed swiftly, but he was still plagued with the nightmares that had begun as we started our voyage. Or perhaps they were not nightmares, but they were unsettling to him and perplexing to the rest of us. Melchior was convinced that they contained a message, or perhaps more than one message, since sometimes dreams can have very complex meanings. Balthazar was far from certain.

Again, it was some days after the attack, when we were awakened at about five o'clock for another night of travels. We had perhaps an hour before setting off again, and the women brought us our evening meal. We had all grown much closer after surviving the attack, and so the women of the caravan were less reticent than they had been before. We were sitting by the fire, and there was no wind, and so the tiny plume of smoke rose above our campsite and headed on into the sky, almost in a straight line between ourselves and the star.

"Each time that the dream returns to me," Balthazar explained, "something more is added. I do not mean that it unfolds like episodes in a long story, but rather that it is repeated with more detail each time. Perhaps I notice something new every night that was always there, or otherwise something new is added each time. I do not know. And no matter how many times that I dream it, the vision never becomes familiar, or rather it never becomes less disturbing even with repetition."

We asked him to describe the dream once more. It was as he had said earlier, with the raven-haired woman brandishing a sharp sword. "But her eyes are not eyes," he said. "The pupils are holes, little dark holes reaching back into nowhere, into emptiness from which stream thin shafts of piercing bright light. Wherever she turns her head, they seem to lead her gaze like beacons." He looked at the ground and spoke slowly.

"And in her hand was the same deadly sword, but this time I could see that she stood in a pool of blood as deep as her ankles. And it swirled in patterns like the tides." Balthazar shuddered, shaking himself rather as a dog shakes off water after a swim.

"I rarely get nightmares," he added, forcing a smile. "Almost all my dreams involve good food and sunny places for naps, and of course lots of beautiful ladies." At that moment Yasmine let go a long low growl from where the camels were tethered. "But only one lady camel, my love," the king called to her. Whenever he grew tired of a topic, he tried to distract us with his wit and cheer.

"Does any of it mean anything to you?" asked Melchior. "An image on the sword hilt, a garment, a colour? Does she speak?" Balthazar shook his head.

"This dream is uniquely bothersome," he said. "I have had dreams, otherwise, throughout my life and they have meant nothing. They are only dreams after all."

"Possibly they appeared to mean nothing, because you thought that they meant nothing. You never wrote down details to go back and check, did you?" chided the old man. "You promised to teach me about camels. I think we scholars need to teach you about investigation."

"I am as ever, all eyes and ears, my lord," said Balthazar playfully.

"King Balthazar," said Bilquis. "If you wanted me to, I could ask Usar, the old lady who makes the medicines for the caravan. They say that she is very good at interpreting dreams."

Balthazar looked up in feigned horror and held up his hands. "My dear," he replied, "my condition is still far too delicate. No matter what that old woman came up with, I do not believe that I could stand the smell." And with that, everyone laughed, and he succeeded in redirecting the conversation.

We gathered our last few belongings, and then we saddled up and then we rode. We spent another night chasing our star, and another morning brought us closer to our objective. It was a few days later, perhaps, that we passed the other caravan.

We had begun to make camp, when we heard the sounds of a caravan in the distance. Over the whistling desert wind, we could hear the camel bells first, then occasional sounds of the animals and then the human voices and the rest. We paid little attention, being hungry and tired, until of course it passed by near enough for us to see. We had passed two caravans on the first few days out, but since then we had seen no one else save the bandits.

It was a large caravan, somewhat bigger than ours. And in it were perhaps one hundred men in chains: old and young, strong and weak, healthy and sick. They wore leg irons linked to fetters on their wrists, and, wherever metal met flesh, were angry seeping wounds. Some walked, and more staggered, but, apart from the clanking of chains, all were silent, as were the guards who walked alongside, hard men with stout wooden clubs. Neither the prisoners nor the guards nor the caravaneers nor the other travellers appeared to even look at us as they passed. They stared ahead, silently, as though nothing else existed but themselves and the desert and somewhere a destination. And of course we said nothing, mostly because we were so surprised by the sight of it all.

We were simply unaccustomed to such things and went to ask Daoud, but, when we found him, he stood watching them pass with tears running down his cheeks. His fists were clenched, and the muscles stood out on his neck in well-defined chords, as though they were carved of wood. These prisoners were *Yehud*, he explained, Jews, as was he. They were slaves.

I asked him who had captured and sold these people, since we were so close to the land of the Jews, where they could have taken refuge. He answered that it was Herod, the Jew whom the Romans had made king of the Jews. He had broken Jewish religious law, contravened the Torah, their holy book, and begun selling local criminals as slaves—selling his own people to foreign governments, there to be worked to death, rapidly if they were lucky. Daoud fairly trembled with anger, but there was nothing that either he or his men could do. It became clearer, said Melchior later, why he pinned such hopes on a star.

After the caravan passed us by, sleep remained impossible for a while, and so the traders called a meeting. Now was the time to turn the caravan to the south, they said, and Daoud listened to them carefully, for they were nearer than before to their own familiar territory and safer from bandits.

The traders explained that Herod's government was rumoured to have erected three new tollbooths on the roads that we ordinarily might have taken to Jerusalem, roads which passed by Galilee. And the tollbooths were likely to be armed with soldiers and possibly cavalry.

In the past few years, Herod had trebled and quadrupled taxes, to construct the many new cities and pagan temples that he was building to please his Roman masters, they explained. These were both expensive and expansive, among them Caesarea, and Sebaste, which was the Greek name for Augustus. There were also Phasaelis, Antipatris, and others. And they were full of the most expensive statues, such as you might find in a pagan temple, declaring this Roman emperor to be the equal of Ahura Mazda, in other words, of God Himself. In his maddest, most egotistical moments, even our own appalling emperor would never have entertained such a thought. Had he done so, his own Parthian guards would have cut him down before the public had its chance.

"No, Herod tells us that Augustus is superior to the one true God. So even the Creator is now a subject of Rome," one of the traders complained. And the others nodded in a mixture of anger and sadness. It seemed so unwise to us, Herod imposing punitive taxes on his own people, to build what were effectively temples to the faith of an occupying army.

"If only it stopped there!" complained Daoud. Herod's government had taken over—stolen, Daoud called it—the trade in spices, and so no one was allowed to import cinnamon or peppercorns or spikenard or other spices under pain of death, except for those who had paid enormous taxes for the privilege, on top of even bigger bribes to the corrupt officials empowered to issue the licenses. Families that had spent generations in the spice trade were made paupers overnight. Daoud said that his own family was one of them. But they fared better than one of his neighbours, who complained and thus had been sewn into animal skins and fed to a pack of dogs in the public stadium, another royal policy that horrified the people.

And so our travelling companions begged Daoud to take another route, to avoid Herod's troops and tax inspectors. For those who had spices, being caught meant losing everything and quite possibly being sent back the way we came, but chained to one hundred others, like the poor souls who had passed us earlier.

"That is the way of the kingdom of the Jews," said one *Yehudi* trader. "Our king bribed Marc Antony to be made tetrarch, and now bribery is our national sport. Hail Caesar." The others, Jews and Gentiles, sullenly concurred.

Daoud did not seem surprised by their request to change direction, although it entailed risk, but he only promised to think about it. What settled the matter, I believe, was a hillside display that we passed on the next day. Four wooden crosses had been erected alongside the road, and from each hung what I thought was some strange leather sculpture, until we drew closer, and I recognised that each was a human corpse. They had been alive when they were affixed to these wooden devices, and then they struggled, fighting a losing battle against slow asphyxiation, until they died and were baked black in the sun. Their leather lips were stretched tight over their bared teeth in a hideous rictus of death, and their every muscle was pulled and twisted into unnatural prominence, as though it were made of a wire cable. There was a wooden sign nailed over one of them, which a businessman translated for us. It said that the dead men had been spice traders. Presumably spice traders without permits or, as the merchants believed, without the ability to bribe the police.

To get past the guard posts, Daoud explained, we would have to be clever, heading for a spot east of Jerusalem, but stopping early enough that the traders could make their own separate ways into the city. Otherwise, the police would demand bribes worth more than the spices themselves.

The businessmen agreed, and so we broke from the appointed path and bore south earlier than we had planned. And we kept to our nocturnal timetable, until Jerusalem was but a few more days away.

"Tonight we change our routine for the last time," Daoud declared, "and we stop travelling by night." Everyone knew why, of course. It would look suspicious and attract the attention of any passing patrols or, more likely, of any snoops who thought they could inform the authorities in return for a share of the cargo. On the road, everyone travelled by day, and so would we.

We had sympathy for the traders, and the route made little difference to us. We were not trafficking in spices other than Melchior's mysterious myrrh and frankincense, and those only in tiny quantities. Changing tack only meant that we would enter Jerusalem, a city we had never before seen, from one direction instead of another. But it also gave us a longer respite than normal, as we waited through the long night to reverse our times for travel. It was a welcome rest.

We passed some prosperous *Beddou* shepherds with large flocks late on that day, and some of the more generous businessmen bought sheep that were slaughtered for an evening feast. The women marinated the legs with yoghurt and spices, to make them as soft as butter in the mouth, and then roasted them whole, while the remainder was cut into chunks, put onto skewers, seasoned, and cooked over hot coals. Since we were in no hurry, they could take the time, as well, to make rice, which was always too time-consuming when we travelled. Most of us pre-ferred rice to bread, whether we were Turks or Thibetans, from Africa or from Arrakhan.

Since many of the women of the caravan came from Persia, they cooked the rice in the Persian style, which everyone agrees is the best method on earth. You know the kind, where the rice is rich in butter, and a crust forms on the bottom of the pot, deli-ciously golden brown and crunchy. And some merchants contrib-uted a few precious spices, particularly cumin from the kingdom of Orissa to the east of Hindustan. It was a luxury that we could never afford at home, not on the stipend of a student or the salary of a professor.

After weeks of perfectly edible, but admittedly uninspiring, stew and unleavened flatbread, this was a feast to be remem-bered. Indeed it is remembered—by me and perhaps by Balth-azar as well—and it has been nearly fifty years since our journey.

Then one of the merchants produced some Persian wine for those who wanted it. Indeed, by the end, we were so completely and deliciously sated that few of us had any intention of moving anywhere at all, except for Balthazar. He gathered the women, the cooks, and camp followers after the meal, saying that he intended to recite a poem—an epic poem indeed—on their culi-nary abilities. "Missus Attar's roasted goat," he rhymed, "Warms the gullet and soothes the throat. While Missus Allam's fine *pilau*, Will be remembered years from now." And he made up a dozen more similar couplets. As we applauded, he kissed the hand of the oldest crone, and you'd think he had given them each a gold stater.

He was a great charmer, Balthazar, and it is no surprise that everyone loves him. He was still a middle-aged man then, and full of enthusiasms. He must be well over ninety years old by now, somewhere down that sunlit, perfumed coast of his. And I would wager that he is full of life even still.

As we rested on our blankets and belongings, for the most

part concentrating on digestion, Balthazar turned to Daoud and asked him why they did not rise up against the Romans. Daoud looked somewhat surprised at first. Such conversations are far from prudent in a place where so little as a whisper from any of your enemies could land you in Herod's dungeons. But Daoud was perhaps as rash as Balthazar, and he was even better with a sword, and, if he had any reason to fear being overheard, he decided not to let it intimidate him.

"Kill the Romans?" he asked. "Why, we would in a moment, as soon as we were through with their puppet, Herod. Every one of us. Jews and Gentiles, Turks and Beddou nomads, Hindus and Gandharans and Afghauns and everyone who works with caravans and who suffers under this monster."

"He has no supporters?" asked Balthazar incredulously.

"Those on his payroll, of course," said Daoud. "But it was not so many years ago that ten were found plotting to kill him. The palace torturers spent at least a week killing them, cracking their long bones and dislocating their joints. But, eventually, the people of Jerusalem came to know who had betrayed the plot. Within a few hours a crowd formed outside of the informer's house. They literally pulled him to pieces like a roast chicken and threw the bits to the dogs in the streets. That is how much people want Herod dead. The palace guard were called out to recover his corpse, but they could not get within half a mile of where he lived. The people of Jerusalem would not let them pass."

Daoud turned to Melchior. "Did you march with Antigonus?" he asked. "Were you among the Five Hundred?"

"Alas, no," the old man replied. "By then I was no longer a soldier." It was about ten years after Persia defeated the Romans at Carrhae, he told me later—and only a few years after our new emperor Phraates drove the Romans out of the lands of the Medes. It was then that a Persian army of five hundred marched to Judea to support a man named Antigonus, who was the last of the old Jewish kings from a royal house called the Hasmoneans.

Once more the Persians had risked their lives to free the world from Roman tyranny.

"Herod was a usurper, elected king only by the Roman Senate, not by any Jew," Daoud explained. "He stole the throne from our rightful kings and murdered their families. And you nearly made it. You Persians nearly saved us. We Jews were so close to freedom," Daoud continued. "Nearly overthrown, Herod went on as if nothing had happened, starving our people with his taxes, killing our priests, and filling his temples and theatres with costly statues to Augustus, whom he calls the God-Emperor."

"Perhaps your newborn king will change all that," said Balthazar after a while.

Daoud spoke softly. "I hope so," he said. "It is all that we pray for. That and revenge."

When he spoke of revenge, the old man looked sad and turned his head away, looking up toward the star that we had followed for so long. It seemed a lot to ask of a star, so new and so very far away. And it seemed that almost everyone demanded something of that star, except perhaps for the old man and Balthazar, Bilquis, and me.

The nights had grown colder with each passing week and also clearer, as though we could see further and deeper into the Heavens. We went for a walk that night, the old man and I. Most of the others had gone to sleep, wrapped tightly in their cloaks and blankets. We just walked and occasionally sat on a rock, and then walked some more. Melchior said that, after half a century of practicing astronomy, it felt strange to watch stars and not be surrounded by paper and brushes and ink, furiously scribbling notes and marking positions.

"Now," he mused, "I just watch them. I do believe that I like this better."

We sat still for quite a bit longer, until the cold overcame us, and he stretched his old bones and pulled his cloak tight about his ribs, and we slowly began to make our way back to the camp. I asked him why he had me buy the spices, the myrrh and the frankincense. It made an odd state gift, particularly for a monarch, but it was too little to sell for profit, even if we could manage to circumvent Herod's proclamations. Melchior took a long look over shoulder, as if he were about to share his secret with our star and me.

"An experiment of course," he said. And even in the dark I could see his eyes twinkle almost like the star itself.

"It could hardly be a state gift!" he laughed. "Had I asked the government to provide us with one—as of course we should present to a newborn king and a potential ally of Persia—they would have thought and talked and formed committees and written reports and taken testimony and drafted budgets and sent messages back and forth to the emperor, before permission would have even been considered. And it would have filled three caravans full of windbags and bribe-takers and soothsayers and secret police and temple priests and guards and pillow-carriers and gift-bearers and court musicians to accompany it there. By the time that had all happened, the newborn king would have grown as old as I am now. No, it is to be an experiment, just as I told you, as we walked to Bahram's palace. Investigation."

I asked him how we could use these two rare essences to investigate anything at all.

"Three. Three substances," he continued. "Gold, frankincense, and, of course, the myrrh. Three of them. You see, messiahs and the saviours of a nation are scarcely born every day, and there is no tradition of who they are, or how they develop over time. It may be a completely unique experience, or if it is not, it is a very rare one. So I have devised an experiment. It may not be a very good experiment, but it is the only one I could think of thus far. It is very simple, as such things go. We offer the child his choice among the three items and see which one he chooses. That, I figure, will tell us more than all this ancient prophecy will ever do."

"And if he chooses the gold?" I asked.

"Yes," said Melchior, "if he chooses the gold, he will be precisely as predicted, a great and powerful emperor. He will be a master of men, a commander of armies, a potentate of immense wealth and power, and nations will tremble at the mention of his name—that sort of thing."

"If, on the other hand, the child reaches for the frankincense, he will be a mystic," he continued. "Then we will be dealing with a very different kind of being entirely. He will be the sort of spiritual leader who can transcend the borders of nations and perhaps even empires, a leader who perhaps does not even need an army. History has seen those before, and, as we know, the Holy Zoroaster was one of them. The frankincense, then, proves that we are dealing with a creature of an entirely different order of power and magnitude. Now if the child chooses the myrrh, what will that suggest? Think, and then answer."

We were hundreds of miles into the desert. We were not even completely certain in which kingdom we were, and the old man was inadvertently teaching again, bless him. He had always said to students, "think, and then answer." So there was little else to do. I thought and then I answered.

"An *hakim,*" I said, "a healer."

"Good!" replied Melchior, and I almost expected him to award me points. "They are different than seers and mystics and holy teachers. These are the miracle workers, somehow channelling power from God or from the Heavens. I do not know. But they are not unknown throughout history and they are neither great, conventional emperors, nor are they prophets or teachers. But they can lead millions—for when they work their cures and alleviate suffering, the people love them for it. At least they love them for a time, until the crowd forgets and becomes bored and finally turns nasty, as it inevitably does. Can you think of a fourth type? We can add another substance and present a fourth choice to the child."

I could not, and I tried, as we walked along in that chill night. "A proper experiment will spare us," I said, before we went to our beds, "from having to pay too much attention to the most hopeful guesswork of this new king's most devoted followers." I pointed to where Daoud lay asleep, and then touched my finger to my lips.

"Precisely," whispered the old man. "We call it investigation. Have good dreams tonight." And so we went to sleep beneath a single star that signified what was for us all that mattered.

For some days the land had grown increasingly hilly. And so it was, more than halfway through the next day, that we began to pass beneath small watchtowers on the tops of the smaller and nearer hills. They were built in a makeshift, slapdash way, with pieces of flat limestone or shale stacked one on top of the other. They looked, from a distance, rather like beehives with a small window in each. As we passed the first one, someone came outside and blew on a trumpet of some kind, presumably to warn the others further along. Daoud later said that they were sheep's horns and called *shofar*, or something similar. He further explained that there was a desert settlement ahead, and there we would spend the night in safety. They were a pious community, and sufficiently ornery that even Herod thought them better left alone.

These, we learnt, were people who called themselves the Essenes. They were particularly religious *Yehud* who had fled Roman control and Herod to live freely in the desert. They were not armed and active revolutionaries, said Daoud, although he maintained that salted throughout the mountains outside of Jerusalem were colonies of those as well.

No, these were the most devout amongst the devout. He noted that we were fortunate not to have arrived on their Sabbath, for, on that day, not only was no food prepared, but it was also forbidden to relieve one's self. Among the Essenes, the Sabbath must have been a very long day indeed. Daoud also warned us against saying anything untoward about some Jewish prophet called Musa or Muses. Our hosts were particularly touchy on the subject, and any such blasphemy resulted in death. This did not seem like an imposition, inasmuch as neither Melchior nor Balthazar nor Bilquis nor I had ever heard of the man. Anyway, what civilised person would ever criticise another man's gods, particularly to his face?

After passing several hilltop pickets, we were met by two of them, Saul and Sami, I believe, who escorted us to the huts and caves where they lived. Both were dressed in long white garments, which they apparently donned as some formality on our behalf, and they carried small spades made of metal. These, Daoud explained later, were used to bury their excrement, so that it did not give offence to the sun, which they revered as something that was not quite a god, but almost as good as one. This made them unusual monotheists, to say the least. But their attitudes toward purity were not completely unlike those of our own Zoroastrians, who work to keep land and fire and water and air free from polluting one another. However, as we know, the Persians do not go about carrying little spades.

We were also told not to touch any of the Essenes, for that would pollute them, but neither should we feel inferior in any way, because Essenes also became polluted when they were accidentally touched by other Essenes who were of lower rank. It seemed a complicated way to live.

And it seemed almost churlish of me, a guest and one coming in from a long and uncomfortable trek through the desert, but I wondered how these people might conduct other matters, common relations of an interpersonal nature, if for example they were married. The answer is that they almost never do such things. It was very rare that Essenes married, because, as one of them put it, "women cause strife and upheaval, and we tend to like it quiet here." It was fortunate that Bilquis was not around when that part was explained, or it would have been, as the man predicted, not as quiet there. They replenished their numbers, apparently, by

adopting orphans or by recruiting middle aged or elderly men
who had grown tired of life in the larger world without. And they
took great pains to explain that the decadence of Roman Jerusalem, and Herod's oppression, made their numbers grow apace.

There were several hundred of them in this community, at a
guess, and I gather there were several Essene communities elsewhere. They were required by their god to wash six times a day,
which meant that they spent a lot of time carrying water. This
was helpful, because there was nothing that our company
needed more than washing after more than a week since our last
large oasis. Sami or Saul—I forget which one, since they looked
quite similar—directed us to a cow pond, the use of which would
not pollute the area, and it did the job nicely. Even our legendary
hospitality would be tested sorely, if a caravan of more than one
hundred and fifty people asked to wash at my home or yours.

And then, rather generously, they invited us to eat with
them, of course sitting safely far away, on the other side of a long
series of rough cloths spread out on the ground. About fifty of
them came to join us, and we ate the simple fare on which they
subsisted day after day, year after year, which was flatbread and
one dish of food, usually vegetables of some sort, or pulses.

They had already eaten their noonday meal, they explained,
which was a sort of daily sacrament and hence one to which outsiders were never allowed, because we would, as you have
undoubtedly worked out already, pollute the rest of the community with our presence. So this unscheduled meal was an act of
charity for us visitors.

Sami, or possibly Saul, sat across from us and explained their
daily routine. They arose before daybreak, forbidden to speak
until the sun had risen, for fear of polluting the sun. Then they
worked until eleven o'clock, when they met to take a ritual bath
to cleanse away any newly acquired pollutants, donned sacred
white garments, and then went for the sacramental silent midday
meal. In case they picked up the odd additional pollutant coming

out of the bath, the meal was preceded by a few special prayers. Then they ate, had more prayers, took off the white garments, washed again, put the work clothes back on, and continued toiling until perhaps five o'clock, when it was time to wash yet again, in order to remove any newly acquired pollutants.

They ate little, drank less, and, from the looks of them, lived to great ages. More than fourteen in this community alone, said Saul or Sami, were more than one hundred years old.

"Is that due primarily to the prayer or to the diet?" asked Melchior, and the Essenes thought it a good question.

They explained that they spent a great deal of time collecting desert herbs and studying their effects, and so their various cures were in great demand near and far. But these medicaments were not sold by individual members, they explained. Money was forbidden to them, apart from what was held in common by a committee, and thus the communities sold the medicines and awarded their members new clothes, when the old ones had completely worn out. From the looks of Saul, or possibly Sami, they did not replace their garments frivolously.

But medical skill was not the whole of it, they insisted. They grew their own food in some way that minimised pollutants, but none of the land around us looked sufficiently moist or fertile. The critical ingredient missing from most agriculture, they said, was neither fertiliser nor water, but rather piety and, of course, avoiding life's many pollutants, which was best done through a vast collection of their rituals.

"Are there women Essenes?" asked Bilquis. I regretted that we had not told her this part earlier.

Our hosts went silent for a while. "Not in this community," they explained as evasively as they could.

"So there are other Essene communities made up of women, or of men and women together?" she asked.

"It is possible. We are not certain," they answered evasively. Bilquis did not believe them, but she was too polite to say so.

They rapidly shifted the conversation to a major works project which seemed to involve the entire community. They were preparing a vast library of their songs and texts, rules and regulations—the latter of which were considerable in number— and they had hollowed out a cave in the soft stone of the nearby cliffs to act as a repository. But, as you might imagine, they were forbidden to show us either the cave or the scrolls, because we would have carried with us various unwanted pollutants.

After the meal, we set up our campsite a few hundred yards from the outer periphery of their community. And several Essenes joined us in the evening, but most retired early, in order to be ready to arise well before dawn. Of those who remained, apart from their displeasure with the corruption and materialism of Jerusalem and the vigour with which they concocted and enforced a near endless litany of monastic regulations, they had little to say worth remembering.

Theirs was, I am afraid to say, a regimented and dreary life, and to this day I am not fully certain whether I would prefer such hard liberty before the easier yoke of servility under Herod, although I suppose I would grudgingly select the former.

But I promised to tell you about the anchorite, did I not? It was on the day after. Our caravan moved along, until we were maybe eight or ten miles beyond the religious community, in the midst of a vast sea of desert scrub, when we came upon an old Beddou nomad standing stock-still beside the path, leaning on his stick. If you ever imagined someone who had spent a lifetime as a desert hermit, it was he. Dressed in rags, he was, and burnt from many years in the sun.

Daoud had ordered rest from our travels, and the women served up a light collation of items mostly prepared the night before. Melchior and I dismounted and walked to where the old nomad had stood, but he had seen us ride past and had turned his back to the road and was walking off into the desert, presumably from whence he came. I called to him, and he turned back. I offered him my water bottle, but he refused, politely touching his breast.

"Do you live here?" I asked. One of the caravaneers translated, and the hermit began to chuckle. Melchior smiled as well, and in retrospect it seemed to have been a silly question.

"Of course! Here. And elsewhere too. Sometimes I live just over there, beside the bush, and sometimes near that rock. But at the moment I am somewhere else. I am here!" he said, making a circular gesture that pointed to nowhere. He smiled merrily: "Before I arrived, there was nothing here. Nothing at all. Now it's filling up. Filling up with emptiness," and he chortled at his own obscure joke.

I tried to clarify my question. "I meant, are you a part of the community back there?" And I pointed towards the Essenes in the mountains behind us.

The man grinned and shook his head. "Poor fools," he cackled. "Built themselves a furnace, and every day it burns them. All they needed was a lamp." And with that he waved farewell, turned, and shuffled back into the desert, shouting something at the sky, leaving me surprised and Melchior nodding and laughing harder than ever before.

Chapter Ten

THROUGHOUT THE NEXT DAY, many members of our caravan made their farewells and drifted off in their own directions. Mostly they wended their way to where they had friends or relations or, lacking those, to wherever they thought that they might walk among the gentle, dusty hills and olive orchards, pass through one city gate or another, and thus inconspicuously enter the bazaars of Jerusalem.

Daoud kindly gave us the names of friends and relatives with whom we might stay in the city, for commercial hostels were few, and those that could be found were commonly believed to be full of thieves and spies. Whatever we said to him, we could not have thanked him enough, for he was far kinder than ever he needed to be and he had come to our rescue so many times in that long journey.

"It was nothing," Daoud murmured dismissively. He took Melchior's hand in both of his hands: "This wise man should join my caravan and command the guard," he added, "or else we could trade places, and I would work for him. *Shalom*, Professor, *Shalom aleichem.*" He spoke in Hebrew, and it was how he wished us peace.

It was then that Balthazar began to bid us farewell. We were surprised. We had forgotten his promise to strike off in a different direction once we reached Jerusalem, a pledge that we attributed merely to his good manners and his reluctance to interfere with our mission. But then, in all seriousness, he announced his plan to leave. Before Melchior could say anything, Daoud interrupted with a look of incredulity.

"This is a joke, yes?" he demanded. "One of your nice jokes?" Balthazar was puzzled and insisted that he was quite serious. Daoud looked this way and that, making little fists and wringing his hands and seeming utterly despondent. "You will ruin everything! Everything!" he complained, looking far more upset than when we were attacked by bandits.

"It was the reason why I knew that you people would succeed," said Daoud. "The major reason why I took the risk to bring you." He turned to the rest of us. "You said it to me. You said this king, this Balthazar, he comes from Sheba."

"I said I am the king of Sheba," said Balthazar, "or at least I once was."

"Exactly!" Daoud continued, speaking rapidly. "It is written! It is written in our prophecies that you will find him, that you will find our king. The husband of Queen Bilquis, the Queen of Sheba, he was King Suleiman, the wisest man in the world. He spoke the language of the birds and he controlled the *djinn*. And he wrote us a book of songs, which we still have. One sings about the coming of our Messiah, our saviour king, and in this book of psalms he declares: 'the kings of Tarshish and of distant shores will bring tribute to him; the kings of Sheba and Seba will present him gifts.'"

Daoud scowled thoughtfully, but never slowed his rapid delivery: "So you are part of the prophecy, whether you like it or not. You must be there for it all to happen. So it is no longer your choice. God does not need to ask your opinion. The programme is fixed. It is written. Finished! Decided! Simple as that!" Daoud then crossed his arms and thrust his chin into the air, as though there could be no more discussion.

"Done!" he added, just in case it required one more word.

Balthazar was dumbfounded. "I had always thought of myself as a free man," he puzzled, "and now I appear to have been kidnapped by someone else's prophecy."

"No," Melchior interrupted, "you still have a choice. You are invited by friends." The old man spread his arms: "Balthazar, stay with us a while longer. Come, follow our star for just a few more days. It will inconvenience you little, and you can have the distinction of being the first monarch to welcome this newborn king. Besides, good friend, it would comfort me not to bid you farewell so soon."

Balthazar smiled thoughtfully. "It is tempting, Melchior. But the prophecy demands that I give gifts to this king," he said. "And I have brought none to give."

"I will find you something," said Daoud hurriedly. "I have a friend with a shop. It is in the Old City near the temple. He has carpets. I will make him give you one. For free. A nice one."

"No, thank you, although you are as kind as ever," said Melchior with finality. "King Balthazar will present the newborn monarch with frankincense."

"With what?" asked Balthazar incredulously.

"Never mind," I told him, "he will explain later."

"And besides," said Bilquis, "you don't have my permission to leave. Speaking as your nurse, your shoulder has not quite finished healing and you said it yourself. Kings are very fragile creatures indeed." And with that Balthazar laughed and surrendered.

"You are bringing frankincense to the *Messiah*?" asked Daoud. "Yes," I answered, "and gold and myrrh." The caravan master shook his head at the mention of such curious gifts, but he reached into the neck of his shirt, pulled out a small leather bag, and thrust it into my hands.

"Then give this to the king as well," he said. From its weight alone I could tell that it contained far more gold than we had paid for our journey.

So we bid a temporary farewell to Daoud, and he gave us details of where we might find him, so that we could join him for the return trip, were we heading back in a fortnight or so. And, with that, we set off in the direction of Jerusalem.

It took us but an hour to come within sight of the city walls.

Jerusalem is a place of about thirty thousand souls, and it is not wholly unattractive; mostly but not wholly. Everything is built of the same, tired, honey-coloured stone, up and down the dry hills over which the town is laid out. There is no great river to speak of, so one wonders why people settled there. It is a rather pointless place in which to live, so it must be a result of prophecy.

Dusty olive trees and scrubby bushes are dotted here and there. They do have spacious bazaars, and their streets seem to be well drained, although it never rained while we were there, so we had no chance to see whether they were properly engineered. It is not, however, a place that one associates with good food like Ctesiphon or wine like Shiraz or the best fruit like Mashad. Or with a cosmopolitan culture like Damascus. Nor can it be likened to Herat for its music or Ispahan for its scholarship.

There is no great learning in Jerusalem at all, unless you are concerned about the mysterious and esoteric workings of the *Yehudi* mystics, and—believe me—there is plenty of that. There are people called *cabbalists,* who are possessed and haunted folk, rather like the Essenes. They try to decipher secret messages from God by counting all the adverbs or nouns or adjectives in their holy book and dividing by prime numbers; people building furnaces when all they need are lamps. As for poetry or science or painting or music or even architecture, you might as well stay home and spare yourself the trip.

Nonetheless, there was a great deal of building going on. Along with innumerable and rather vulgar pagan temples, as well as cities and theatres and *stadia* all dedicated to the Roman god-emperor, King Herod had finally promised build the downtrodden Jews a temple and, over the past ten or twenty years, he went about it, but only after a fashion. The people of Jerusalem said that the proportions were perhaps fifty to one, or fifty pieces of their gold were squandered glorifying Rome for every one spent according to the wishes of the people who paid the bills.

When we passed by the temple—which looked expensive and rather garish—we saw that it had two new towers, one said to have been named for a favourite wife of Herod's whom he had murdered and preserved in a glass tank full of honey. Jerusalem is not a place that one visits for pleasure.

We made our way toward Damascus Gate, where Daoud's friends and relations lived, and we initially found them to be most hospitable, but otherwise of little practical help. No one had warned us of this infernal census.

King Herod had decreed that everyone in his kingdom must travel to whatever town he had declared to the government to be his birthplace. Usually this meant a traditional family seat of some kind rather than merely the place in which you happened to be born. It filled the nation's roads with travellers rushing back to one place or another in time to fill out innumerable forms and pay endless fees for the privilege. I correct myself. They first had to bribe the officials. Thus, privately satisfied, the officials would then charge them lesser, official fees to fill out the forms that they were already required by law to submit. Without the initial bribe, Herod's scribblers stopped you from complying with the law, which left you at risk of being fed to jackals in the town stadium. Charming people, these officials; the public had to pay one set of jackals to escape another.

Apparently, this immense public inconvenience served three purposes, in addition to lining the pockets of Herod's police and his foul bureaucrats. Or at least this is what the local people told us. Herod wanted to report back to his masters in Rome that he governed large numbers of loyal subjects, larger numbers than expected, in the hope of having his imperial status somehow upgraded. This was contrary to logic of course. Usually a colonial puppet administrator tries to make the population appear smaller, for then the imperial power demands less gold as tribute. Herod, however, wanted to exaggerate the size of his fiefdom, in order to aggrandise his position with the Roman god-emperor, and, if that meant bleeding his subjects dry, he would do it. Indeed, he was doing it already.

And so, of course, in addition to being counted in this appalling census, the head of each household was required to swear a loyalty oath to Augustus. This would have gone down better in Rome than amongst the Jews, whose religion quite clearly forbids doing such things.

Time and again, this Herod passed pointless rules and regulations that flew in the face of practice, tradition, and religious law. If this was intentional, it was an example of astonishing cruelty, and, if not, it was monumental stupidity. Perhaps both. Indeed, Balthazar rather dryly suggested it could only be due to an oversight that this horrid Herod failed to make his subjects eat cold roast pork.

The last reason for this vast nuisance of a head-count was that Herod wanted to raise taxes again. He probably wanted the money to put gilt-bronze statues of Augustus in the public lavatories.

So this colossal interruption of normal life, this census, not only filled the streets and hotels with travellers, it filled them with angry and resentful travellers as well as with every seedy and greedy policeman, cowardly soldier, and meretricious bureaucrat in the land, looking to empty the pockets of the unwary, not to mention strangers and anyone who lacked important relatives who could save him. It was not, you see, an ideal time for our visit. But, I suppose, we did not choose the time. The star did that.

We tramped through those tiny streets for hours. Our feet hurt, and even our camels complained, as we pulled them along behind us. And finally someone ran to find us—a small boy with news.

Perhaps the third or fourth house we visited, on Daoud's recommendation, was owned by a cousin of his named Ruth. And their house, like all other houses, was already crammed full of visiting relatives. So they offered us some buttermilk and condolences, and we forged ahead. Everyone knew someone else who had a house, of course, and who might have a spare room that turned out to be full of distant relations from Dan or Beersheba or Galilee or some other dismal backwater. They were desperately hopeful people, but the actual help never quite materialised, until this small grubby boy, named Amahl, came running along with the news.

If I recall correctly, Daoud's cousin Ruth spoke to her aunt by marriage Esther, who spoke to her neighbour Rebecca, who found her brother Seth in the market, and he had a friend Yakoob, who was a builder who had knocked together an extension for a neighbour who found us rooms in what appeared to be a chicken coop. Well, it was cleaner than a chicken coop, but Yakoob's carpentry left something to be desired. We never met him, but judging by the doors and walls and window-frames all askew, he might well have had one leg shorter than the other. Yet a roof over our heads was, although we did not feel too joyous at the time, a stroke of luck.

Amahl's mother, who was widowed, lived at the back of Yakoob's neighbour's extension, and we were put—very kindly I might add—into what appeared to be an extension to the original extension. She then set about preparing us far more food than the poor dear woman could afford, and her curious little son poked and prodded his way through every package we carried, driving us mad with questions, until Balthazar gave him some silver and sent him to the market to restock his mother's larder.

"There is a lesson in this," said Melchior while we waited for supper to cook.

"That poor people are always the most hospitable, much more so than the rich?" hazarded Balthazar, reclining in the doorway.

"I meant something else," said Melchior, but, before he could explain, Balthazar had another theory.

"Very well then, let me try again," said the king. "The lesson is that the people here in general are very hospitable, rich and poor alike."

"Yes, I am certain that they are, but I meant…" began Melchior once more, and becoming irritated. Playfully, Balthazar interrupted a third time.

"Then the next time we follow a newborn star halfway across the firmament to a distant city colonised by your nation's most vicious enemies," he mused, "we should do better research on finding good accommodation?"

Melchior could hardly speak.

"Let Bilquis have a turn," Balthazar insisted. "Bilquis, what do you suppose is the lesson in all this?"

"Don't you dare!" Melchior objected.

"The lesson is," she chimed in anyway, "that Uncle Melchior was going to make a donnish point about something or other, and we had better let him go ahead and do it before he has a fit." All three of us suppressed smiles, as the old man continued.

"Thank you!" said Melchior, shaking his head. "I am simply trying to make a point about the reception which we have received so far. Dressed conservatively, in homespun travelling clothes, even still we attract a lot of attention. Not just from relatives of Daoud. Look at this boy Amahl's eyes as he watches us. We look like a circus to him."

"I thought it might be that I gave him a piece of liquorice from my box, and he was hoping for another," said Balthazar.

"Undoubtedly," Melchior agreed dryly. "This is not a town accustomed to visiting Persian academics and their elegant young nieces or well-bred, young Gandharan students or, for that matter, enormous, liquorice-bearing African monarchs. We ought to bear this in mind."

"Do you mean to watch out for spies?" asked Bilquis.

"Precisely. And mind how we present ourselves," Melchior explained, but at that point Amahl's mother began to bring in far too many dishes, both hot and cold, both sweet and savoury, accompanied by two kinds of rice and various breads leavened and unleavened, plus home-made pickles of assorted kinds, the sight of a mere portion of which would have sent our Essene friends scurrying into their deepest caves in horror. It was delightful. And very filling. And none of us had any idea of how tired we were from all the additional walking through a strange city and worrying about where we might find a place to stay. We were, in a word, exhausted.

Balthazar let out a low, soft, anguished moan, and we looked over at him with concern. "There remains one small, single, lonesome puff pastry, filled with goat's cheese and tarragon," he declared, pointing into a dish, "and come the morning it will be pitifully soggy and tragically limp." We shook our heads, too tired to chew. "Well, we must not insult the mistress of the house," the king declared, popping it into his mouth. He sank back onto the cushions and smiled beatifically.

Before we went to bed, we walked outside into the dark street, to see the star once more. While trees grew here and there, and their branches oftentimes hung over the narrow lane, most were skeletal, having shed their leaves weeks before, as winter closed in. The buildings were no more than one or two storeys tall, so there was mostly a clear view of the sky. In the distance, we heard pariah dogs barking, but everything else was silent. We looked into the sky, where our star continued to lead us, this time appearing towards the south.

"It cannot be too far, can it?" asked Bilquis. "This is but a small kingdom, and this king is meant to be born inside of it."

"That is just what I was thinking," said Balthazar. "We cannot be far off now, not if there is any truth in the prophecy."

"We will soon see," Melchior said. "Meanwhile, I want us to move out of Jerusalem as swiftly as we can. I feel uneasy here. I cannot describe any more than a deep sense of foreboding."

We would have been wise to heed the old man's advice. But

morning came, and even the smallest lanes began to fill with vendors hawking their wares and people bustling from one place to another. And, of course, more people turned up to help us. By then, it seemed as if half of the Old City was either related to Daoud or knew someone who was. And all of them were hospitable people and, because Amahl's mother expected relatives to arrive imminently, all of them, or most of them, seemed to be busy trying to find accommodation for us.

And they were interested in us for another reason. Our presence alone seemed to prove, illogical as it might seem, that their hopes would be fulfilled, that the old prophecies were coming to pass, and the people would soon have their Messiah. Or so it seemed to me, without specific proof.

They said little, I suppose, as oppressed and occupied people anywhere would curb their tongues, particularly among foreign strangers. But they made their feelings clear. There was a very old woman named Shulamit, who insisted on cooking us an enormous breakfast and who kept offering a litany of prayers that we might find, in her intentionally ambiguous phrase, "whatever we were looking for."

She kept laying her hands on Balthazar's forearms as a gesture of blessing, so often that he found it hard to eat, and each time she would make the same wish or pronouncement—and each time she managed to stop the food from reaching his mouth. Finally, he managed to lean down and crane his neck over her hands, taking a bite, while she stared heavenward and carried on in Hebrew.

There was also a middle-aged man named Simeon, who had a deep baritone voice and the good looks of a professional actor. His whole focus in life, said his neighbours, was praying for the Messiah and waiting for the Messiah, and he suddenly grew very optimistic and followed us around for hours, simply watching and smiling expectantly—not in any simple-minded manner, but as though we were part of some preordained appointment to which he was privy and we were not. Indeed he told Bilquis that he was promised, in a vision, that he would not die without laying eyes on the Messiah.

But nobody mentioned the star. Indeed hardly any direct reference was made to our mission, and this was the point explained by Raqib, the old man who finally sheltered us in his tiny guesthouse. Some of the local people had tracked him down and requested his hospitality, for he was regarded as a wise old soul and a more appropriate host than some avaricious, brothel-keeping hotelier of the sort that we would have blundered into on our own.

He met us in the early afternoon and took us through the city bazaars on our way across town to his small stone house. Daoud, as well as Amahl's mother and some of the others, had pointedly wished us well on our quest. As I said, they seemed to know what we sought and they wanted us to succeed. But they had few details, fewer answers, and Melchior, ever the scholar, wanted to investigate further. Again and again, he had short conversations with shoppers and shopkeepers and stallholders along the way, deftly probing and trying to determine if anyone had sighted anything new in the heavens or if gossip touched upon prophecy. If it had, no one admitted to it.

"Being good businessmen, most said that the heavens portend bargains, but only if I bought their linen or horseradish or garlic or henna," Melchior recounted with some amusement. "But two of them answered me in Latin and nearly spat on my feet. Clearly they thought that I was a Roman spy merely disguised as a Persian astronomer, trying to ferret out disloyal subjects of the god-emperor. So people are aware of something in the heavens, I should imagine. But meanwhile, we only hear circular conversations…" And here he fell silent.

Finally, up the third or fourth narrow lane, we reached Raqib's house, and one of his sons led our camels on to a nearby stable, where they could be fed and watered. Raqib was a Gentile of some sort, perhaps of Philistine descent. And although he had made his living as a cloth merchant, and later an occasional hotelier, he was a learned man, both literate and well read. So he and the old man had a lot in common.

Melchior and our new host spent hours going through the man's library. In no time at all, they had unrolled so many scrolls that the room filled with dust. The afternoon sunlight burnt shafts of light through the oiled parchment windows, and, within each golden column between the windowpanes and the pounded earthen floor, a million motes would circle and spin like tiny heavens each with its own stars and planets. But the two scholars did not even begin to notice, with such a wealth of learning before them.

Of course, they could both read anything in Latin or Greek, and our host had an unusually early and clearly transcribed work of Diogenes that Melchior had not seen before, and another on humours of the liver. Then Raqib used his local knowledge to translate some of the older texts in Hebrew and Aramaic. In turn, he was delighted that the old man could crack the more complex phrases and allusions in classical Persian, as well as a goodly amount in our Kushana language from further east of here, not to mention the Kharosthi script, which always proves so confusing to outsiders.

"Yes, yes, King Melinda again," said Melchior, peering at the scroll. "You can find copies of this in Persia, if you know where to hunt. But they are probably scarce as emeralds out here. He was a southern Bactrian satrap with the Greek name of Menander. He interviewed a Hindustani holy man named Nagarjuna about two hundred years back, and this was their conversation."

"So it is Buddhist then?" asked Raqib.

"It is a seminal text among Theravadans, Sarvastivadans, the whole lot. Old Nagarjuna converted the king on the spot," Melchior explained, "or that is the legend. All those Greek gods were sent up the flue like smoke. Later on, we can puzzle it out together, if you like." Then he looked up and turned to me, pointing at the text: "Caspar, what is that word there?"

I looked. "*Dhamma,*" I said. "From Pali, the language of the Buddha. It means a law of cause and effect. It has an element of destiny, but also justice."

"I thought so. Caspar is a Gandharan," Melchior explained, "and so these languages are not so arcane to him. Although I am rather impressed by his knowledge of Pali. Goodness me. Pali indeed." I smiled bashfully.

"We could use some justice here," mused Raqib.

Raqib's wife brought us a pitcher of some kind of citrus juice, which was sweeter than the bitter *naranj* to which we are accustomed here in Persia. Melchior asked for seeds to bring home with us, to see if they would grow in his garden.

"I wonder if some Hindustani holy man could convert Herod," mused Balthazar, who had looked over the scrolls with interest.

"Convert him to what?" asked our host.

Balthazar smiled. "Convert him to Judaism for starters," he suggested. Raqib seemed to find it an amusing idea, but hardly the sort of thing to repeat in public.

"His forbearers are Edomites, descendants of Esau. So the king of the Jews is nominally Jewish," said Raqib, arching his eyebrows. "But of a decidedly hybrid sort." Melchior smiled. They both shared the educated person's taste for understatement.

Bilquis and Raqib's wife went around the corner to the market to buy food for supper, and Balthazar and one of Raqib's teenaged sons went to where we had lodged the camels, to see if they were being fed and rested and then to pay the stablekeeper. Meanwhile Melchior and I relaxed, while Raqib showed us his collection of maps.

"You will be heading there, I suppose," Raqib said, pointing south of Jerusalem. "That is obviously your destination."

"How would you know?" I asked.

"Easily. It is Bethlehem," our host explained.

"Do all new stars automatically go to the same place?" Melchior teased, and the landlord smiled.

"Only this one, at a guess," he said. "All the *Yehudi* prophecies, at least those about their Messiah, indicate Bethlehem. It is the city of Daoud or David, one of their ancient kings. Their saviour will come from the house of David, in royal David's city. That is what they all say. Everyone would know that."

"No one has mentioned it so far," the old man added.

"Here, there are few rewards for volunteering information to strangers," said Raqib.

Melchior leaned forward and squinted at the map, which was rather small. "It looks nearby," he said.

Raqib agreed: "It is a little town, scarcely more than a village. And only about a short walk from here. I mean that I do not pretend to know about new stars and newborn kings of Judea, but it is hard to imagine such a thing happening anywhere else. Unless you were looking for some messiah of the Assyrian people; that would be some way north and far to the east, I should imagine."

Our host's wife, who was named Shahla, was an enormously fat and humorous woman and, judging by her eyes and her smile, she must have been a great beauty in her youth. She and Bilquis brought us an early supper consisting of fresh flat bread and a vast and appetising array of various salads made from fresh herbs, then crushed beans and roasted aubergines and olive oil and nuts from the pine trees up in The Lebanon. We began eating, certain that Balthazar would return in a moment, for he was not much given to missing meals.

"Have you found our destination yet?" asked Bilquis. Melchior nodded.

"Bethlehem," he said. "Rather Raqib-*jan* has found it for us. If the star follows the prophecy, it will lead us to Bethlehem."

"I will get you blankets and sheets for the ground," said Shahla. "You can bring them back, when you come through

Jerusalem on your way home. If you think that it is hard to find accommodation here, in a big city, Bethlehem is a small town and it will be crammed with people returning for the census. I hope it won't be too cold," she added, unconvinced.

It was obvious even then that it would be too cold, and indeed it turned out to be far too cold, since Bethlehem is at a somewhat higher altitude than Jerusalem. We thanked her for the generous offer, which would undoubtedly be welcome when we got there.

"Why," asked Melchior, reaching for another fig, "is not everyone else there already?"

"In Bethlehem?" asked Raqib.

"Precisely," the old man continued. "I have my own notions, but I want to hear yours. We are not the only people who can see the star. It is up there in the sky for anyone educated enough to recognise what he is seeing, and there must be a lot of those people here. And it appears to fulfil their prophecy. And, frankly, it comes at a time when a messiah might be rather welcome. One might think that everyone under the Roman yoke, or the *Yehud* at least, would be flocking to Bethlehem."

"Perhaps some are unaware of the star," Raqib said. "Perhaps their *rabbis* are telling them to be prudent. But mostly I would imagine that the Jewish people are doing what they and what everyone else always does here, keeping their heads down, trying not to attract attention and, in particular, keep out of sight of the Romans. Merely arriving at the birthplace might itself be seen as an act of open rebellion."

He had no more than finished speaking, when his son burst in the door, out of breath and gasping out some urgent message in Aramaic, of which we scarcely understood a word. We did, however, know the words for Romans and for King Balthazar.

Our landlord grew ashen-faced. "Roman troops," he explained. "They appear to have arrested your companion. They have taken him away."

chapter eleven

IT TOOK BUT A FEW MOMENTS for the lad to grow calm enough to tell us what had happened. He and Balthazar were walking back from the stable, when a small detachment of palace guard, Romans, rounded the corner in formation, seized Balthazar, and declared him to be under arrest. When the boy tried to follow, they boxed his ears for his inquisitiveness. Then he ran back to tell us what had happened.

I am not sure what we would have done next without Raqib, but together we went to the local police station. There they were loafing and sleeping and doing what policemen usually do and, of course, they had little knowledge of, or interest in, what had happened.

"How much is it worth to you?" asked one, taunting us. But another said he had heard that Roman troops had arrested a black man and taken him away.

"He claimed to be a king, of all the nonsense," chuckled one of them stretched out on a bench. "He'll get the royal treatment in the dungeons tonight," he added, and the other policemen laughed. I wanted to attack the lot of them, but of course I remained silent. Meanwhile Bilquis strode up to them.

"I am his daughter and I have the right to visit him," she insisted.

"His daughter?" they mocked.

"I am normally darker, but I've been out of the sun for awhile," she explained, and at this they fell about in merriment.

"Try the palace gate on the Jericho road," they suggested, and we made a rapid exit.

"I knew that would work," said Bilquis under her breath, adding the word "bastards."

We tried to convince Raqib to go home immediately and let his son take us to where we could see the palace, and then we would go ahead on our own. In that way, the Romans would not necessarily associate him with us, and it might save our hosts from difficulties later.

"I am sure that the Romans have figured it out already," Raqib insisted, "and, living in Jerusalem for so many years, my son has already had enough lessons in cowardice." He led us out of the bazaar and down the hill to the palace, and then to the appropriate gate at the back. Ironically, and it was a fine night for irony, the guards ordered Melchior, Bilquis and me inside and left Raqib at the gate, closing the door in his face. Honestly, I was relieved for him.

The palace guards looked up from their benches. These were strong men, who gave the impression of being better trained, brutal, and quite unlike the neighbourhood police. "The African told us nothing so far, but we figured that you would come eventually," said one of their officers, an enormous and very pale man with a lantern jaw. Melchior later said that he was a Briton or something similar.

"Are we under arrest?" demanded Bilquis, and the officer made a funny face at the others.

"Of course not, my lady," he mocked. "You are guests of King Herod, of course." He threw a ring of keys to one of his deputies. "Take them away," he said. We had little option but to follow. He led us up some stairs and then along the exterior wall, then down a staircase in one of the towers and across a small open area, perhaps a small parade ground, and then into a sort of a keep and up more stairs. At the top of a landing, two armed guards opened a pair of doors, and we were pushed through, with the doors slammed shut behind us. The floors were marble, and so were the walls. On the far side, on little pillars, stood portrait busts of Augustus and Herod. They might have been marble too, or possibly alabaster, which is cheaper and easier to work. A yellow-haired teenage boy in a white toga proffered a silver tray of Alexandrine crystal glasses full of something yellow that seemed to match his hair.

"Cypriot wine," he purred. "I hope you like it." We each took glasses, and he pivoted on his heels and disappeared into another room.

The three of us were dumbfounded. We followed the sounds of conversation up another few marble steps, which led us into a much larger room containing perhaps twenty or thirty people. We had expected iron bars on the windows and prisoners in rags. Instead the walls were hung in expensive cloth, and the women were dressed in silks, with one or two specimens resembling the finer stuff we saw in the caravan. Even some of the men wore silk, if you can believe such a decadent thing. And, in one corner, surrounded by four or five of people, stood Balthazar with a rather large tumbler of what looked like the same wine that we had just been served.

"And then I drew my sword," he explained, raising one arm into the air dramatically. At that point he noticed us. "Hullo!" he called, converting his gesture into a dainty wave, waggling his fingers over the heads of his audience. "They said that you would be coming along shortly. I'm telling them how we repulsed the bandits."

Bilquis rushed to his side to see that he was unharmed, which he was of course, and she gave him a great hug of relief. "This girl was going to kill eight or nine of them before supper," he continued, "but unfortunately for her, we fellows got to them first. Now, have any of you ever been attacked by a man with a giant axe?" His audience was spellbound.

Meanwhile an older, white-haired gentleman rose from his divan and approached us, and the four or five people standing around him followed. He spoke to Melchior in a language that I had not heard before, and my teacher could scarcely contain his surprise.

"I am so very sorry," the stranger apologised to the rest of us. "It is frightfully rude of me. But I am a Greek, and it is so rare to find a fellow Hellene in Jerusalem nowadays, especially a Persian. We do so love Persians here, but we get so little opportunity to see them anymore, don't we?" His small circle nodded and murmured in equally insincere agreement. The man introduced himself as Nicholas, a Damascene Greek, and said that he served as the court historian.

"In turn," said Melchior, "we apologise for being underdressed. We have only recently arrived in town, and the invitation came, well, somewhat sooner than we had expected."

"We understand," said Nicholas, smiling indulgently. "His Majesty can be playful at times." The small group continued smiling. "But you travel so lightly," he continued. "Every other time that Persians came to Jerusalem, it was always with an invading army. And it took us absolutely forever to clean the carpets afterwards!" In addition to being an historian, he was apparently some sort of palace wag. His retinue giggled dutifully, and Melchior smiled weakly in return.

"How peculiar," the old man replied. "It wasn't so hard to clean my uniform after Carrhae. We always found Roman blood to be thinner than the normal kind. Do excuse me." And with that he went to find Balthazar.

There was another yellow-haired slave boy—they must bleach them somehow—with another silver tray, into which Balthazar peered intently.

"You really must try these, you know," Balthazar said to me around chewing and swallowing. "Small, um, bird's legs of some kind. You can eat them bones and all, but I don't," he explained. "And these here appear to be… mmmmm… tiny fishes dipped in batter. Simply marvellous. Take two or three at a time. Now where was I?"

"You had slain five of the Parthian bandits," said a woman with silver-foil leaves in her hair.

"But more were coming on horseback. It must have been frightening," added a perfectly round, fat fellow, who looked to be a bookkeeper.

"Ah, then we are coming to the best part!" Balthazar continued, and from a small distance Melchior smiled and shook his head indulgently.

Bilquis had been dragged off by some of the women to meet a princess of some kind, I believe she was the king's sister. Balthazar later said that Bilquis did a fine interpretation of a curtsey, especially for someone unaccustomed to it, since it is hardly a Persian custom.

The princess reclined on another of these daybeds or divans. It is how Romans deport themselves at dinner parties, I believe. It certainly seems to be nothing about which our *Yehudi* or Gentile friends had ever heard. Anyway Salome, for I think that was her name, was of what we might call a certain age. Her looks had begun to wane, but she appeared not to know it; mutton dressed as lamb, we say. I rather wish I had heard the earlier portions of their conversation.

"Do they have any arts in Persia?" asked the princess archly. Pretending to have missed the calculated insult, Bilquis smiled as innocently as anyone could.

"Oh, yes, Your Highness!" she replied, playing the peasant convincingly. "Particularly onion farming. We consider it to be a great art back home, although, of course, it takes time. And our menfolk sometimes wrestle with bears."

"I meant mosaics or encaustic paintings in wax, or classical dance," scowled the princess. "I am still regarded as the leading practitioner of Graeco-Roman dance forms here in this country."

"Then you should come to Persia and teach us," Bilquis replied sweetly, and the princess beamed. "Many of our older ladies would love to learn how to keep so limber," Bilquis added, and Salome's smile evaporated, but, before she could speak, yet another blond slave boy—they must have imported them by the gross—bade us all rise for the arrival of Herod.

Accompanied fore and aft by pairs of Roman centurions, the king looked like nothing I had come to expect. First, and it was only due to my own ignorance, I had not expected his advanced age. He was well into his seventies. Nor had I imagined that he would be so nearly an invalid.

Herod was an immensely fat man, and he walked leaning heavily on a stout stick. Indeed, once or twice, I thought that one of his bodyguards would need to grab hold and steady him lest he topple over. He made difficult work of crossing a room and he had enormously swollen feet and lower legs. They almost resembled pieces of wooden furniture rather than parts of his own body. It must have been quite painful. And similarly, he was constantly short of breath, wheezing like the bellows in a smithy. Well, he died not long after we met him, and none of us was even remotely surprised.

I had rather expected him to wear a purple toga or something grand, but he dressed in a fairly unimpressive white one of ordinary Egyptian linen. Either it was plain or had a very simple border design picked out in silver thread. I cannot remember, since it was so long ago. But, had you seen him on a street, you would have thought him a retired restaurateur or successful building contractor rather than the king of the Jews.

He nodded to his guests one by one and greeted them hoarsely, as he tottered into the room. "Nicky, Salome my dear, Michael, Livy…" And each of them bowed or curtseyed. The centurions attempted to steer him towards one of the divans, which had obviously been kept empty for the king, but he waved them away as though they were a nuisance, and he slowly made his way through the group, until he reached Melchior.

Melchior dropped onto one knee, pressed the king's hand to his forehead, and muttered something that again I could not understand. Obviously it was in Greek again. From the reactions of the audience, this was not a greeting in the expected style, but the show of foreign manners seemed to impress them.

"A Hellene!" observed Herod, clearly surprised. "Marvellous. Next, you will tell me that you are an Achaemenid as well."

Melchior rose to his feet: "From the house of Demetrios, Your Majesty."

"Splendid!" replied Herod, smiling. "How lucky we are! Stay here and help me civilise these damned people." His guests smiled as well, but their eyes betrayed a measured concern. They had not foreseen how the king would greet his foreign enemies, and, if they had, this was not what they would have predicted.

"Help me civilise the lot of them!" Herod continued. "Except for my sister of course. It's her job to civilise me. Graeco-Roman dance forms. Important things like that!" And with that he laughed, until his laughter degenerated into a fit of coughing. Two of his bodyguards moved to support him, but he regained his composure and waved them away. Throughout it all, Salome smiled with her lips alone; her eyes betrayed no emotion.

"It was kind of Your Majesty to invite us," said Melchior, "especially on such short notice."

"Yes, indeed. My little trick," admitted Herod. "I did not want you to leave Jerusalem without us having a chance to meet." He paused, as if to collect his thoughts. "We are a small backwater in a great empire," he explained. "It would be such a tragedy to be visited by a Persian nobleman and an African monarch without you coming to see me, this simple old king of the Jews."

"The pleasure is purely ours, Your Majesty," said Melchior, and Herod's eyes narrowed only slightly.

"And to what do we owe the honour of your visit? Can you tell me that much, Your Highness?" Herod asked, pointing to Balthazar. He knew very well why we had come to Judea, for his spies in the bazaar had surely told him. What he wanted to see, of course, was the evasive skill with which we might reply.

"We have invited our august friend here to be the ambassador plenipotentiary to the royal court of Sheba," lied Balthazar, adopting the royal 'we' for the only time that I ever heard him use it. "And almost precisely halfway between Persia and Sheba is, well, this palace of yours. So what better thing is there to do than to pay court to Herod the Great? After all, everyone in your entire country prays daily for the king of the Jews," he added ambiguously. Then Balthazar bowed deeply, rose, and broadcast an enormous smile. His answer was neither informative nor particularly diplomatic, but even Herod's audience smiled at the display of cheek.

Herod turned to his sister and gestured behind him. "Salome, my petal, please see to our guests. These visitors and I have some diplomatic business to discuss. Brief diplomatic business." Then he hobbled ahead to a side room, with his bodyguards behind him, and we knew that we were meant to follow.

Herod sat down in a wooden chair and motioned to his guards, who brought two divans for the four of us. A servant— oddly enough a brown-haired boy this time—brought us fresh drinks and then retreated behind a closed door. Herod kept his hands folded in his lap, and he stared at them while collecting his thoughts. Then he looked up and smiled, almost sweetly.

"My sources made their reports. I know everything," he said.

"How fortunate, Your Majesty," purred Melchior. "I've been a scholar for nearly seventy years and I still don't know everything. Perhaps you could tell us."

"About what?" asked Herod. "The smuggler's caravan? Your revolutionary travelling companions? Your visit to the Essenes? Entering the city through Damascus Gate? Where you stayed in Jerusalem? But, come to think of it, I do have a question."

"What is that, Majesty?" asked the old man.

"Wine!" he barked at the guards, and they brought back the boy to fill the glasses. "It eases the pain in my legs," Herod explained, taking a large draught before returning to the discussion.

"You have done nothing to hide your origins," he continued. "You were not disguised as Armenian merchants, which is what Persian spies normally do. You are even still wearing your Parthian trousers. Then you saunter brazenly through my bazaars and along my streets, asking my people where you can find the king of the Jews, and the one place you never look—the one place you never visit, or even enquire about—is here. The palace of the king of the Jews. Am I uniquely fortunate? Is there some particular reason for this calculated insult, or do you intend to visit every kingdom in the region and mock the rulers one at a time?"

It was Melchior's turn to choose his words carefully. "Very well. We will explain. We have heard that somewhere in this kingdom was recently born an infant Messiah, a newborn king of the Jews. We have come to see him."

"Really? Is that all?" asked Herod. "I think that I heard one of those stories every two or three years since I was made tetrarch, and that was more than forty years ago. Another king of the Jews, eh? Guards! Just a little more wine."

After they refilled his glass, Herod had them bring a footstool, and they helped him to lift his heavy right leg on top of it. His breathing was difficult, possibly more so than before.

"Do you know the point of what I am trying to do here?" he wheezed. "Not what the idiots say in the bazaar. Not what the Essenes think, carrying around their little trowels and burying their turds. Not the lunatic rebels who live in the desert and pray for the end of the world. They say that I want to ingratiate myself with Rome. For what? For pretty slave boys? I am far too old for that any more. For gold? I have more than I can spend. For imperial honours? I am too old to make the journey to see the god-emperor. Ten years ago I would have done it one last time, but today it is impossible. Do you know why I do these things? Why I build the temples, the theatres and all?"

"Please tell us, Majesty," Bilquis answered.

Herod cleared his throat and wiped his lips with the end of his toga. "Destiny!" he croaked, "and I do not mean my destiny. I mean Rome. The gods have created this empire for the express task of civilising the world. Our political system may not be perfect, but it is the best that mankind has created thus far. And it is our destiny to clear away the backward tendencies, the retrograde movements—to crush the little religions, the little nations, the sects that stand in the way of making everyone in the world a good Roman citizen. Secretly, they all want to be Romans, you know. Everyone does."

"Or they may just say that to be polite," said Melchior tartly.

The king ignored him. "What the world needs is consistency. Uniformity," Herod continued, "and building a portion of that is my final ambition, to stop these little people from interfering with progress, to stop them from oppressing others."

"Who were the Essenes oppressing, Majesty?" asked Balthazar. "They seem to live in their deserts voluntarily."

"Essenes! A mere trifle!" Herod scoffed. "No one will miss them!"

"I am certainly no scholar, Majesty," replied Bilquis. "But it seems that a lot of people prefer their own ways and wish only to be left alone."

"Then they are oppressing themselves and their families," said the king, waving his hand as though it were a minor detail. "They should be working in the bazaars, holding down decent jobs, worshipping the civic gods, venerating the emperor, paying gold into my treasury, and going to the amphitheatre with their families. Instead they waste lives that should be supporting the state and the civilisation."

"Their very existences are corruptive influences," he continued. "In time, they will disappear. Either naturally, as people choose to become good citizens of Rome, or we will clear them away with only as much force as necessary. From Londinium to Nubia to Hindustan and Cathay—that is Rome's destiny. It is the march of human progress. Not these revolutionary loons in the desert or these monthly messiahs. Augustus understands this, but people here do not. At least not all of them, not yet. But they will. I can assure you of that."

Melchior smiled. "In parts of Persia, Majesty, this may be easier said than done."

Herod laughed. "It won't happen in my lifetime or yours, my *Achaemenid* friend, but perhaps in the lives of your young charges here," he said, pointing to Bilquis and me. "And it will happen. Persia will fall to Rome, and the lands beyond it. It is inevitable. It is the iron law of progress. Guards!" And the guards came and helped him to his feet.

"Go find your messiah, then," he laughed. "Find all of them and bring them back here for supper. My kitchens can feed thousands of messiahs."

"Thank you, Your Majesty," said Balthazar, with a gracious nod. "Then we shall continue to follow our star." Herod stopped dead and turned back to us.

"Star?" he asked. "What star?"

Herod had clearly not heard of the star; perhaps his astronomers had feared to tell him and risk his wrath. Not surprisingly, it mattered to him immensely. Balthazar had said more than he should have, and now there was nothing else to do but to describe the star to Herod. The king appeared fascinated. He asked Melchior about the star's locations in the heavens and its astrological movements, and then its position in relation to the earth.

"And so this sign, this newly made star, is over Bethlehem? Over King David's city? You did not say that before. Hmmmm. It might well be worthy of attention. We Jews have our prophecies you know." Surreptitiously, Herod nodded to the captain of his guard, who nodded in return, listening with care to what was being said.

"Do an old man an act of kindness," urged Herod. "If you

find this newborn king, come back and tell me. Then perhaps, if it is not too far, and if my legs are not troubling me too much, I can go there to worship him."

"Certainly," answered Melchior. "But why would one king of the Jews wish to worship at the feet of another?"

Herod laughed and clapped Melchior on the shoulder. "Because I shall not be king much longer. I will be food for worms," he replied. "What is one fat old man compared to sacred prophecy? And another thing: should we encourage my replacement to cooperate with destiny? Or ignore him and run the risk of him falling in with the trouble-makers and the smugglers and the idiots in the desert?"

"Safe travels to you all. Hail, Caesar!" said Herod, and he left to rejoin his dinner party. The one remaining guard closed the door behind the king and led us across the room and out through another way.

Chapter Twelve

WE WERE GIVEN AN ESCORT out of the palace, and, rather disconcertingly, the soldiers followed us most of the way home. When we finally reached the guesthouse, Raqib and Shahla were relieved to see us, and one of their sons was dispatched to the bazaar for some roast lamb and fresh bread and pickled garlic. When we told him what had happened at the palace, Raqib said that we were very lucky to have left unharmed.

He thought that we might have escaped disaster because Herod could never be certain of Melchior's status back in Persia. It would not benefit him to become involved in a diplomatic incident, especially one that might involve Augustus Caesar and the Parthian court. Raqib found Herod's response to news of the infant king far more confusing. He had expected Herod to explode in jealousy, for the graveyards were said to be full of competitors to his throne. "But they say that our king is like a mirror," Raqib concluded, "and whoever looks into it sees himself peering back. It is one of Herod's skills. Perhaps you saw no malice, because you bear none yourselves."

We resolved to set off in the morning for Bethlehem, and after supper Shahla brought us some warmed goat's milk to help us sleep, then we made our way to our beds.

In the morning, two of Raqib's neighbours came to report that a dozen Roman cavalrymen were stationed at either end of our narrow lane, saying that they had orders to escort us to Bethlehem.

"Whatever for?" asked Shahla. Her son explained that it was

ostensibly for our safety. He had spoken to the Romans, and they claimed that there were bandits on the road to Bethlehem who hoped to prey on travellers heading home for the census. The guards were there, the troopers explained, to ensure our safety and nothing more. None of us believed them, of course, and none of us wished to travel with an armed force of Romans. But there seemed to be no other way, until Shahla brightened visibly and asked Raqib if he recalled a game that they used to play as children. She pointed one finger into the air. Raqib looked us over, as if to study us, then smiled and nodded.

"It might work," he agreed. "Although most of us are getting a little too old and fat for it. You and me at least." His wife stuck out her tongue at him and then grinned.

"All right, everyone!" said Shahla, clapping her hands. "You boys collect the camels from the stable and take them to Aunt Farida's. The rest of us are going up onto the roof!" And with that, we mounted two flights of stairs, and then used a ladder to climb through a hatch onto the flat roof of their home. In every direction were other flat roofs at various heights; some with laundry drying, some full of pots in which their owners were growing kitchen herbs, some containing goats or chickens or pigeons or firewood, and some, of course, empty. In the far distance we could see the towers of Herod's temple, and in another direction the roof of his palace, then in a third the domes covering one of the major bazaars.

"This way! Follow me!" Shahla declared, and she led us across their roof, and then lowered herself down a short distance onto the neighbours' roof, reaching up to give us a hand. Then she led us across another roof, around some chickens, to a place where we had to climb up a few feet. For a rather rotund old girl, she was remarkably agile.

"We used to do this as children," she recalled, "my sister and I, and all the youngsters in Raqib's house. And the neighbour kids. All of us. We grew up around here. We used to brag that we could go from anywhere in Jerusalem to Temple Gate without taking two steps one after another on any single street."

After we had gone halfway down the row, she leaned over the wall and shouted something to people on the ground. In a moment or two, they came upstairs and opened the hatch onto their roof, and then led us down a ladder through their house to the ground again.

"This is Missus Hasan," she said, pointing to a short woman pounding laundry in a great metal bucket and splashing water everywhere. Missus Hasan waved and smiled amiably, as though strangers clambered down through her house every morning. Then Shahla led us across the street and up several more flights of stairs. She was right, we never took more than two steps onto any street, for the lanes were narrow in the Old City, and the houses were crammed tightly together.

It was not, I must say, an efficient means of travel, for we spent an inordinate amount of time coming and going up and down various people's stairs and clambering onto their roofs. But Balthazar explained that it was a wonderful way to make new friends—and all of them were initially fascinated and then charmed by the courtly black giant getting tangled in their washing lines and stumbling over their boxes of onions and beetroot, horseradish and spinach.

"God bless you, Madam!" he muttered as he barged through home after home. "Splendid place you have here, Sir!" he declared. "My goodness, what a wonderful bedroom for the goats. Do they keep this all to themselves?" he asked. And on and on we went.

"There is an important lesson here for home, if we ever get back there," said Melchior. "Think of how much satisfaction we are having escaping from the Romans, and remember it when your students play other tricks on you."

I think we must have received seven or eight invitations for lunch, when we finally arrived at Aunt Farida's, where food was already waiting, particularly a delicious soup made with white beans and lemon juice. Aunt Farida explained that her daughters would be back with our camels in a few moments and that we were right around the corner from the city walls. Within moments we would be through the gate, out of Jerusalem proper and safely on the road to Bethlehem.

Bilquis looked worried. "What will you tell the guards, when they finally get tired of waiting and come looking for us?" she asked Raqib.

Shahla declared: "We will tell them that you are Persians, and so you unrolled one of your magic carpets and simply flew away!" They laughed and laughed, and that did nothing to diminish their bravery.

Soon thereafter, her daughters came to the door and announced that our camels were waiting outside. We thanked Aunt Farida and bade farewell to Shahla and Raqib. "You may have made the difference between our success and failure," said Melchior.

"Come back someday, and we'll work through my library together," Raqib offered, "perhaps under the reign of a new Jewish king!"

Our camels were rested and fed, and Yasmine clattered her hooves on the paving stones and roared with delight, as soon as she laid eyes on Balthazar. Neighbours joined our hosts, crammed into the narrow street, and it seemed like half the town turned out for our departure.

Someone I had never met pushed a bundle of hot, fresh flatbreads under my arm. Another handed a bag of oranges to Melchior, and someone plucked some posies from a window box and pressed them into Bilquis's hand. Spectators leaned from upper storey windows or peered over rooftops to have a better view of us. Small children demanded that their parents lift them high into the air, so that they could kiss Balthazar on his cheek. It was, as we say at home, a real *tamasha*. Fortunately, the Romans were more than five streets away, peering intently up either end of an empty alleyway.

"*Shalom, shalom aleichem!*" cried the neighbours who were Jews.

"*Salaam, salaam aleicum!*" called the neighbours who were Gentiles, for the similar phrases convey an identical blessing of peace.

And so, with that, followed by laughing strangers whose rooftops and attics we knew better than our own, surrounded by exuberant friends whom we would probably never get to know, we rounded the corner in a great mob, but left them all waving behind us, as we rode through the towering iron-shod gate, past the local policemen sleeping on their benches, and out into the green olive groves and dusty hills beyond the city walls on the high road to Bethlehem.

And so we rode. Over and around the gentle hills we went, as the walls of Jerusalem and even the battlements of Herod's highest temple towers receded and finally vanished behind the tops of the dusty green trees and the hills of honey-coloured stone. And when the midday sun began its slow descent, and as the shadows began to lengthen, Melchior made us stop and open our bundles and remove our travelling cloaks and put on our best apparel, for soon we would find, he said, what we had travelled so very far to see.

The old man carefully unfolded his pale blue velvet cloak, shook the wrinkles out of it, and drew it over his thin shoulders. He said that it was welcome, for the afternoon was already chill, and the night would be colder yet. Balthazar wound around his head a sumptuous silk turban of gold and midnight blue and crimson. He had a similarly elegant wrap for Bilquis, something African and emblazoned with green and yellow. And Melchior lent me his own shawl, the Kashmiri one with all the fine needle-work. And we remounted our camels and carried on, pursued by the encroaching darkness.

From time to time, over the next several hours, we came across farmers or families by the roadside. Once or twice, there was a small shop. Melchior or Balthazar asked them if they had seen the star, or if they knew of the birth of a king. And every time the local people gave no reply, or we heard the kind of mumbled answer given to small children or to the hopelessly senile.

"It may be," said Balthazar after a while, "that we have failed. Or that the star is further than we imagined. Or perhaps the child is not yet born."

Melchior asked me for suggestions, and I had none. "I do not know how we could even rephrase the questions," I confessed. The old man rode silently for a while, until it grew nearly too dark to travel.

Bilquis looked high above her at the star, which seemed to hang motionless, shining at the very centre of the heavens. "It may start to move again," she said, more in hope than because she really expected it to move.

Melchior rode silently for a while, deep in thought. "We are asking the wrong people," he said finally. "We ask those who fear, those who have something to lose by speaking the truth." But, before he could finish, Bilquis interrupted him, pointing.

"There, Uncle! We can try them!" she cried, and Melchior looked ahead and smiled. There on the hill were three children, young shepherds watching their flocks. We could only see their silhouettes against the darkening sky and the flicker of light from their tiny campfire.

"Precisely what we want! They'll give us honest answers! Well done, girl!" cried the old man. He nudged his camel with his heels and darted ahead of the rest of us, as we hurried to keep up. Stopping beside a stunted olive tree, he dismounted in a trice, threw his reins to Bilquis and stalked up the small hill, from where the young shepherds watched him most intently. We followed a little more slowly, for it took some time to tether the camels. When we reached the top, he was helping them feed the flames with small twigs.

"And these are my friends," he said, gesturing towards us. The two boys and a girl nodded sombrely. "That one is a king," he added pointing to Balthazar. The golden threads of his turban glimmered in the firelight.

"Hello," said Balthazar, in his deep voice, and the children stared intensely.

"Do you know why we are here?" Melchior asked, and they shook their heads. He spoke slowly and with gravity. "We have come to see the mysteries. We have crossed vast deserts. We have been attacked by enemies. We have travelled half the earth to come here to Bethlehem and see the mysteries. Have you seen the mysteries?" And one by one the children nodded.

"Yes," said the smaller boy. "We saw them. Are they coming back?"

They had heard the voices, or parts of voices, beginning some weeks before we arrived. The voices had echoed back and forth in snatches of conversation which the children heard reverberating across the night sky like half-remembered songs from trumpets or the reeded flutes called *shawms*. The voices, they explained, had started as soon as the star had come out.

"The stars?" asked Melchior, using the plural. No, they meant the star, the one star. Our star. They pointed to it.

For some time there had been these snatches of strange song in the heavens. And night by night it grew louder, until, twelve nights before, the sky had filled with lights, and the lights seemed to move and gather until they formed the images of creatures shimmering above them, so spread across the night sky that one could not tell if they were as big as houses or as big as galaxies. Their images were woven together and intertwined, said the children, so that the night sky became black waves of hair, and the reflections of the stars became eyes, and white flesh of the moon became skin. And out of their eyes streamed narrow beacons of

piercing light, which followed wherever they looked and illuminated wherever they directed their gaze. Melchior glanced at Balthazar, who nodded sombrely, for the children had described his
recurring dream.

"Did they carry anything in their hands?" Balthazar asked.

"Like what?" replied the girl.

"Like a sword?" answered the king.

They conferred amongst one another. No, they said, the
creatures carried nothing. And what would they want with
swords?

"What did they say to you? Could you understand them?"
the old man asked.

Not until twelve nights before, said the children. That was
the night on which the baby was born. Earlier the sound was
incomprehensible, first like pounding wings and wind, and then
over that came sounds like musical instruments talking. But then
it became clearer, and so very loud that they could not tell if the
sound was emanating from inside or outside of their heads. And
everyone came from the town, and from the little hamlets and
clusters of cottages and from the huts of the herdsmen.

"And we all stared into the sky. And the creatures, they said
hosanna," said the elder lad. "It means praise."

"They said 'Hosanna to God in the highest, and peace to
men of good will,'" corrected the girl who was slightly older than
the others. "The king was born, and the angels had come to
praise him. Everyone said that they were angels."

"But he is just a baby," said the smallest shepherd boy. "He
doesn't look very much like a king to me."

"And how did the people respond, your father and mother,
for example," the old man asked.

"At first they kept us inside, as though there was a bad storm.
But the sheep need looking after. So they came with us," said the
older boy.

"And they looked a lot more afraid than we was," said his
brother.

"And the other grown-ups? What about them?" Melchior continued.

"When the angels made themselves visible," the girl answered, "before we could understand them, people started to come and watch. At first, they hid alongside of stone walls or behind trees, where they thought that they could take shelter. But soon they realised that the angels mean no harm. So they came and watched here with us."

"Will you take us to see this newborn king? We have brought Him gifts," said Melchior. The children looked uncertain, until one of them ran up and over the hill to what must have been the village of Bethlehem nearby. Above us the stars were all out, and as you might have imagined, the newest of them all hung directly over our heads. It had brought us to our destination and had no more directions to provide.

A few moments later the boy returned with three adult men beside him. They were burly fellows, probably shepherds or herdsmen or farmers, and two of them carried stout sticks, but not because they were lame. Two of the men stood with their feet well apart, holding their clubs with one hand and tapping them into the other palm as though they expected a fight.

"My name is John, this is Mordecai and Joshua," said the first man. Melchior answered in kind and told them a brief version of our story. They looked at one another uncertainly, until John nodded. "You can come up," he agreed, "but Mary says she needs to feed the baby and put him to bed, so we had better be quick. I hope you don't mind the questions. We need to be careful."

"We understand," answered the old man. From the pockets of his gown, Melchior took out three small bundles. Two were wrapped in cloth and bound with the green ribbands that he used to tie his astronomical charts, and the third was Daoud's small leather bag of gold coins. He handed one package to Balthazar and another to me. "Frankincense and myrrh," he explained to us. "We've been through this before. Do as I do."

Meanwhile Bilquis tried to make conversation with the lanky herdsmen, as they walked together. "And how is the baby?" she asked, taking two steps for their every one.

"Small," muttered John, and the others nodded. They were not very talkative.

"He is a small baby, is that so?" she asked rather unimpressively. "Is he healthy?" They said nothing for another dozen paces.

"Eats and sleeps mostly," grumbled Mordecai. "Babies is like that."

But Bilquis could be single-minded, although she took a few moments' pause before trying again. "Have you had a lot of visitors?" she continued.

"Nope," said Joshua. We walked on up the hill.

After a few more minutes, John added: "Had some angels. They must be gone home now." Mordecai made a peculiar noise that appeared to signify agreement.

"And so this child, this newborn, is the child of prophecy, the king of the Jews?" asked Balthazar. The three men stopped, turned, and looked at him rather coldly and analytically, as though he might be a fool.

"Yeah," said John. The others nodded, turned, and continued leading us up the hill.

Right on the very edge of the town, overlooking the pastures further down the hill up which we had climbed, was a pleasant, if small, stone cottage from which shone welcoming lights. But they led us past it and around to the back, where there was a small barn of some kind, dug into the hill.

"Don't be too long," warned John, and Mordecai made another of his incomprehensible noises, this time a kind of a sniff and a grunt done at once. John followed us, while Mordecai and Joshua waited patiently outside. While we were in Bethlehem, I grew to like those three herdsmen. They were protective of the child and his family, and proof, said Melchior, that people can be perfectly good without being remotely articulate.

We later learnt that it was as Shahla had suggested back in Jerusalem. The child's parents had come to Bethlehem for the census, but there was nowhere to stay. There were only two full-time taverns or inns in the village, both of which were small and both full of paying customers. Even the small stone cottage that we passed, which was owned by one of the newborn child's second cousins, was full of paying guests. So the extended family had made the barn as comfortable as possible and kept bringing food and hot water and cloths and such things up from the house, while the child's mother, Mary, had her baby. I did not think it a very propitious beginning for a great monarch, but Melchior thought exactly the opposite.

The stable, or barn, had been well prepared, or made as good as stables can be made to look. There was a quantity of warm quilts and clean straw, and someone had brought a small iron brazier full of charcoal, over which a gaunt middle-aged man warmed his hands. He rose to greet us and introduced himself as Joseph. His wife, Mary, was at the manger, in the back of the stable, changing the baby's linen and then rewrapping Him in swaddling clothes to keep out the chill. When she came to greet us, she seemed young and small, but with very large brown eyes that fairly danced with brightness and interest. She looked quietly vivacious, and first impressions were true. When John, not quite correctly, introduced us as three kings, she curtseyed and, reaching behind her, tugged on her husband's sleeve until he took off his cap.

"Would you like to see him?" she asked. "He's ready for bed, but a few moments won't hurt, especially since you have travelled so far." Melchior nodded, and she scurried to the back of the stable and returned with a small bundle of clean, white, woollen strips, from which protruded a small pink face and one even smaller hand.

"His name is Jesus," she explained, as the baby grabbed hold of his mother's finger and smiled. There was a splendid feeling of calm there, and all of us commented upon it thereafter. It felt oddly still, as though nothing else could ever possibly matter.

"And is he the king of the Jews? If so, we have brought him something," said Melchior. Mary smiled and began to answer, but I never heard what she said.

The only thought in my head was that I could never remember getting ill so very rapidly in all my life. It came on instantly, much faster than food poisoning for example. Of course, I was younger then and spent much less time being ill, but this promised to be devastating.

My pulse began to race. I could feel my heart fluttering in my chest and then pounding. And next, in one of those sorts of odd, inchoate realisations that one has between sleeping and waking, I recognised that it was not my heartbeat. It was an incessant pounding and rushing in my head. At first, I thought I was having a stroke, but then it seemed more like the beating of wings. Once I identified the sound as that of wings, I began to panic. Then I heard the voices start, as if wind instruments could speak. I was hearing what the children had described. The strange sounds were stretched into words, which were slowed down and drawn out into a long, a very long *hosanna*.

Whatever else they said was confused. The room began to grow dark. Mary and Melchior and everyone else began to recede, as though they were moving away from me in some sort of tunnel. And all the time, the sound of wings grew relentlessly and the chorus of voices grew louder. I expected to fall onto the floor insensate, but then I heard someone almost shouting, "Are you all right? Are you all right?"

It was Mary, but she was not speaking to me. Rather she was holding Melchior, who had collapsed onto the floor of the stable. In an instant, I found that the sounds in my head had disappeared and, although I was shaken, I returned more or less to normal.

"Yes, yes, fine," blurted Melchior, who seemed embarrassed.

Joseph helped him up onto a pile of straw, and John brought him a dipper of water from the earthenware jar.

"Most amazing," said the old man, once he had caught his breath. "A rush of wings and a chorus of voices. Positively deafening it was. Voices like trumpets of some kind. Definitely wind instruments. They said the same thing over and over again. They said…" and Mary interrupted him.

"*Hosanna*," she said. "They normally start with that. Those are angels. They came almost every other day when I was first pregnant. You are very fortunate you know. Angels don't talk to everyone."

Balthazar tapped me on the shoulder and pointed to his head. "Did you?" he whispered. I nodded and then looked at Bilquis, and she nodded too.

"These are gifts for the child," said Melchior. He motioned to us, and we each left a small parcel at the foot of the haystack where Jesus rested. The baby smiled at each of us or else at everything in general, but, so far as the gifts were concerned, he paid them no attention whatsoever.

"I think you need something to eat," said Mary. "You are probably tired from all that travelling. If we were home in Nazareth, it would be different, but our hospitality is a little constrained here in Bethlehem. But Joseph's cousin Sarah is a dear, and she lives next door, and she always has something on the fire, doesn't she, darling? She makes lovely soup."

Joseph nodded, as his wife continued: "Could you take them next door and see if Sarah can come to the rescue?" She turned back to us: "And I have to put my son to bed. So we will see you all in the morning?" We thanked her, and she followed us to the door, talking to Bilquis.

"Now do you have enough blankets?" Mary asked. "Are you sure that you don't need to settle in here? There is plenty of room, you know. There's only three of us, and this stable holds about three donkeys and a pair of oxen and as many goats as you could ever possibly want as housemates. And none of them mind sharing either." Mary laughed at the thought. Bilquis properly assured her that we would survive in relative comfort.

I wish that it were true, for I doubt that all the quilts in Bethlehem could have warded off the winter chill that night. I wore all of the clothes that I had brought with me, and we wrapped up in every spare blanket or quilt that we had originally or that Shahla had managed to provide.

Periodically, I peeked out of my cocoon and saw the old man, in his thin cloak, sitting on a rock slightly further down the hill. I thought that, were it not so cold, I might have joined him. But then, as I thought again, I pulled myself out of my blankets, sucked in a breath against the numbing cold, and made my way down the hill, picking my way among the stones by starlight. Before I even reached him, he spoke as though he knew who I was, yet he had never turned back to look at me.

"I abandoned the experiment," he declared. I sat down beside him on the small boulder. "There was no point, of course," he continued. "Our common experience is something very strange indeed. Possibly even wonderful. Shepherds. *Apsaras*, or what they call angels. A king born among goats. Fascinating."

I remained there awhile. "This child is no normal king or healer," he said after some minutes.

"What is he?" I asked.

"Possibly greater than anything that we presumed. But beyond that, I do not know," the old man replied. "I need to think some more."

I climbed down off the rock and went back up the hill to bed, leaving the old man alone with his thoughts and his stars.

Chapter Thirteen

WE SPENT ONLY ABOUT two days in Bethlehem, and it was a most interesting time. Moreover, the people there were remarkably patient with all of our questions and tolerant of our ignorance too. What they simply took for granted were things that we had scarcely imagined; these *apsaras* for example, what the *Yehudi* people call angels.

Bilquis spent much of those few days with Mary, and they became friends by the end of it. I think she learnt more than the other three of us put together. Mary told her that the angels had first appeared eight or nine months earlier to tell her that she was pregnant and carrying the Son of God, the future Messiah. It was most remarkable.

Everyone hears about these prophecies—*Yehudi* prophecies of their Messiah, *Zardasht* prophecies of Mithras—but it is quite another thing to find yourself in the midst of one. These are things that we only read about, and frankly that is just how it should be.

But this exceptional young woman was given very little warning—and given it by angels as well. It was all good enough for us to see or hear these angels. By the time that they appeared to us in the stable, just about everyone for miles around had seen or heard them already; stable boys and shepherds and sweepers and even that nasty old woman who did the cooking for Sarah's guesthouse. All of the farm animals had seen them too; and apparently they made the dogs bark like nothing before. In other words, we had the experience of others to guide us, to soften the

shock. But the angels came to Mary unannounced and unde-
fined. Had they appeared to me as a complete surprise, I would
have assumed that I had a brain tumour or that I was going mad.

So the angel had informed Mary, and it came back repeatedly
bearing the same message. She said that she grew less upset over
time. She approached the matter as analytically as one could, but
eventually, she explained, you either have to believe it or not. She
did of course. She had to make a choice and she made it.

"It must have been difficult," Bilquis said to her. Mary apparently answered, with innocence and sincerity, that these things
are made difficult intentionally, and what is important is only
how we respond. She was full of answers like that; issues more
complex than a city map and answers as simple as breakfast.

After hearing the angels, Mary broke the news to Joseph,
which was another problem entirely. She had to explain that,
while still a virgin, she was pregnant with the Son of God. You
can imagine how any man might have reacted. If she was lying,
mad, or mistaken, she bore the child of another man. Yet, if he
refused to help, she may be stoned to death in the village square.

But he was far from ordinary, Joseph—quiet and reflective
and, of course, older than she. I quite liked him. Bilquis said that
he had kind eyes and the patience of a saint. He was a carpenter
of some sort, and probably a good craftsman. About the only
person to whom he talked at any length was Melchior, and Melchior said that they spoke chiefly about wood and not even a
great deal about that.

But I get ahead of myself. Mary said she knew that Joseph
would trust her and stand up for her. And so she told him of the
angel, and he asked no more questions and he supported her
completely. I do not know whether this was primarily born of
some marvellous gallantry, or whether it was his faith in Mary's
revelation, or something else entirely. But the more that you
think about it, the more remarkable he seems.

Ultimately, I suppose, Joseph realised that her declaration

could only have been one of two things: either the most appalling lie in history or the most astonishing truth. But it was never easy for him.

Then there was the travel. Their own families were content to keep her at home, to deliver the baby in a small town called Nazareth, somewhere off the King's Highway. But the angels apparently commanded Mary to deliver the infant king in Royal David's city, for so it was written in the prophecies. Then, as far as Mary was concerned, there was nothing else to say. And, as you might expect, Joseph cooperated.

It was neither the country nor the time of year in which to take a pregnant wife travelling. But they came to Bethlehem. Some days later the baby was born, and twelve nights thereafter we made our way from Jerusalem.

They were candid people, the child's parents, perfectly straightforward. But, on two occasions, they had remarkably little to say, and this did not make our investigation any easier, I can assure you. Or at least that was my impression at the time.

We were having lunch. Sarah had sent us yoghurt of some kind and some green olives and fresh salad leaves and oil and bread. People eat very well in Bethlehem, much better than in Herod's palace, if you ask me. Anyway Melchior's question drilled to the very heart of things, as you might expect him to do, and when Melchior asked those kinds of questions, is was impossible to take offence. There was no malice in him, and you could see that quite plainly in his eyes.

"So why do you think that you were chosen?" he asked them. And within his question were hidden more questions still. Why not a couple who were richer, or poorer? Or more or less free from sin? Or prouder or humbler? It was a question that probed why they had been chosen, but it also asked why *they believed* that they had been chosen. Their answer, then, would tell us a great deal about their expectations and values—whether the couple could articulate them fully or not. He was very clever, the old man.

Mary had just finished feeding the baby and had turned her back to us, as she laid him on the clean, sweet-smelling straw, wrapped this time in linen. When she looked over her shoulder, her eyes danced, and she answered as light-heartedly as ever anyone could.

"I don't know," she almost chirped. "It wasn't really our decision, was it?" And she turned back to adjust the bedding around her child. And that was all that she ever said on the matter. And those two sentences were two more than Joseph said either.

Initially, I was not sure what to make of her reply, but the old man fairly beamed with pleasure. I had only seen him look like that on the rare occasions when students dazzled him with answers that he had not expected them to know.

"Yes," he said softly. "Of course."

The other surprising answer came later from Joseph. Balthazar was helping him bring wood for the fire, he said.

"I asked him how he planned to raise a boy who was destined to be a king and maybe a good deal more," Balthazar recalled. "I explained that even in insignificant countries like mine, royal courts go to a great deal of effort and expense. Needless to say, it required efforts that these two people would find hard to replicate. I merely wondered what Joseph had in mind," said the king. "It was," he added, "one of my stupider questions."

"Joseph made a little shrug, as he dumped the firewood onto the ground with an enormous clatter," Balthazar continued. "Then he turned, wiped his hands on his shirt, and said: 'I don't know. But his real father might have something in mind.' And with that he went back to the woodpile for another load. He referred to *Ahura Mazda*, or *Yahweh* or *Allah* or the Creator, as though he lived in the house next door."

"What do you suppose lay behind Joseph's answer?" asked the old man. "Mary's too for that matter?"

Balthazar thought carefully.

"Belief in prophecy, and in the angels," he answered. "These people have very strong faith."

"And you?" he asked Bilquis. "Think, and then answer." He was unconsciously teaching again. She said revelations from the angels, and I offered nothing better. "There is something else," muttered Melchior, almost to himself. "There is something else, and I don't yet have the words for it. And whatever it is does not like words." The old man remained quiet after that for most of the afternoon.

It was on that same second night that the angels, or *apsaras*, returned for the last time. It was several hours before dawn, and I am quite certain of that for reasons that will become clear in a moment. I was sound asleep, out of doors of course, and wrapped in not enough blankets. And dreaming. First I heard the pounding of wings and the rush of wind. Then there came the strange musical voices coalescing into something intelligible. Indeed, I heard the sound before I saw anything in the dream. I am certain of that.

"Do not go back," it said. "Return home another way." The voice said that again and again—or the voices, for it was always hard to tell if it was one or more of them due to their strange musical timbre. Then I remember looking down and noticing that I was standing in water, but, when I looked closer, it was blood. It was repulsive, to put it mildly, and the crimson blood felt warm and thick and fresh, as it swirled around and around my ankles. I looked for somewhere higher and drier onto which I could climb, but there was nothing but a flat, shallow ocean of blood as far as I could see. And storm clouds roiled endlessly over and above it. And, in the distance, there were flashes of lightning partially hidden by the clouds. I remember thinking that I was somehow transported into Balthazar's dream. But the message was different. And all the time the voice continued reverberating: "Do not go back. Return home another way."

Then I turned and saw it, or rather saw her. The angel looked as Balthazar had described her. Unearthly, pale skin beneath white, pleated linen, with masses of inky black, curly hair spread out across the sky, until it merged into the night. There were wings beating somewhere, but I am not certain that I could see them.

I really could not tell you, to this day, whether she stood before me or simply filled the entire sky. She turned and, above the dark purple weepy rings beneath her eyes, her pupils were dead empty-black holes from which shone needle-sharp beams of bright light. And they swept across the shallow ocean of blood, coming closer and closer towards me. I felt that, when she finished facing me, the beams might pierce through me like arrows, but, when she turned, I felt nothing worse than a dread fascination.

"Herod plans to betray you and murder the child," she intoned. "Leave swiftly and return home by another way."

I started to speak. I was asleep, and, in a half lucid way, I knew that I was asleep, but I tried to ask her some questions. I wanted to know who she was, or rather what she was. I wanted to know why she held the sword and who had shed the blood that swirled around our ankles. Was it a sign of something that had happened already or a warning of something dreadful yet to come?

But every time that I opened my mouth, no sound came out. And every time I opened my mouth, her voice returned, droning that same message again and again, as though it were spoken by trumpets. Finally, I awoke and sat bolt upright in my blankets with the beating of wings and the angel's message still throbbing in my skull.

It was night—judging by the stars, the darkest time a few hours before the dawn. And it was silent. Down the hill and up towards Bethlehem, the cottages were dark. The people inside them were asleep. Nearby, the sheep were asleep. Everything was asleep. But looking more closely, that was not true. Twenty feet away, cloaked in darkness, Bilquis sat upright as well, looking straight at me. I made a half turn and saw Melchior behind me, gazing into the heavens, lost in thought.

"Did you…" Bilquis whispered. I pointed up into the sky and nodded. She nodded back. Melchior heard us and touched a finger to his lips to tell us that Balthazar was still sleeping.

"Don't bother," sighed Balthazar, as awake as we were, but lying with his head propped against his valise, as if it were a pillow. "As our friend Mary would say, we are always so fortunate when the angels come to call." He sounded less than convinced.

Later, when we compared experiences, our four dreams had been identical, like our simultaneous vision at the stable. But it was still late at night. I lay there and thought and half-dreamed and let my mind flow through those many mental states between sleep and wakefulness for which we have no words at all. There are no geographical terms for the twilight lands between daylight and darkness. No nouns for that period of inaction halfway between the conscious and the unconscious. If there ever were such words, our masters caught them and pulled them apart and dashed them into a thousand pieces to keep them from us, because it is in those indefinable moments that we have our single, small, only chance of seeing the truth.

Towards dawn, perhaps, I dozed, but, when I finally steeled myself against the cold and crawled out from under the blankets, Bilquis and Balthazar were already loading the camels.

"Packing up?" I asked unnecessarily. They both nodded and kept on working. There was, as Mary might have said, nothing more to discuss. Melchior was initially nowhere to be seen, but soon enough he came loping down the hillside from the stable. He was very tall, and for someone whom I tended to think of as old, he could move quickly and fluidly.

"They are going to Egypt," he announced, "on instructions similar to ours, apparently. From on high, one might say. They've been told to leave immediately. Apparently Herod is more jealous than he seemed."

"I am thinking of our Roman guard from Jerusalem," warned Balthazar. "King Herod might well be in a mood for vengeance."

"Precisely," Melchior replied. "The angels told Mary and Joseph that there is no time to spare. Meanwhile, two of the shepherds said that they will join us on donkeys or mules. They have fast ones that can keep up with our camels. They will take us east into the deserts, deep enough that we can circle far around Jerusalem and not risk being spotted." We had never even thought to plan our departure, so thoroughly had we absorbed and obeyed the angelic instructions.

"So that is it," I said. Our journey was truly over, or so I believed. I felt regret because there was so much more to be learnt in Bethlehem.

"I wish we had more time with them," complained Bilquis. We all nodded, or rather Balthazar and I nodded. Melchior shook his head and smiled.

Not long thereafter, we walked up the hill, leading our camels behind us, and made our way to the stable for what would be the last time. Mary and another woman were bathing the baby, who laughed and splashed about in a large earthenware pan.

"We've come to say goodbye," said Bilquis.

"To you and Joseph. And to Jesus of course," I added, pointing to the baby in the bathwater.

"This is his cousin. He's eighteen months older," Mary explained. I was young then and did not know one infant from another. She wiped her hands on her apron. "His name is John, and I have never seen a baby who so enjoys the water." She went to the manger and lay down beside her son, who woke and stirred gently.

"Did the angels tell you too?" she whispered. "We are going to Egypt. Won't that be exciting? I have never been to Egypt." He reached for his mother's face and smiled contentedly, and she reflected the self-same smile. And for a moment, Bethlehem or Egypt or Nazareth or the moon and all the planets simply ceased to exist for the two of them.

But no moment lasts forever. "We beg your leave, my lady, and so we would like to thank you now and bid you farewell," said Balthazar. He reached out to the infant, who grasped the king's finger in his tiny hand. "He is strong," Balthazar observed, "and that is good in a king."

"There are many kinds of strength, Your Majesty," Mary replied. "God knows he will need them all." She kissed the child, then rose and thanked us for coming. As she saw us to the stable door, she asked us for our prayers. "You will never be forgotten," she added. "Your generous gifts will see us all the way to Egypt, and I do not know how we could have otherwise afforded to make the journey."

"The gold comes from a businessman," Balthazar explained.

"Then thank him for us. And tell him what a difference he has made." And she brightened at the thought.

"We will," promised Balthazar.

Then Mary took the old man's hand in both of hers: "And you will always be remembered as the first to visit my son and the first to pay him tribute." Melchior smiled and corrected her.

"We came second, my lady," he said. "They were the first." And he pointed through the door of the stable into the yard, as the first strong rays of morning light shone in. There stood the families of shepherds and farmers and cooks and cleaners, the old and the young, women and children and men, who had all seen the angels, who had protected and comforted the Holy Family, and who gathered now to bid farewell to us visitors, whom they called the three kings.

Bilquis looked troubled: "I hope that you aren't being made to leave Bethlehem because of something that we told King Herod."

Mary smiled and touched her cheek affectionately. "Silly," she said, as though it were some private nickname that she had for Bilquis. "You're part of the plan too. We all are. And once we know that, we know enough."

Mary embraced her, as the rest of us mounted our camels, but finally it was John who broke the silence. "We could stand here all morning," he grumbled. And so Bilquis climbed aboard Sahar, and we started off. Balthazar turned in his saddle and left them with a warm smile, Bilquis with lingering glance that continued until we had ridden out of sight of the town. Only Melchior looked forward, silent and deep in thought.

"Did you notice," I asked Bilquis, "that last night the star was gone?" It had disappeared just as suddenly as it had come.

She looked at me, smiled and shrugged her shoulders. "Of course," she said. It was an answer that I could have expected from Mary.

Mordecai and Joshua rode along with us, and, so as you might expect, the conversation lagged now and again. We were scarcely to the bottom of the first hills, when we left the road and took a tiny footpath east through the olive trees and then through the scrub and finally out into the barren desert. Our guides knew their way.

We kept riding, until it grew quite late. Samuel wanted to get us as far away from Jerusalem as rapidly as possible and take us to the caravan path leading to the northeast and safety. So we ate day-old bread on camelback, munched dates, and handed the water bottles back and forth amongst us, but we did not dismount until nearly midnight. We were dead tired and sore, and so were the animals. When we finally made camp, Yasmine nearly wept with exhaustion or pent-up irritation, and she pouted until Balthazar personally brought her the feedbag full of fresh barley from Bethlehem.

"I am only too grateful, my darling, that you aren't in the mood for a massage," laughed the king, "or else I would be up until morning." He scratched her gently on the nose, and Yasmine closed her eyes and made the wet, blubbering noise that among camels passes for a sigh.

We ate sweet oranges and drank tepid buttermilk and sat in the darkness. "Most remarkable, those people of Bethlehem," Melchior observed, "they live in a world where prophecies come to pass without a moment of concern—where the supernatural is experienced, observed, and then treated no differently than the natural."

"They accommodate it like the weather," added Balthazar, and Melchior nodded in silent agreement.

It was part way through the next morning that Balthazar left us. Our guides brought us to a small desert town and found us some men with donkeys who were heading north and who would take us to find a larger caravan for the longer crossing to Persia and the east. We thanked the men of Bethlehem and bade them farewell. It was then that Balthazar discovered in the bazaar some spice traders heading south beyond the Dead Sea, over the deserts and onward across the Gulf of Araby. It was his intention, he told us, to finally go home.

"There were no angels and no swords in my dream last night," he explained. "No blood and no trumpets. Only sunlight. I was in Sheba overlooking the coast, and it seemed exactly as it did when I was a boy. It was green and overhung with bougainvillea that grew up the trunks of the tall palms. It was lush with mango groves, and those fat ivory blossoms hung heavy among the jade-green leaves of the frangipani trees. White ibises flew overhead, and grey parrots with scarlet tails chattered from the thatched rooftops."

"I was in a coastal garden terrace that once belonged to my father," he recalled, "and people had come to see him, as they always used to do. They were dressed in flowing garments of a hundred colours and a thousand patterns, because that is our way—the very old with their eyes still sparkling and their minds alert, the children so impeccably polite and inquisitive, as they always are on the African coast, the women gentle, yet outspoken and proud. I could hear the birds singing and the sounds of the surf. And the sky and the sea matched one another in those luminous shades of blue unknown anywhere else that I have ever been."

"Is it really like that?" asked Bilquis.

"It was like that long ago," Balthazar replied. "And it was like that in my dream. They were waiting for my father and they kept calling for him in their gentle, musical voices. We all called him father, not just his children, but everyone. That is our way, along the coast of Africa. In our lands, the king is regarded as everyone's father. And their hands stretched out to welcome him. I remember so many hands of so many colours and varieties. Calloused hands and soft ones. Hands of the very old and the very young. Burly, muscled hands and delicate, manicured hands with long, slender fingers. And I kept looking for him over my shoulder, until someone tugged on my sleeve and tried to lead me among those people in the garden. Only then it became clear. It was me for whom they were waiting. The name that they had used for my father they were using for me."

"And so I am going home now," he said softly. "It seems the time to start listening to my dreams."

He took from his finger a heavy golden ring, set with a rich green stone that he said came from the very heart of Africa, and he slid it onto Bilquis's finger and kissed her gently on the forehead. "Keep making up your own mind, Queen Bilquis," he said, and he climbed aboard the back of Yasmine the camel.

Then he leaned across and took my hand. "Caspar, you saved my life once and now you must save theirs. Please get them home safely," he requested, and I promised to do my best.

For a moment, we waited in silence, and all that we could hear was the whistling desert wind. Finally Balthazar spoke again, laying his hand across his breast. "God's speed, Melchior," he said to the old man, and Melchior gave the same reply.

"God's speed, my friend."

Then the King of Sheba clicked his tongue, and with a spirited roar Yasmine obeyed his command and lurched to her feet. They rose up together, until he towered above our heads, and then they set off at a stately, measured pace to join the little caravan bound for the fabled spice isles and perfumed coast of the Erythraean Sea beyond. And, as he rode, he sang in the ancient language of his people, as we had not heard him sing since he bathed in Melchior's rooms on the eve of our great journey. And his voice was deep and strong and full of joy. And it rang out over the desert long after his towering frame, slowly rocking to and fro on his lofty saddle, had finally disappeared behind the farthest dune.

Melchior said nothing, and he stood on the road, and he leaned heavily on his staff, and he watched the horizon until long after Balthazar had passed from sight. Then he wiped his moist eyes with his sleeve, perhaps to cleanse them of sand, and then he spoke. He said, "Let us go home."

Chapter fourteen

I WAS IN THE PRISON CELL, when I heard them come for the old man, and I thought that my heart would break. Then, when I looked at Bilquis, and when she looked back at me, I knew that it would break, if indeed it had not broken already.

Even far along the corridor and down the row of cells, we heard that imperious pounding of fists on the heavy oaken door. Nobody apart from an official makes such a noise trying to get into a gaol; trying to get out may be another matter. But we heard the blows echo through the nearly empty prison, then the hurried steps of the gaoler shuffling across the stone floor, awakened no doubt from one of his opium dreams; and then the removal of the heavy wooden crossbar, the creak of the iron hinges, then the low rumbling of orders being given and the silence of orders being taken, and finally the unmistakable tramping of at least a dozen men in heavy iron-shod boots.

Bilquis and I stirred, as though there were somewhere to hide him in that tiny, square, unfurnished cell. But Melchior smiled faintly, and he raised up his hand as if that might somehow calm us. Then as the footsteps drew nearer, I saw the blood. In a desperate attempt to keep from crying out, Bilquis had bitten into her trembling lower lip and a fat, single drop of crimson crept slowly to her chin.

There was no question of why they had come. They had managed to suppress much of the public outcry that day at the trial, and everyone knew that the verdict would be a foregone conclusion. So carrying out the sentence before the sentence was officially pronounced was perhaps a small procedural matter, but of some convenience to the state.

I beg your pardon? I have already told you of the trial that day, have I not? Oh, dear. I sometimes get ahead of myself. And do please help yourself to the buttermilk. Otherwise I grow distracted, wondering if your cup has gone dry. And she's brought us goat cheese again, but unfortunately not the kind that I like. But do have some, if you want. Now where was I? We returned from Bethlehem, where our guiding star had vanished, presumably gone back from whence it came. But I told you that already. Of course I did.

Then we said farewell to King Balthazar on the road, and we joined a small caravan that would carry us home to Persia. It was not one of Daoud's caravans, but of course they knew him. I think that Daoud was liked and respected by everyone in the caravan trade between Latakia and Ladakh. Or maybe further, because most of the travellers were bound for the silk bazaars on the westernmost edge of Cathay itself. The traders had sold their goods in Jerusalem or Alexandria or Palmyra, and now they journeyed east again to repeat the endless process. Of course, this meant that the passengers were as rich as the caravan was small.

Oh, yes, they carried some luxury goods to sell off in Persia or Gandhara, in Hindustan or Cathay: light, tiny, wondrous things such as painted glassware from Alexandria, or fine Egyptian embroideries, or small Roman gilt-bronzes—*fibulas* and the like. These did not take up much space or require many camels. Of more interest to me were their saddlebags, presumably stuffed with gold earned from the sale of silks and spices and the rare medicines of the East. Or at least we assumed that their bags contained gold. The businessmen certainly would not have left it behind.

But they understandably never spoke of their treasure and, moving swiftly in our much smaller caravan, we shaved at least a week off of the time it took to make the outward journey. So we were safer, less exposed to the risk of robbery for a much shorter period, and, and, mercifully, there was not the slightest indication of bandits.

We talked along the way home, the old man and Bilquis and I. We spoke of what we had seen, or I suppose that we did, but it was all so very long ago. Nowadays it all runs together in my mind—what we spoke of on the way there, and on the way home, and then at the trial. You know, sometimes my teacher seems like a shadow to me, like a dream half-remembered at morning. And other times he feels so vivid and so near that I almost expect him to walk into the room and send me off on an errand. If you live long enough and meet people worth remembering, I suppose that this will happen to you.

And then what? We came home, made our reports, and returned to life as it had been before. Or so it seemed at first.

Of course, the old man scribbled some notes, and we went dutifully to the Palace of Elders. By then old Bahram, the High Priest, had died and his scheming young secretary, Keshvari, had been named the temporary replacement. Emphasis was put on it being temporary, of course. Even had Keshvari been ten years older and a more obviously successful administrator, he had no background in Zoroastrian theology or canon law. So everyone assumed that he was a sort of a human bookmark, indeed a rather unpleasant one, soon to be replaced by someone older, better educated, better connected, and frankly better mannered. But throughout all the empire, this was the beginning of a difficult time, a period of decline that plagues us still, and with it come distinct advantages for the ambitious, the shrewd, and the unscrupulous.

I suppose that there might have been as many as twenty elders at the meeting, not quite half of the total, and at least ten of the twenty gazed vacantly out of the window or toyed with their cups or dozed intermittently as the old man spoke. One of them was almost one hundred years old and as deaf as a snake. To be fair to them, however, they were mostly an unexceptional sort of clergymen, and the farthest that their interests could be stretched, in this world at least, ran from the local temple to their vegetable gardens and back again.

Indeed my teacher said something to that effect, as we walked home from the meeting. It was an oddly warm winter's day, the earth smelled green and fresh, and we carried our cloaks slung over our shoulders, well aware that this was a false spring, but enjoying it nonetheless. "If Mithras does come down from Heaven to save us," Melchior said, once we were sufficiently far from the palace not to be overheard, "unless he lands in the temple forecourt or in one of their spinach patches, the elders may miss him altogether."

So, in that early hearing, Melchior spoke, and Qazi Kamran asked thoughtful questions, and Keshvari said little and did less until midway through the meeting, when he seemed to have been seized by an idea. Thereafter he scribbled furiously until we adjourned.

I thought it remarkable that the spymaster was nowhere to be seen, now that we had returned, particularly given his interest when we set off on our journey. But when I asked the old man, he scowled. He said that Sattar would trust the information much more, if he could get it second-hand by bribing or torturing someone who had heard us in person. This was the way of intelligence services everywhere, my teacher explained. Then, once their advice proves inadequate, as it almost inevitably does, they can protect themselves by blaming their sources.

If there was any official outcome of that single meeting, we were unaware of it. Qazi Kamran said afterwards that the minutes would be sent to the capital and that, so far as he could determine, it would take at least a couple of decades before any infant *Yehudi* Messiah, real or imagined, would be old enough to make trouble for Rome or for the puppet administrators of its colonies. Throughout the formalities, if I remember correctly, Keshvari merely nodded and mumbled in barely audible agreement.

Apart from that, we spoke about the journey to friends and family, as one does when one returns from such an adventure. And of course Melchior answered, after his formal lectures to be sure, those of his students who asked him what he saw. But there were neither public speeches nor clandestine meetings nor any of the other sensational activities of which the old man stood accused at one time or another.

This is why we were so surprised when Melchior was arrested, or why we were so surprised initially. Eventually, it all became clearer. Our emperor slept the sleep of the poisoned. He was in the final weeks of a long coma, and his rightful heirs were virtual hostages in Rome, while his wife, the Roman whore Musa, stood waiting at the imperial deathbed with her spineless son. In Khorasan, to the east, a bandit had taken the name of our first Parthian emperor, Mithridates, and threatened to lead the people in revolt. And, in the capital, our leaders frittered away their time, pondering how the empire might be made more modern, more patriotic and its subjects more malleable and less— shall we say—encumbered by their rights, their traditions, and their pocketbooks. Within this atmosphere, Keshvari saw his chance.

I told you that half of Melchior's forbearers were Achaemenidae—Graeco-Persians—and the others were magians, priests by tribe and by vocation. So, to Keshvari, Melchior's Achaemenid half represented the old classical culture that our masters had begun to attack as unpatriotic. His more ancient magian half—and his having been ordained—might also provoke a weakened clergy, eager to take offence at any scientific observation that challenged the orthodoxy. And were the temporary High Priest successful in his own ambitions, executing a purported enemy of the state, especially a scholarly aristocrat, would attract attention in the capital and, in enough circles, admiration and perhaps promotion. Minor details, such as the truth and the old man's innocence, could be removed from the court record long before they came under scrutiny. And as High Priest, even a temporary one, Keshvari had the power to do it.

The old man's trial was set to begin in the middle of *Nauroz*, presumably in hopes that the town would be distracted by the New Year holiday. But, even at the vernal equinox, winter remained with us exceptionally long that year, and, although we had passed the middle of March, there was no relief from bitter winds and leaden skies. Even our traditional first visitors of spring, the crocus and the *nargis*, what Romans call the narcissus, thought it wise to remain beneath the ground, while such unpleasantness raged above.

If you continue with your studies here in Persia, as you ought to do, and certainly if you stay on to teach here, as I have, you may eventually plumb all the complications of the Iranian New Year and perhaps even the meanings of their many traditions. Most of the Persians have no idea why they do half of these things, most of which date back further into prehistory than anyone could guess. But they make even our own merriest holidays back home seem rather austere.

Now, the old man paid no more attention to holidays than good manners demanded, but Bilquis always seemed to come alive at *Nauroz*. And well before the first of the thirteen days, she collected the *haft sheen*, the seven traditional ingredients. She had prowled the bazaars to find an exceptionally fine *sherab*, wine in this case from Shiraz; and a fat yellow beeswax candle for the *sholeh*, the candle flame; and *shookoofeh*, blossoms from the garden that she raised with her own hands. I think that they were those small yellow tulips from Turkestan, but I am no longer certain. It was long ago. That sort of tulip was very fashionable once, and everyone wanted them.

And then she acquired the sweets and the milk and the book of poetry and the rest. She had a special plate, left to her by her mother, which was only brought out at New Year. She always put it by the door, full of lentils and water to make them sprout. At the end of the festival, as you may have seen, the *Zardasht* hurl the fresh greens into the river, symbolically casting away sins for the new and presumably holier year to come.

But, throughout it all, Melchior was in gaol. Still, a few friends and family visited the tower, and Bilquis went to see some of them in return. This tradition of reciprocal visits, called *deed va bazdeed*, made the old man's absence feel even greater than it did already. He was snatched from us even before he died, and soon enough we would lose him completely and forever. But, being a good Persian girl, Bilquis kept the traditions and, being my teacher's niece, she carried it off with quiet dignity. But now and again I would snatch a glimpse her when she thought that no one was watching, and it was only then that she allowed herself to weep.

In the days before the trial, in and around bringing him his meals, Bilquis carefully prepared the old man's best clothes, and she refused to let the *dhobi* lay a hand on them, insisting on washing and pressing them herself. On the day of the trial itself, she rose before dawn and brought them to the prison with an enormous breakfast that was more than Melchior had ever eaten in a week of mornings. She said that he was in good spirits, as indeed he had been throughout the days since his arrest and imprisonment. He had grown ever quieter, it seemed to me, but even in long periods of silence his eyes continued to twinkle as brightly as ever.

So, after she returned from delivering his clothes and his breakfast, still early on that chill, gray morning, Bilquis and I wrapped ourselves against the wind, left the old man's tower, and walked to the Palace of Elders. Here and there along the way, some of our neighbours left their homes and accompanied us, or else they offered words of encouragement and fond hope. We were perhaps eight in number when we reached the palace and rounded the corner and saw to our surprise that there were more than one hundred people already waiting outside the towering double doors of the court. The wind whipped them mercilessly, but they pulled up their collars and turned their backs and waited patiently for the carved wooden doors to be opened.

I recognized some of them, of course. There was Hashem, the schoolteacher, with about a dozen of his young students in uniforms so clean and stiff with starch that they looked as if they were going to the temple next door. "If there is justice here today, I want them to see it," said the old man's student, and his young charges nodded somberly. Bilquis asked the children for their prayers, and a small, bright little girl declared, rather proudly, that Ahura Mazda had been sent dozens of them already.

Our local butcher was there, along with his angry, red-faced wife, but she seemed less irritable that day and she even smiled at me. There were twenty or more of his current students and any number of former ones; the old man had taught so well and for so long that nobody knows how many there are, undoubtedly many hundreds.

I spotted a distant cousin of Melchior, an elderly, lantern-jawed woman who walked with a limp. She was someone whom I had met only once before, but we recognized one another and we waved over the heads of the crowd. Hassan the copyist was there with his teenaged son, the crippled boy who was so swiftly learning his father's trade. And there were at least five men from Daoud's caravan, but they came unarmed or at least they appeared so. Indeed, there were so many people that it was impossible to identify them all, but Bilquis and I agreed that the turnout was most heartening.

We edged through the crowd and reached the double doors, as the captain of the palace guard came out, flanked by four of his larger deputies. These we had encountered when the old man first took me to see the High Priest, and they were dressed in the same leather armour and armed with short swords.

"There's seats inside for fifty," said the captain brusquely, "an' everybody what gets in needs a token. Right! You then!" He turned to me.

"This is the niece of the accused," I explained, indicating Bilquis, "and I am his personal assistant."

"Sorry. No ticket, no seat. Move aside!" A short balding man behind me proffered a clay ticket stub, a kind of a flat bead sometimes handed out at sporting events. He was someone whom I had never seen before. The captain let him through and turned to me: "I don't make the rules, but I gets paid to enforce 'em. Take my advice and go quietly."

"But my father is on trial," pleaded Bilquis, "on trial for his life!"

I interrupted her. "Look!" I nearly shouted. The captain had raised a single finger, and two of his guards had reached for their short swords menacingly.

"Want to see how far I'll go?" threatened the captain. He took another ticket from an elderly lady. "Look, smart boy, take the girl home," he added.

"Do you know him?" Bilquis grasped the old woman's arm and asked her urgently. "Do you know my father, Melchior? The man on trial."

The white-haired woman shook her head. "My husband is the deputy tax collector in Charasia," she said, referring to a small village about three miles away. "But he is too sick to come, so they said that I should go in his place." The guards parted and let her into the courtroom beyond the great wooden double doors.

Neither Bilquis nor I had noticed the growing reaction of the crowd behind us. The ones near the front had heard what the guard had told us, and soon enough all of them realized that the courtroom was to be packed with employees of the state. Apparently, none of us who knew my teacher would be allowed to see or hear the trial; and we began to suspect, not without reason, that the verdict would be similarly engineered. A sound of quiet urgency arose from the crowd, resembling the tense tone of a colony of bees when they feel threatened.

Standing on the steps as we were and looking behind us, by now there seemed to be about two hundred people outside of the courtroom, although I suppose that some of them were government workers following orders. Then someone shouted out an obscenity, a rather foul one, and a clod of earth struck the door high above our heads and rained dirt and gravel onto the palace guard. The captain looked at his men, nodded, and one of them darted back inside, presumably to bring reinforcements. Then we heard the clatter of hooves and saw the cavalry round the corner from the prison. Presumably, among their mounts, was Melchior on foot.

The angry buzz of the crowd grew louder, and the horsemen stopped, and through the double doors came thirty palace guardsmen, each armed with a knout or a truncheon. They began to clear a path through the crowd, and initially people seemed determined not to give way. There was shouting, and some were beaten. Then, just in front of me, one of the guards dashed an old woman to the ground, and I scuffled with him until she had time to collect her belongings and scramble to safety in the crowd. Along with many others, Bilquis and I were backed up against one of the long railings between the temple and the Palace of Elders, as the cavalrymen maneuvered their increasingly skittish horses toward the double doors.

Among them, we could see the old man in his finest blue velvet cloak and new woollen trousers. Initially, the crowd cheered, but then the voices fell, when they saw what the gaolers had done to him. They had manacled his ankles as well as his wrists, and both were chained to a horse and rider preceding him, jerking him this way and that. He still managed to raise his arms enough to acknowledge their cries of support. But you could see, even from so short a walk from the prison, that the bands of iron had badly abraded his wrists and his ankles. Nonetheless, he wore the expression of a man out walking for his health.

He was sent inside, and then they closed the double doors behind him, and the captain of the guard ordered the rest of us to disperse. Of course, hardly anyone obeyed. One of the red-haired twins, the strapping young giants who were our neighbours at the old man's tower, had found himself a good-sized cobblestone. He looked ready to hurl it at the head of the nearest palace guard, but Bilquis spoke to him kindly but forcibly, and he set it down. Narrow-eyed and tense, two of Daoud's men looked at me quizzically, but I shook my head. Bilquis was right; violence was not what the old man wanted.

And so, for nearly three hours, we waited, stamping our feet and rubbing our limbs against the cold. Some of the crowd surrendered to the weather and went home, and no one could blame them. Some asked the remaining few of us to let them know as soon as there was news, so that they could return. But nearly thirty of us stayed, with no definable objective, a tiny knot of people bound together by a faint hope.

In the middle of that most depressing morning, when we were cold almost beyond words, a raggedy man rounded the corner with a heavy wooden *karachi*, one of those pushcarts containing a charcoal brazier and a brass pan of roasting nuts. He brandished an iron poker before dramatically stirring the coals and sending a pillar of smoke and steam and glowing red cinders high into the chill air. "Free nuts today!" he called, "Get 'em while they last!"

We needed no second invitation, and the small packets that he gave us warmed our hands and our stomachs and our hearts. "Do you know my uncle?" asked Bilquis.

"The old professor? Why, of course," the man replied, scooping more shelled nuts into his pan with his charcoal-blackened hands. "Him and me, we's professional colleagues," he explained, as though he were a professor of medicine. "Of course 'e's a customer of mine," he continued. "All the best people are. But after 'e buys 'is groundnuts, or sometimes almonds, we talks philoso-

phy. So we's colleagues on two accounts; on account of roasted
nuts and on account of 'igher learnin!'"

I had never noticed him before, but his name was Salim, and
I think that he kept pushing that cart through our neighbourhood until he was well past eighty. But none of us ever passed
him again without making a purchase.

It was sometime past noon when the court adjourned for
lunch. Some of the spectators presumably remained in their
seats, where they must have either fasted or eaten food that they
had brought along with them. Others left in search of local eater-
ies, few of which were near the palace, but they would not have
known that, since mostly the spectators were ordered in from
distant villages and towns.

I was about to suggest to Bilquis that we return to the tower
and came back later in the afternoon, when the palace guards
snapped to attention, and a small figure dressed in black
squeezed through the double doors and around the guard and
rushed, breathless, down the steps toward us. It was Qazi Kamran in his judicial robes.

"I am so glad that you haven't left!" he gasped. "It took me
some time to work out why you weren't there and why the
courtroom was full of complete strangers. By then, of course, the
trial had already begun."

"What is happening? How is my uncle?" Bilquis demanded.

"I shouldn't be seen here, you know. I could be in a lot of
trouble—judicial impartiality, you see. But he's fine. It's not
going well, but he's fine for now." As he spoke, Kamran's hands
fluttered like the wings of captive doves.

"Look, when we reconvene, give the guards this note. At
least the two of you can get inside." He thrust a scrap of paper
into my hand and started to go, but then he turned back and
smiled an odd, wistful sort of smile. "I do so wish that I had been
one of his students," he added. "I've never heard a better lecturer.
It's all a pity, such a pity!" And with that, he lifted the hems of his

black robes, as an old lady might hike up her dress to cross a puddle, and he sprinted up the steps and through the tall double doors, which made a great hollow sound as they slammed shut behind him.

Most of the well-wishers went home, since they were not going to be allowed into the courtroom. Bilquis promised that she would get word to them somehow, when anything happened or whenever they were needed. We gave Kamran's message to the captain of the guard and we entered the courtroom with the petty officials and found ourselves places on the hard wooden benches along the back wall, about six feet above the courtroom floor.

One row below us, two government clerks fretted and gossiped in low whispers that were nevertheless clearly audible. "But if what he says strengthens the rebels," suggested the first one, "then he is a danger to us all." Wide-eyed, his colleague nodded vigorously in agreement. At first Bilquis could scarcely contain her disgust, and then she simply chose not to contain it.

"What utter rubbish!" she declared, looking straight at them. They ducked their heads and fell silent.

The morning had begun, we later learnt, with Keshvari reading a long litany of supposed crimes committed by Melchior: that he had knowingly strengthened anti-government rebels and intentionally weakened the empire; that he had given state secrets to Roman officials, maligned the state religion, impugned the veracity of the sacred texts and Heaven knows what else.

No witnesses for the prosecution would be summoned, because, he declared, they all feared retribution, although it was never quite clear from whom. Moreover, Keshvari said, in many cases revealing their identities would dangerously weaken the empire in its state of war against purported legions of enemy insurgents. And, of course, anyone of potential help to the government had already given his testimony beforehand and in private.

But neither, Keshvari had decreed, would the accused be permitted to call witnesses for his defence. That was considered to be a costly waste of time, when the beleaguered state, set upon by enemies within and without, could least afford such procedural luxuries. So, somehow, the old man had to answer charges that were listed but unexplained.

Thereafter Melchior told the story of the star and the journey and, so far as we could ascertain, answered genuine questions from Qazi Kamran and parried hostile barbs from Keshvari. The third triumvir was a deputy chief of police who did not look as though he understood a word.

"He's done a splendid job here today, the dear old boy. And what an adventure he had, going all that way to wherever it was," said the old wife of the deputy tax collector, as she reclaimed her seat next to Bilquis and removed a bundle of knitting from a straw bag. She obviously had no idea that Bilquis and I had made the same journey. "He looks so much like my own father," she continued. "Same snowy beard and same kindly eyes. Of course, my father's eyes weren't blue."

"I am worried that the trial might be stacked against him," said Bilquis, but the old lady smiled and touched her forearm reassuringly.

"Don't worry, dear," she replied. "Those judges work for our government. So they have our best interests at heart." Bilquis managed to force the faintest of smiles, as the three justices re-entered the court.

First came Qazi Kamran, seeming even more jittery than normal, nervously averting his glance to avoid looking directly at anyone in the courtroom. Behind him came the policeman who had grown his eyebrows together in the middle, as was the fashion, above a pair of small beady eyes that already seemed too close together. He was possibly not an idiot. Behind them came Keshvari, and I was astonished at the change that had overtaken him in less than a year.

He had found some elaborate chain of office that old Bahram had probably lost in a drawer somewhere; at least nobody remembered ever seeing the old High Priest wear it. It appeared to have convex enamelled links the size of small cups and a gilt dinner plate hung in the middle. Then he had either chopped his collar-length hair or pulled it back severely, which made him look even more gaunt than he really was. And most of his fingers appeared to have acquired golden rings, or rings plated with gold.

Beneath the chain of office, he wore a heavy robe of wine-red velvet, and I whispered to Bilquis that it was likely made up of Bahram's old curtains. Beneath that, he wore his traditional black. But despite my amusement and general disgust, the over-all effect was by no means comical, for above it and below it and throughout it all was Keshvari—and if he had done nothing else since the old man and I had met him in the palace, he had culti-vated his sneer and made himself vastly more dangerous and powerful than he had ever been before.

Behind the High Priest came the remainder of the palace guard, at least forty men strong, armed with halberds and sharp-bladed hangers and dressed in leather scale-armour fortified with iron studs. They fanned out across the back of the room, two men deep behind the judges. By making it appear as if the judges and the spectators needed such protection, Melchior was made out to be a threat. Shallow but effective, such is the psychology of the state.

Behind the guard, solitary and silent, stood one of the men who had visited our garden with Sattar, although he was in plain-clothes and left midway through the old man's story, just after Melchior answered a question about us fending off the bandit attack, but before he explained what we saw in Bethlehem. It was typical of our state functionaries then as now, and now as then.

Yet the dramatic entrance of the High Priest and his guard so captured the crowd's attention that we utterly failed to notice the arrival of Melchior, led quietly up the stairs and into the wooden dock where prisoners are made to stand. So he seemed to simply appear, to materialise all at once like a kindly spirit. And he stood quietly and politely, and he looked serene enough, but whiter and paler than I had ever seen him before. Indeed, I would hardly have been surprised, had he simply and slowly grown more and more pale, until he completely vanished into thin air.

Keshvari whispered to one of the court clerks and then folded his hands and smiled savagely at the old man, whom he refused to address by name. "If we remember correctly," he began in a flippant tone, "when we weren't suffering from the effects of a heavy lunch"—here some spectators laughed—"the accused was making a great effort to tell us something about death." His tone altered, and his eyes narrowed: "That is a subject worthy of consideration by all enemies of the state. Pray continue." Almost in a whisper, he made the last two words sound as though they were spoken by a serpent.

Melchior waited for a long time before he spoke; waited until the audience craned their heads toward him, lest he answer in a whisper; waited until Keshvari began to fidget with one of his many rings, twisting it around his finger in irritation.

Melchior then answered in a voice as clear as a bell. It was the voice we knew from the lecture hall. "I said, my lords, that, by the grace of Almighty God, I travelled far and lived to see two remarkable things: a great birth and a great death. Or what I believe to be the end of a great birth and what may be the beginning of a great death."

Keshvari rolled his eyes theatrically. "A portentous message indeed," he sneered. "Had you a question, Qazi Kamran?" he asked the tribunal's sole theologian. The small bald man shook his head and looked down at his hands. "Well, I do," Keshvari continued. "Would the accused say that this newborn, this supposed god-child, was more or less powerful than the Great Parthian, our own emperor of Persia?"

"Does your lordship mean the one who's in a coma?" asked the old man, and Keshvari's eyes flashed with anger. Some of the spectators concealed smiles. "At the moment, neither king can feed himself nor change his own soiled linen, but we expect the younger one to learn some new skills as he grows older," Melchior added.

The High Priest sneered: "You talk too fast. Earlier you said it yourself: this infant king has no palace, no retainers, no army, no trappings of state, and so you, the accused, have no credibility."

"Oh, that," said Melchior dismissively, as though he had stumbled onto a specious argument in class. "If the child's father can create entire planets out of nothing and make stars appear from nowhere, precisely what rank of Persian civil servant does the child need to impress?"

Keshvari swiftly looked away, scarcely able to contain his irritation, but nor could the audience fully suppress their enjoyment. It had apparently been much like this throughout the morning.

Qazi Kamran had clearly kept as quiet as possible throughout most of the trial, but he interjected in order to head off yet another direct confrontation between the witness and his persecutor.

"You would have us believe," the judge began, "that Ahura Mazda has sent the world his son. Lord Melchior, can you tell us how you draw this remarkable conclusion? And another thing—even as a matter of speculation, my lord—why didn't the Creator send His son here to Persia, as He sent His Holy Prophet Zoroaster? Has God lost interest in us?"

The old man smiled warmly and shook his head, as though gently correcting a mistake made by a favourite student. "My conclusions are based on scientific observation, My Lord Justice. At least fifty independent observers, including me, saw and heard the angels, who are some sort of *apsaras* apparently. Each of the witnesses seemed sane, or at least as sane as any judge in this country. And their testimony was consistent in every key regard."

"However, as experiments go," he added, "I admit that it was not perfect, for it cannot be easily replicated, unless of course the acting High Priest wields unexpected influence in very important places indeed."

Keshvari scowled and barked out a reply before the audience had time to respond. "There are limits to your insolence, Melchior, just as there are limits to your so-called science, and most of us will benefit from both."

Melchior failed to suppress a smile. "My Lord Keshvari," he asked, "does our faith take a position on the human senses?"

Unschooled in theology, Keshvari had no idea, and so he had no choice but to respond in anger, and his voice rose accordingly. "We shall ask the questions here! The judges, not the accused," he began, but Kamran raised both his hands.

"Let him go ahead," the justice conceded. "Just for once." Keshvari scowled, but folded his hands as a gesture of long-suffering patience and nodded to the old man in the dock.

"My lord, who gave you your eyes?" asked Melchior. "Think and then answer." He was teaching class again, and, had his former students been allowed into the gallery, they would have recognized the phrase immediately.

"Ahura Mazda, Almighty God," sighed the High Priest in feigned boredom.

"Then how angry will he be, if you refuse to use his gift? He gave you a brain as well, although your eyes are rather easier for us to appreciate. Do you use these gifts, my lord?"

"Be careful," warned the High Priest. "We are also informed by scripture," he began, but Melchior continued.

"You must think that the Maker of the Universe is an astonishing clot," the old man continued. "You appear to believe in a God who designs intricate human eyes and creates powerful human brains and gives us the power to reason, but then forbids us from using the gifts that he made for our use. Real science is no threat, Keshvari. Observation and analysis mean putting God's gifts to use as he intended."

"Abuse not use, Melchior! And I have had quite enough of this!" declared the High Priest. "You have been tested by God and you have rejected him in public!"

The Chief Justice, ever the peacemaker, interjected again. "Lord Melchior did not answer my question—why were not these angels sent here to Persia?" repeated Kamran. "You yourself believe that the Creator himself has promised us a messiah in the form of Mithras, if indeed you still believe your vows of ordination." Keshvari saw the potential for apostasy in Melchior's answer, and his eyes narrowed in anticipation, but he did not need to wait long. The old man turned to the far side of the judicial bench.

"Colonel Afshar," asked Melchior, "have you any children?" The policeman, the third triumvir, looked up, startled that anyone would bother to address him directly.

"I have three girls, my lord," he answered.

"Are they bright, lively girls? Do they sometimes talk a lot?" the old man asked. The colonel smiled bashfully and shook his head in the affirmative.

"And no doubt you speak to them in Persian, because your family is Persian," the old man continued.

"Yes, of course," said the policeman haltingly, fearing a trick where he might become the butt of a joke. Or worse yet, a joke that the others would understand but that he would not, for that is among the greatest fears of the slow-witted.

The old man craned his head and spoke gently: "But had you spent years in Cathay, where no one speaks Persian, and had you a second family there, you would love your other children just as much. And you would speak to those other children in what? In a language that they could understand." The policeman nodded, less guardedly than before.

"Colonel, is it possible that Ahura Mazda does the same as you would do? And so there may be one God and one message, but many languages and perhaps many messengers. Maybe one for each of his families of children?" asked Melchior.

No longer intimidated, the policeman smiled and nodded, as the old man continued. "On one day, God may choose to speak in Persian; then on another in Latin, the language of our Roman enemies; and someday perhaps in the language of the Beddou nomads or even another tongue." Melchior turned to the spectators: "One path may be straighter than another, but all of them can take us home." Keshvari scowled, as everyone else pondered what the old man had asked.

Melchior turned back to Qazi Kamran: "My Lord Justice, am I still true to my vows?" he asked. The judge stared at his notes.

"That decision is the task of this court," snapped the High Priest.

Kamran paused. "You have told us much about the great birth and the arrival of a king." He spoke in a quiet voice that could scarcely be heard. "Now what of the second part? What of this great death?"

Melchior stretched his long arms far out in front of him, grasping the wooden rail, staring at the swirling wisps of multi-coloured cloud painted on the beams of the ceiling and thinking for a long time in silence. One or two of the spectators followed his gaze into the rafters, as though the answer might be found written there. And they waited patiently, until even Keshvari fixed the old man in a long and steady look of uncertainty.

"There are several kinds of truth," began Melchior, much more softly than before, almost as though we had disappeared and he spoke to himself alone. "Some factual types of truth thrive under scientific investigation. They grow clearer as a result of chopping and parsing, defining and redefining, testing and discussing."

"Yet another kind of truth defies being qualified or quantified," he continued. "It is killed by conversation. It is fed by silence and contemplation. Yet this truth, begun in Bethlehem, may prove to be more a revolution than a revelation."

Keshvari's eyes brightened at the mention of revolution, for it was a word that could be made to do useful things. As with many people capable of nothing deeper than politics, words and ideas were to the High Priest little more than cudgels, blunt instruments with which to bludgeon his opponents.

And so it went on. The old man spoke of how we saw demonstrated, in Bethlehem, a way of making self and selfishness disappear. It was, he said, a way of being that converted self-absorption into almost pure function. We saw it demonstrated most clearly in Mary and Joseph, but also in the shepherds and their families.

"Simply by imbibing that atmosphere," he said, "we were drawn into a world where angels spoke to children, sometimes on a nightly basis; where God could dare to be a man, even an infant; where the Divine chose to become commonplace, yet was all the stronger because of it."

"It was a strange world for the likes of us, but it was real enough," the old man recalled. "Where words conveyed little, and the silence between the words held all the meaning. It was a world that was superficially identical to our own, yet completely different." From this, he said, comes revolution, but a bloodless one to be fought within.

"If it takes hold," added Melchior, "and if one by one men start to scale and conquer the citadels of their own hearts, the war will be led not by a soldier-god like Mithras, not by some military messiah, but by a helpless infant and his young mother. And by changing peoples' attitudes and the protocols through which mankind interacts with God, it can alter how each man interacts with the rest of mankind. It might," he concluded, "return us to Eden by returning Eden to us."

Some nodded. But I am afraid that, for all that the majority understood of what he had said, Melchior might as well have spoken to them like King Suleiman, in the languages of the birds or the *djinn*. Those simple witnesses who may have wished to understand seemed unable, while those with sufficient intellectual capability were for the most part intentionally deaf to his message.

Indeed, we spoke of this in his cell after the trial. After several hours more, Keshvari called a halt, saying that in the morning the court would reconvene to pass judgment or to continue its questions as it saw fit. And so Melchior was returned to his cell, where Bilquis and I brought his supper, including what was probably the last pomegranate in the entire province. It was somewhat shrivelled by March, but it was indeed a pomegranate, and it cost me almost a day's wages.

"Today I was on a fool's errand," Melchior murmured after a while. "After realising that my case was lost, I wanted to use the trial as my last chance to educate. And then what did I do? I tried to use words to describe something that does not want to be described by words, something that actively resists words, something that is simultaneously elemental and sacramental. But see? I am using words again!" He shook his head wryly, taken by the irony of it all.

"We all felt it when we were in Bethlehem," Bilquis agreed. "But there is no way to bring the courtroom there or to bring Bethlehem here."

"No, and if their revolution is to succeed and these skills are to spread, it needs some kind of transmission, person to person," the old man mused. He was on trial for his life and yet so easily distracted by the challenge of how to spread an idea. "They will need to replicate the experience of Bethlehem and then send their graduates out into the world. I see no reason why it cannot be done," he continued, but then he paused deep in thought. "Indeed, it is perhaps possible to keep the movement from being strangled by its own talk." Here his voice grew ever so slightly wistful. "But I rather wish that I could live to see it," he added.

He seemed to read our minds, for we all feared that the end was fast upon him. That memory still seems so clear, you know. So very clear.

Again Caspar nodded off to sleep on his favourite cushion, with his head tipped down onto the soft white nest of his beard, with his breathing shallow, but gentle and unlaboured. Once more I pulled the dun-coloured shawl up over him. Then I told the old servant woman that he had fallen asleep, and I returned home to my lodgings.

chapter fifteen

IT WAS ON THE NIGHT after our first day in court, I am quite certain. We were in the prison, and I gave Bilquis my handkerchief to mop the blood from her chin. We do very silly things in times of crisis—she had not noticed, and it really did not help much. Then, as the tramping of the soldiers grew closer, she held on to me, trembling, but the old man rose up and walked slowly to the cell door, as though he were going to meet a welcome guest. I suppose that I was never so brave as Melchior, for, when the wooden bolt was removed from the door, I thought that my heart might stop. Yet I was even more astounded when I saw that it was Qazi Kamran, accompanied by about ten palace guardsmen still in full leather armour.

His treachery made me furious, almost insensate. We expected neither justice from the trial nor vocal support from the cautious Kamran, but neither did we dream that the Chief Justice would, himself, lead the team of state executioners. Who knows, I wondered, what else Keshvari had accomplished by bribes or threats? So I started by holding Bilquis, and then she began to restrain me lest I fling myself at the old man's betrayer. Perhaps I was braver than I thought, or more likely I was too angry to think.

However, Melchior merely shook his head sadly and held out his hands in welcome. "So the unpleasant task falls to you, Kamran," he said. I noticed that some of the men had drawn their short swords.

"Yes, and we haven't got all night," the judge answered curtly.

"It should not take long," replied Melchior. "Am I first permitted my prayers?" My teacher's voice was even, and, like his hands, his gaze was steady.

The Chief Justice looked first perplexed and then angry, without the slightest hint of his characteristic dithering, and I wondered if his public appearance had been no more than a charade. "You can do that afterwards!" he snapped. Then he stopped and looked up suddenly, with the startled expression of a man who had been run through with a blade. "Oh no," he gasped, and then stammered for what seemed to be an entire minute, before he regained his composure.

"Y-y-you misunderstand me! We are going to my private c-c-compound!" he blurted. "These men are loyal to me. And believe me, we are risking our lives taking you to safety. We are c-c-c-committing treason, you know." He had come to rescue Melchior.

No sooner had Bilquis understood what he meant than she flung herself onto the little man, kissing both his hands and sobbing with relief. I began to thank him profusely, but my teacher interrupted, speaking almost in a whisper.

"No, Kamran," he answered. "It must not be done like this. Your father was a brave man, and you are every bit his equal. But not in this way. Take your people home." Kamran was astonished at the old man's refusal. He had certainly risked his life in coming there.

Once it had grown clear to him that Melchior would be found guilty regardless and then sentenced to death, Kamran had hunted out every member of the palace guard who had descended from old family retainers or for whom he or his father or even his grandfather had done favours. Each of those armed men behind him, together with their kinfolk, represented a century or more of mutual loyalty to Kamran and to his forebears, for that is how things are done here. And because of those family ties, the guardsmen had little choice but to join him and, had their mission failed, they would have gone to their deaths satisfied, knowing that they had acquitted themselves properly. But rescue and treason were purely Kamran's initiative, and so a court justice had risked his life to stop an injustice.

"You know what my compound looks like," Kamran argued. "You have seen those walls. With a handful of men, we could hold out for a month. Maybe two. And it only takes three days to send a messenger to the capital. They would listen to me and they would move the trial. Come, we have little time!"

Melchior sighed and rested a hand on Kamran's shoulder. "When I was first imprisoned, and when Caspar came to you for advice, you told him a wise thing," the old man explained. "You said that people need to believe in the integrity of their traditions. You were correct. We must not take that from them, Kamran, nor can we by our actions encourage every hot-headed young Persian to resort to violence. Go home with our gratitude, Kam-ran-jan. Leave tomorrow in the hands of God."

Kamran argued a while longer and then pleaded, but to no avail.

"There is another thing I said to Caspar on that day," the justice said bitterly. "I said that, even by Achaemenid standards, you were obstinate. Often foolishly so."

"Yes, Kamran," Melchior chided him, "but that thought is so very obvious that it earns you no marks at all." My teacher smiled faintly: "Think," he said, "think, then answer. All my life I have been a teacher. Now, if we do as you suggest, we would make a mockery of my life by trying to save it."

The judge thought silently and then he nodded sombrely, and the old man embraced him: "Go now, while you and your men are safe. God's speed, Kamran-jan, and God's blessing."

"And God's blessing to you, my lord," said the Chief Justice, who bowed as he backed out of the cell, making no effort to conceal the tears coursing down his cheeks. He had scarcely gone, when the old man turned to me.

"Have you brought a brush and some ink?" he asked. I nodded. "Then we have work to do," he said, and I sat on the floor, folded my legs, and began to take notes, as he dictated his last will and testament. Hashem would be given his best velvet robe, because he could otherwise never afford one, with five daughters to raise on a schoolteacher's salary. Madame Soraya, the elegant Afghaun lady who had struggled so hard to teach the flute to Bilquis and failed, would be given a Chinese bronze pot that she had once admired.

"The scrolls go to the astronomy department," he said and then corrected himself. "All but one of them. The one of Saturn with the wine-stain on the bottom. You'll recognize it. It's where you first showed me our star. I want you to have that. I was going to give it to you for *Nauroz* anyway." I felt a lump grow in my throat, but I continued writing. "And in my bottom drawer you will find an exceptionally fine sundial. Small enough to fit in a pocket, it folds up into itself like a gilt-brass tortoise. It was made by Ajmar in Nishapur almost a century ago. He was the best, you know. It belonged to my grandfather. Wait a few weeks for appearances' sake, and then give it to Kamran with my thanks."

It occurred to me, and perhaps to Bilquis as well, that he had almost disappeared into functionality—as Mary and Joseph and some of the others had done. Where some condemned men might have lapsed into regret or self-pity, and where others could easily be forgiven a final night of bittersweet reminiscence, Melchior threw himself outside of himself and went ever forward.

Of course he bequeathed the tower and the land to his only close relative, Bilquis, as well as a small orchard that his father had planted at what was once the edge of town and was now nearly in the centre. It was valuable too. And there was family jewellery, including some fine gold work purportedly descended on his mother's side from one of Alexander's generals.

After that, he had me record a long list of requests. Several students deserved commendations that he wanted brought to the attention of the academic authorities. Then there had been some arguments within the faculty over next year's curriculum, and he wanted a particular course repeated. Things like that, prosaic things, banal things. A new bitumen roof for the tower. He wanted to pay for the education of Jamil, the neighbour boy who helped Bilquis around the house. "Otherwise he will grow up to be like his mother," grumbled the old man, "and I am not certain that the universe can withstand another of those."

I cannot remember them all now. Insignificant things they were, but at the time they seemed almost sacred, because they were of the moment and important to him.

Finally, he declared that it was time for him to sleep. He embraced me and then Bilquis and said little apart from simple thanks. Then the gaoler was summoned, and the cell door was opened.

"I shall see you both tomorrow. Tomorrow will be interesting for me," he said, and then he added: "But tomorrows have always been interesting for me. Good night to you both." He was an Achaemenid, and his simple farewell was not restrained so much as austere. And it conveyed meaning enough.

After the gaoler locked the door behind us, I peered through the window, until Bilquis tugged at my cloak impatiently. The old man had not lain down to sleep. He sat upright, staring into the middle distance, calm, half-smiling, and deep in thought.

Bilquis paid the customary tip to the gaoler, and we began to walk home in pitch darkness, but we were not far from the prison, when she began to sob and collapsed into my arms.

The next morning, we went early to the courtroom, and this time there were almost no spectators. Indeed, the rainy streets were nearly empty. Lancers, in pairs, patrolled the environs on their muscular black mounts, and there must have been a hundred palace police within two hundred paces of the court. A woman pushed a cart, selling fuel for that night's festival, for it was the last Wednesday before the New Year, but two of the guards hurried her along. Another pair of them swaggered up to us, preparing no doubt to send us away, until one of the officers recognized us as Qazi Kamran's guests from the day before and he gestured that the others leave us be.

Inside the courtroom were perhaps twenty people, one or two of the old man's students who had been driven away earlier and a larger group of low-level government functionaries who were paid to attend. But anyone who could reach the courtroom through the patrols of cavalry and palace police was apparently free to watch and wait. And so we did, as one hour moved into the next. There was no indication of a trial. No announcements and no notices of adjournment. There were no guards, no justices, no scribes with their green caps, neither pallid, petty officials nor ruddy policemen, neither parchment scrolls nor heavy bronze seals, nor spirit lamps nor wax, nor coming and going. Over the next two hours, more visitors trickled in and found seats, possibly bureaucrat stragglers or perhaps the simply curious, but, whoever they were, they were given precious little to see.

I was mystified. Bilquis began to suspect foul play, and for a moment we considered whether she would return to the prison, while I went off through the palace grounds in search of Kamran. But we remained, and in the afternoon some of the lesser court officials started to arrive, and spectators trooped in to take the remaining seats. Outside, we heard the clatter of horses, and, presently, Melchior came up from the cells below and entered the dock, as policemen filed in to stand along the back walls.

It was then that Bilquis grabbed my arm and pointed urgently into the crowd, where Qazi Kamran sat on a public bench near the front, as though he were a common spectator. He did not wear his formal robes and had entered without any of us noticing. Then I spied the third justice, the policeman, sitting two rows behind Kamran on the other side of the room among the crowd. Where they sat did not matter. The significance lay in their absence from the judicial bench.

We said nothing, but others started to notice it too, and whispering began in earnest. When the troop of policemen marched through the great inner palace doors, as they had done the day before while preceding the justices, they were no longer palace police. Those had been replaced by harder men in almost featureless black uniforms that were quite unfamiliar to me.

Finally, the nearest ones lined the doorway and stood stock-still, as we heard a faint noise, a kind of clattering and dragging sound that grew louder. Then we clearly heard wheezing. This all continued for some time, until I could barely make out, coming slowly down the distant corridor, a tall, hunched figure dressed all in black, hobbling along painfully on two sticks—two silver-headed sticks that glistened in the few shafts of sunlight that here and there illuminated the long, otherwise sunless, hall. It was Sattar, the spymaster.

The soldiers parted for him. Of course, then I recognized them. The uniforms were not precisely what Melchior and I had seen in his garden, but they were similar. One of them helped Sattar up the single step onto the platform and into the chair that Keshvari had occupied on the day before. Sattar pulled a handkerchief from his sleeve and wiped his good eye, then cleared his throat.

"I shall make this brief," he snapped, looking at no one in particular. "High Priest Keshvari has been called to the capital on a matter of the utmost urgency. Until he returns, I am to head this court of inquiry, which hereby adjourns until the accused can present a thorough report of his claims. A very thorough report in the interests of *investigation*." And here he looked straight at Melchior, as he put extra emphasis on the last word.

"Meanwhile, preparation costs will be under-written by this court at a rate of two gold staters per month," he said, and then he banged one of his canes down on the tabletop. "Court adjourned!" he barked. "Bailiffs, clear the room!" Sattar had never introduced himself.

He waved a gloved hand, and the troops began moving along the rows of benches, herding the spectators before them. One of the senior guards looked to Sattar, who nodded, and only then did he unlock the fetters from Melchior and then, with a gesture towards the door, he indicated that my teacher was free to go.

Most people were astounded by the announcement as well as confused by the haste in which it was delivered. They hurriedly grabbed for their belongings, as the soldiers jostled them along the rows of benches, then down onto the courtroom floor and towards the double doors that led to the street outside. But Bilquis hopped nimbly over two rows of benches upstream through the flow of spectators and threw her arms around her uncle, nearly squealing with pleasure. Then more of his students and friends came from various corners of the courtroom to greet the old man and celebrate his unexpected reprieve.

I was equally delighted, of course. Moreover, I was surprised at the decision. But I knew that I would now have plenty of time to see Melchior, but perhaps only one chance to find out what had happened and why. For that I needed to speak to Sattar and, if I missed him that day, I knew that I might never have the chance to see him again. And indeed I was correct, for after that day I never did see him again.

But I was young then, as you are now. And like a show-jumping pony, I cleared the benches, one at a time, and then I muscled through the crowds on the courtroom floor. I ducked down and nearly dived under the arms of the two guardsmen sweeping people ahead of them, reaching the enormous doors seconds before two burly soldiers slammed them shut. At the last moment, four of them blocked me, and Sattar was already halfway down the long corridor, hobbling away, hunched over so many legs and sticks that he resembled a great black spider. Just as one of the guards thrust the gloved palm of his hand into my face and began to push me over backwards, I shouted out Sattar's name. The others clustered around me, as one soldier kicked me hard on the shin. Then, suddenly, the nearest guard stopped, and then they all stepped aside, presumably obeying a command.

Through the half-closed door and far down the tiled corridor stood Sattar, who watched me and beckoned with a single gloved hand. I pulled myself together, brushed the soldiers aside, and walked down the corridor through the three or four bars of sunlight that fell through the tall, narrow windows, illuminating the length of the hall, each containing a million golden motes of swirling dust, as though an entire cosmos whirled between us.

I had ten, twenty, a hundred questions to ask him, but all I could manage was to croak out a single word, "Why?"

The corner of his lip curled upward in amusement, but only infinitesimally, and then he laughed or snorted—it was hard to tell which. "Some problems don't need solutions," he replied. "Then again, if you choose not to solve one problem, you sometimes solve a different one quite inadvertently." He could tell from my expression that I did not understand.

"You're too young!" he snapped. "Not foolish, just young! Time will take care of that. It usually does." He slowly turned to go, leaning heavily on his sticks.

"Keshvari," I started to say, intending to ask what would happen when the High Priest returned to renew his persecution of Melchior. The spymaster made a half-turn and spoke over his shoulder.

"That's the problem on the roads these days. Nobody's safe anymore. As your teacher told the court, bandits are everywhere." He smiled bitterly and continued down the hall. I watched him struggle on, and finally I turned back towards the courtroom, where my teacher and Bilquis waited to return home to the tower.

I had taken no more than a half-dozen steps when I heard Sattar shout after me, calling my name. And his voice echoed down the empty corridor and clattered on the windowpanes and the hard tiled floor. I turned to see him point at me with one of his sticks, fixing me in a one-eyed stare.

"He turned me down!" he cried out. "But he would have been good in the service, you know. Maybe the best! Maybe better than me! He sees things that the others miss." He paused for only a moment: "But perhaps so do you. So consider it. While you're still young." And with that he disappeared, as he hobbled into the shadows. And for a few moments longer I could hear his laboured breathing and the dragging, clattering sounds of him struggling down a more distant passage, until all grew silent.

I found Melchior and Bilquis nearly alone in the courtroom, and we returned to the tower, as the clouds of winter finally began to dissolve into clear twilight, as the weak rays of sun bathed everything in a pale, raking light that made even the barest of trees look golden and capable of sending forth life. Everywhere groups of children gathered bundles of sticks and branches from the hedges along the roadsides, for that night was *chaharshanbeh soori*, the last Wednesday night before the New Year.

The wood was needed, for soon every street and lane, every neighbourhood and village and city and valley and meadow and hilltop throughout the empire would be speckled with bonfires, and the older children would tend the flames, whilst the younger ones, banging pots and pans and making a horrific din, would go from house to house demanding sweets and fruit and small gifts for the New Year about to begin.

And then, when the bonfires burn down to small tongues of fire lapping at the glowing coals, individuals and couples, children with their parents, husbands with their wives, pairs of young lovers, the old together with the young, hike up their cloaks and lift up their hems and leap over the flames. They rush to the edge of the sacred, purifying fire, dashing forward, and then, for a few seconds at least, they soar into the air, as though God had made them into birds. And in a vital act of will and a heartfelt act of hope, they hurl themselves headlong into the future, abandoning old sins and grievances and anger, leaving the past behind them to be invisible and forgotten and gone forever. Such it has been for centuries beyond number, and so will it continue for all time yet to come.

As old Sattar predicted, Keshvari was never heard from again. He vanished somewhere along the road to the capital. I remain convinced that his disappearance had something to do with Melchior reporting the renegades who attacked our caravan, although I could never determine whether they were subsequently stopped or encouraged by the state.

And, contented in his tower, Melchior began to compose his full report, writing and rewriting his account of our travels, adding sections of speculation and portions of analysis, searching the ancient Babylonian texts for the mention of new stars and watching the heavens night after night. And every month, someone would come from the government, someone different every time, who would deliver two gold staters—more in a month than the old man had ever earned from even half a year of teaching. But since no one ever came to tell us where to deliver the report, the research continued.

And every so often, Melchior would visit the *caravanserai* and speak to Daoud or to the other drovers, in case there was any news of the child. There never was, but to him it did not seem to matter.

For, in those final few years, my teacher was consumed by a kind of faith, if that is the proper word. Or perhaps it was an almost palpable certainty. And he radiated this in moments of silence even more than when we spoke. And I was nearly jealous of it. You see, I myself never had it fully and, try as I did, I never managed to develop it. It may be a knack that I failed to acquire, or perhaps it was a gift that I was never given for long. But it has managed to elude me. And yet it is so obvious and so beautiful, surrounding those who possess it.

The old man took a different view, and we spoke of it, as we walked home together following the trial. He said that it was everywhere, but not always visible, neither all of the time nor to everyone at once—similar to the golden motes of dust that we are only permitted to notice when we see them sparkle in a beam of sunlight, but that may be likened to the ordered and endless galaxies of which we are infinitesimal but, according to the angels, still important parts.

And, when we reached home, my teacher led Bilquis and me up the rickety wooden steps onto the roof of the tower, where the old man and I had stood together on that night when we had first seen our Star. And he made a sweeping gesture across the darkness that surrounded us. And far below us, at every point of the compass and across the myriad spaces in between, there shone the lights of countless bonfires, twinkling as though our newborn Star, as well as all of the Planets of the Spheres and all of the Stars of the Outer Heavens, had come down to earth to live forevermore among us. And from out of that night and from out across the land, there came the distant sounds of goodness and laughter.

"It is there," he said with perfect certainty. And on that night I saw it.

This is the account of my teacher and fellow countryman, Caspar, formerly of Nagarahara in the principality called Gandhara in the empire of the Great Kushan. A year after this was told to me, at his instigation, I was invited to join the faculty of modern history as a junior lecturer. Three years later he passed away in his sleep, in his 85th year.

Men of my teacher's generation rarely spoke of personal matters, which were thought to impose unfairly upon friendships, as well as compromising privacy and family honour. Thus, I never dared to ask him what had become of the woman Bilquis, who accompanied the three on their journey. My suspicions were confirmed a few months before he died, when I returned to his tower to collect a scroll that I had left behind a few moments before. Stoop-shouldered by then and heavily reliant upon his stick, he stood in his study beside the old woman who had brought him his meals and who appeared to tend to him so carefully. They held hands, there at the window, together watching the sky darken, as the first few evening stars began to take their positions for the mystical dance that ever follows. And on her finger, just beside her wedding band, was a ring that I had not noticed before. It was a heavy golden ring worked in a fine and unfamiliar manner, bearing a stone that was as rich and green as the heart of Africa, the gift of King Balthazar so far away and so many years ago.

epilogue

TWO YEARS AFTER my teacher died, a stranger came to us, seeking Caspar. We led him to the simple grave, high on the bluff overlooking the city, facing to the west, where the stars always shine the brightest. There the visitor knelt and prayed. He told us that, for more than thirty years, he had been a servant and messenger of the Messiah, whom my teacher had seen newborn in Bethlehem. Now our visitor was on his third voyage to India, and he believed that it would be his last. He took copious notes, as Bilquis recounted the journey that she had made with Caspar and their subsequent time together. The visitor lived among us for nearly three weeks. His name was Tomas, and in a short time he taught me much.

(signed)
JOHN ANDREW
Anno Domini 64
Pax Christi

glossary

Abrashom (Persian): silk. An early and ancient portion of the Silk Road trade route, called the *Tangi Abrashom* or Silken Pass, leads through the Hindu Kush mountains to Kabul, along which the author has discovered Vedic Aryan petroglyphs at least 3,000 years old.

Achaemenid: a powerful and culturally rich Persian dynasty founded by Cyrus the Great in 600 BC, which fell to Alexander of Macedon in 330 BC; a far larger empire than that of the Greeks, but smaller than that of the Romans. They seem to have been the first to codify civil rights, especially for minorities.

Ahura Mazda: Zoroastrianism's wholly good highest being and creator. He resembles the Abrahamic God, except it is not yet decided whether he or the evil Angra Mainyu will forever rule the universe.

Amphora (ancient Greek): large wine jug.

Angra Mainyu or **Ahriman**: in Zoroastrianism, the devil or "the Father of Lies." Zoroastrians believe that our every act, unaffected by repentance and inaccessible to forgiveness, will determine whether Good or Evil eventually rules the universe.

Apsara (Sanskrit, Hindi): a Buddhist or Hindu angel, a celestial nymph.

Arrakhan: a region on the borders of modern Bangladesh and Burma.

Avesta: the holy books of Zoroastrianism, portions of which went missing late in the First Century BC, suggesting some widespread crisis or other reason for a loss of tradition.

Azeris: Turkic natives of modern-day Azerbaijan. Although they settled in the region in the Middle Ages, as traders they seem to have travelled widely long before.

Bactrian satrap: A satrap was a Persian provincial governor, in this case that of Bactria, covering parts of Eastern Afghanistan and Pakistan.

Baksheesh: a bribe, a tip, or a discreet payment serving both functions.

Balkh: ancient centre of learning in north Afghanistan, destroyed AD 1230 by Genghis Khan.

Balouch: a tribe of chiefly herdsmen and farmers who live on the Baluchistan Plateau in eastern Iran, western Afghanistan, and Pakistan.

Baltis: natives of Baltistan, in the eastern mountains of modern-day Pakistan. The purportedly South Asian "balti" cuisine, popular in England, has nothing to do with the place or the people, except that they cook everything in one pot.

Beddou: Beddouins, Arab nomads (Beddouin proverb: "God gives nuts to those with no teeth").

Carrhae: battle in 53 BC, when Persia defeated the Roman Empire.

Cathay: the old European name for China, familiar to Marco Polo.

Chaharshanbeh soori (Persian): a holiday occurring on the last Wednesday night before the Persian New Year. Families and friends jump over small bonfires to symbolize leaving the old year's sins and grievances and unhappiness behind.

Chinar tree: Plane tree, vast and broadleaved, with mottled bark like a sycamore.

Crassus: Marcus Licinius Crassus (115–53 BC), triumvir, richest man in Rome and said to have been the richest on earth, killed at Carrhae.

Ctesiphon: the capital of the Parthian Empire northeast of ancient Babylon.

Dakhma (Persian): Zoroastrian Tower of Silence, on which human remains are exposed to feed carnivorous birds, so as not to pollute sacred fire or earth. In places with Zoroastrian communities such as Karachi and Bombay, dakhma neighbours sometimes complain that passing birds drop gruesome surprises into their gardens.

Dar-i-mithr (Persian): the place of Mithras, used for Zoroastrian ordination and signifying their coming Messiah.

Deed va bazdeed (Persian): part of the Persian New Year, an occasion on which participants exchange reciprocal visits between friends and family.

Dhobi (Hindi, Urdu, etc.): laundryman.

Diogenes: an ancient Greek philosopher (412–323 BC).

Djinn (Arabic, Persian, French): a genie. According to Islamic and other eastern lore. genies are creatures different from angels and humans, made of mouldable elements and able to change shapes at will. They are beings capable of good and evil. King Solomon could supposedly speak the languages of genies, people, and birds.

Farnbhag flame: early and legendary Zoroastrian fire altar based near modern-day Kabul, Afghanistan. Fire altars, tended around the clock, are sometimes first lit from the flames of more famous fire altars.

Gilim or **kilim** (pan-West Asian): a flat-woven carpet, rug, or mat lacking pile.

Gur: molasses candy made from brown and unrefined cane sugar.

Halwa or **Halva**: a popular family of dense, sweet confections in the Middle East and South Asia, rich in flour, butter, and sugar, often with crushed nuts or vegetable purées, roughly the consistency of fudge.

Han: a Chinese dynasty 1100–757 BC, or the largest ethnic population in China.

Haoma or **Soma**: ancient sacramental hallucinogenic drink of the original Vedic Aryans in Central Asia, probably made of Wild Syrian Rue, which is rich in ephedrine. Mysteriously abandoned by Persia's Zoroastrian priests around two millennia ago, and Brahmins in India claimed it cannot be grown there. The author found it drunk socially, not sacramentally, north of Kabul by the Muslim descendants of Vedic Aryans.

Herat: a formerly Persian and now western Afghan city.

Hindustan: a non-Hindu name for India.

Iskandria: Alexandria, the Egyptian city named for Alexander of Macedon, a manufacturer of luxury glass in the classical era and once home to the ancient world's greatest library, with an estimated 700,000 volumes.

Ispahan: major seat of culture and scholarship in Iran.

Jali: Pan-South Asian for a pierced screen, often carved of stone.

Karachi (Persian): pushcart.

Kharegi (Persian): guests or outsiders. Then and now in Persia and eastwards, one's reputation is largely determined by hospitality to guests.

Kharosthi script: used in the kingdom of Gandhara in modern day Afghanistan and Pakistan, a part of the Kushan Empire, chiefly to write in Gandhari and Sanskrit languages.

Khorasan: a region spanning eastern Iran, Afghanistan, parts of Turkmenistan and Pakistan.

Kohl: ancient eye cosmetic made of ground lead sulfide, mascara.

Kushan: a tolerant, peaceful, and artistic empire funded by trade, chiefly Buddhist, spanning Afghanistan, eastern Pakistan and northern India, 30 BC–AD 375; fell to the Huns.

Kushti: the sacred string girdle worn around the waist by Zoroastrians.

Ladakh: a mountainous region of India, near Tibet, on one of South Asia's oldest trade routes.

Latakia: the principal port city of Syria, inhabited since the second millennium BC.

Magian: magus and astronomer, originally a member of the Zoroastrian priestly caste, which lost its sacramental monopoly sometime before the birth of Christ. Saint Matthew refers to them in the singular as *magos*, a Greek term borrowed from older Persian linguistics. It provides our word *magic*, although Zoroastrians oppose sorcery. The King James Bible calls them "wise men."

Mashad: a city of shrines in eastern Iran.

Mithras (Greek for the Persian Mithra): the Zoroastrian Messiah, focus of an extensive, secret Roman military cult 1st–4th century AD. Spanish bull-fighting descended from its taurine sacrifices. He will be born of a virgin, after she swims in a lake impregnated long ago by their prophet Zoroaster.

Nagarahara: modern day Jalalabad, Afghanistan, once a seat of Buddhist learning and ancient science.

Naranj (Persian): a bitter orange, the origin of our word "orange."

Nauroz (Persian): literally. "the new day," meaning the Persian New Year, beginning on March 21. Like some other ancient new-year festivals, it heralds the spring, rebirth and renewal. Attributed to Zoroaster, historians chart its origins to no later than around 600 BC, under the Achaemenids. While pre-Islamic, it is celebrated throughout modern Iran and has also been adopted by Sufi Muslims, Bahai, Alawites, Ismailis, and others connected to Shia Islam and/or Persian culture. The Jewish festival of Purim is said to have been inspired by Nauroz, when the Israelites came under Persian rule in 539 BC. Nauroz contains many traditional activities that tend to centre on forgiveness, purification, and strengthening family or community bonds.

Orissa: an ancient kingdom, now an eastern state in modern India.

Paktues (ancient Greek): the modern day Pushtoon people of Afghanistan and Pakistan, as mentioned by the historian Herodotus in the 400s BC.

Pali: a Middle Indo-Aryan language, now extinct, except in scholarship and for Theravadan Buddhist liturgy. It is either the ancient language of the Buddha or close to it, as well as being used in Buddhism's central Pali Canon.

Parthia: Persian empire 27 BC to AD 224, originally a district of northeastern Iran near the nomadic wastes of Central Asia. Parthia's minor vassals gradually annexed modern day Iran and portions of Afghanistan a century before Christ. While having defeated invaders from as far away as Rome and China, they grew both decadent and weak enough to be overthrown by the Sassanians, minor vassals from southwestern Iran.

Pashmina (various S Asian): exceptionally fine woolen goods knitted from the neck hairs of special Kashmiri goats.

Phraataces: diminutive nickname of King Phraates V, who ruled Persia 2 BC–AD 4. According to Josephus, he married his mother, Musa. Their portraits appear together on coins, but the marriage may have served only to certify the young king's lineage rather than being conventionally matrimonial, but it doesn't matter, because mother and son were overthrown by a disgusted public in AD 4.

Pipal tree: sacred fig tree; "bo-tree" or wisdom tree under which Buddha became enlightened.

Qashkai: a Turkic Central Asian tribe that visited Persia frequently, but settled permanently in Iran 1200 years ago. Nissan has named a motorcar after them.

Qazi (Arabic/Persian): judge.

Sabzi (Persian): greens.

Sahib (chiefly Pushtu, Hindi, and Urdu): sir (form of polite or respectful address).

Sarvastivada: an early school of Buddhism, patronized by the Kushan emperor Kanishka and now extinct. Its central thesis seems to have been the simultaneous existence of past, present, and future dharmas, somewhat resembling the Catholic teaching of God's omniscient view from outside of Time.

Scyths: tribe of Iranian horsemen who ranged as far as Kiev, renowned silversmiths and goldsmiths, 700 BC–AD 400.

Serai or **caravanserai** (many oriental languages): a safe shelter for caravans, offering secure walls and gates, storehouses for cargo, and refreshment for man and beast. Urban or rural along trade routes, these survive from Istanbul south to Arabia, or east through Syria, Iran, Afghanistan, Central Asia, Pakistan, and India. Nowadays they offer parking.

Shalom Aleichem, Salaam Aleicum (Hebrew and Arabic respectively): the greeting, "Peace be With You."

Shamshir (Persian): sword.

Shawm: a reeded flute resembling an oboe or a bagpipe chanter.

Sheesham wood: a relative of rosewood.

Stater: ancient coin, the most common silver versions weighing 7–8 grams.

Tamasha (Hindi, Urdu, etc.): a performance or celebration, colloquially a fuss or commotion.

Theravada: Buddhism's eldest, conservative, and most traditional school. It flourishes in Sri Lanka, Burma, and parts of Indochina, contrasted with the Mahayana or Northern School, commonly associated with Tibet, China, and Japan.

Turkomen: natives of the Central Asian nation of Turkmenistan, also to be found in Iran and Afghanistan. Often nomadic, they are renowned carpet-weavers.

Unani: (Persian word for "Greek.") Achaemenid Persian efforts to conquer the Greek city-states resulted in Ionia trading hands, but they were finally repulsed by the Athenians at the Battle of Marathon in 490 BC. In 334 BC, Alexander of Macedon returned the compliment, crossing the Hellespont near modern Istanbul, conquering the Achaemenid empire by slaughter and intrigue, bit by bit, until the 1329 BC Battle of Jaxartes in remote, modern day Tajikistan. Since Greeks merged into new countries rather than just conquering them, gentle change brought the already highly-cultured Persians new attitudes and ideas in philosophy, sciences, architecture, drama, and the arts.

Ustad (Persian): teacher or professor.

Yasna: the Zoroastrian canon of primary religious texts and related worship.

Yehudi: (Persian word for "Jewish.") Judaism is one of Iran's oldest continuous religions, starting under Persia's Cyrus the Great (600 BC), who rescued the Jews from captivity in Babylon and whose human-rights edict, mentioning the Jews specifically, is in the British Museum. The Old Testament Book of Esther mentions Jews in Persia, and, in modern Iran (despite suffering discrimination and state opposition to Israel), Jews are guaranteed a number of seats in the national legislature as protected religious minorities.

Zarathustra (Persian etc.): the founder of the Zoroastrian religion, born in Afghanistan or eastern Iran anywhere from 1800 to 600 BC.

Zardasht (Persian): Zoroastrian.

Zoroastrianism: A major religion revealed by the prophet Zoroaster, who was probably born in Afghanistan between 1600 and 900 BC, it is said to be the first great environmental religion and maybe is still the strongest, worshipping purity and goodness at fire altars, avoiding disrespect to and pollution of their seven elements of creation: air, earth, water, fire, animals, plants, and humans. Its creator-god, purely good, coexists with a wicked nemesis deity, and, according to its reckoning, our every act will be tallied, determining whether good or evil controls the universe for eternity. It influenced later religions, including Judaism, Islam, and Christianity; for example, it includes a virgin birth. Its European name, not used by its believers, reflects the Christian tradition of calling so-called pagan and heathen faiths after their founders, as Islam used to be commonly called Mohammedanism and Mani's religion Manichaeism, etc.

.

Lightning Source UK Ltd.
Milton Keynes UK
UKOW02f1922131114

241540UK00002B/41/P